INDIAN PIPES

OTHER MARTHA'S VINEYARD MYSTERIES
BY CYNTHIA RIGGS

The Paperwhite Narcissus
Jack in the Pulpit
The Cemetery Yew
The Cranefly Orchid Murders
Deadly Nightshade

Indian Pipes

Cynthia Riggs

THOMAS DUNNE BOOKS
ST. MARTIN'S MINOTAUR
NEW YORK

THOMAS DUNNE BOOKS.
An imprint of St. Martin's Press.

www.minotaurbooks.com

ISBN-13: 978-0-312-35476-3
ISBN-10: 0-312-35476-2

First Edition: May 2006

10 9 8 7 6 5 4 3 2 1

ACKNOWLEDGMENTS

Victoria Trumbull's Hall of Fame, those friends, relatives, and colleagues who have helped to keep her alive and well, include Arlene Silva, who sent me off to Vermont College, which awarded me an MFA; and my manuscript critiquers, Alvida and Ralph Jones, and Ann and Bill Fielder. My two writers' groups are not the least bit afraid to tell me something doesn't work. Members include Jacqueline Sexton, Shirley W. Mayhew, Wendy Hathaway, Carolyn O'Daly, Rev. Bonna Whitten-Stovall (Southern Baptist), Jeanne Hewett, Ernie Weiss, Nelson W. Potter, Ethel Sherman, Rev. Judy Campbell (Unitarian-Universalist), Rev. Mary Jane O'Connor-Ropp (Methodist), and Rabbi Carla Theodore.

G. Miki Hayden went over the manuscript with her red pencil, fixing a lot of stuff that hadn't worked.

Most of all, thanks to Jonathan Revere, friend, plot doctor, cat minder, computer expert, plumber, fire builder, television producer, the quickest wit in the Commonwealth, and the Island's "feared enigma." What would I do without his frequent, "Have you thought of . . . ?"

Thanks to The Bunch of Grapes, *Publishers Weekly* Bookseller of the Year, which stacks my books between the latest Harry Potter and David McCullough's *1776*. Thanks to the West Tisbury Library, which keeps my books on the "hot new mysteries" shelf.

Bed-and-breakfast guests and West Tisbury villagers have been inspiration for story ideas and good and bad guys. I could not have manufactured my characters without their help.

Thank you Nancy Love, my agent, and Ruth Cavin of St. Martin's Minotaur, *the* top editor in the mystery field.

Despite what you may read in the Island newspapers, and despite what the West Tisbury selectmen are saying, my stories are pure fiction, the characters are figments of my imagination, and I've even taken liberties with some of the places.

—Cynthia Riggs

INDIAN
PIPES

———

CHAPTER 1

The fog poured in from Vineyard Sound, driven by a northwest wind that whipped it up the steep clay cliffs, streamers of denseness interspersed with open patches.

Through gaps in the fog, ninety-two-year-old Victoria Trumbull could see the beam from the lighthouse as it swept round and round above them, alternating red and white, warning mariners of the treacherous rocks of Devil's Bridge that stretched out into the sound far below them. Victoria's geologist daughter Amelia claimed the rocks were a terminal moraine dropped by the glacier twenty thousand years ago. Wampanoag legend said the rocks were scattered by the giant Moshup when he emptied his pipe into the waters of the sound.

As the light swept above them in the gathering dusk, droplets of moisture in Victoria's white hair glistened red, then white. She leaned on the stick her granddaughter Elizabeth had cut from the lilac tree, and gazed down. She could hear the pounding surf two hundred feet below her, but she could see almost nothing. The bell buoy off Devil's Bridge clanged. Far away, a foghorn moaned.

"Hiram Pennybacker is the worst bore on this Island," said Elizabeth, who was standing behind her grandmother.

Victoria's wrinkles framed her smile. "He's got some fierce competition," she said.

"We simply wanted to drop off that broken chair for him to fix, but no. Talk, talk, talk." Elizabeth edged closer to the fence. Her arms were summer-tan against her white T-shirt. "You can't see much, can you." Every gesture her granddaughter made reminded Victoria of Jonathan, her dead husband. Elizabeth, who was in her early thirties, was tall and slim and stood straight, like her grandfather.

"Hiram's lonely," Victoria said softly.

Elizabeth shivered. "It's mysterious this time of evening, no one around, and the mist swirling. It feels more like October than August." She turned away from the fence. "Let's go home, Gram, and have a cup of tea."

"Wait a moment." Victoria stared down at the cliff. "I thought I saw something move."

Elizabeth stepped back to where her grandmother stood with her knobby fingers laced in the fence wires, her walking stick in hand.

"Where?" Elizabeth followed her grandmother's gaze. "I can't see a thing."

"Something moved. Look!" The fog had thinned briefly, and Victoria pointed to a wild rosebush that clung to the gullied orange clay below them.

"I still don't see anything. Only poison ivy." Elizabeth wrapped her arms around her body. "Let's go."

Victoria didn't reply. She willed the fog to part again so she could see whatever it was that had moved. The motion wasn't from the wind, it was more like an animal. A dog, perhaps, was trying to get back up the cliff.

"Gram?"

Victoria caught a glimpse again of something, farther away than she had thought and much larger than a dog.

"There!" she said. "See? It looks like a person."

Elizabeth put both hands on the pipe rail at the top of the fence and peered down toward the rosebush. "You're right, Gram. Someone must have fallen."

"We need to get help right away," said Victoria.

"I'll climb down." Elizabeth started to lift herself over the fence.

Victoria shook her head. "Go back to Hiram's, quick. Call the fire department, and get Hiram to come back with a rope. I'll wait."

Elizabeth hurried away.

Victoria kept watch as darkness closed in, as the lighthouse beams overhead grew brighter and more diffuse. She caught only momentary glimpses of the form near the rosebush, no longer moving.

The ten or fifteen minutes it took Hiram to arrive seemed far longer. Victoria's eyes hurt from staring down the slope, trying to pierce through the murk. When he finally arrived, Hiram was carrying a backpack and a fat coil of rope around his right shoulder. He walked with his back bent slightly and his feet splayed out. He was a short, stocky man in his fifties, with a slight potbelly and gray hair worn in a crew cut.

"Thought you had to get right home," he mumbled around the pipe clenched between his teeth.

"I'm glad you're here," said Victoria.

"The fire truck's on the way. Nelson and his boy were at supper. His turn to drive this week."

Victoria was feeling the evening chill. "I haven't seen any movement since Elizabeth left to get you, Hiram."

"I'll climb down." He squatted next to her and secured an end of his rope to the fence post. "This ought to be long enough."

When Elizabeth returned, she was carrying a sweater. "This was in the car, Gram. Thought you might want it."

"Thank you." Victoria leaned her stick against the fence post and slipped her arms into the wool cardigan Elizabeth held for her.

Hiram undid the straps of his backpack and fumbled through it until he found a flashlight. He flicked on the light and aimed the beam down the cliff. "Can't see a thing down there. It's a pea-souper. Seen it coming for a couple of days. How far down is he, Victoria?"

"About a quarter of the way to the bottom, I would guess." She thought for a moment. "Where the cliff changes from a gentle slope and drops straight to the rocks. Right at the break is a rosebush."

"I know the place you mean," said Hiram. "Bad spot." He lifted himself over the fence rail, and, twisting a section of rope around his waist, started down toward the cliff face. Victoria watched him until he disappeared, hunched slightly, picking his way carefully on the slippery clay, stepping through the lush growth of poison ivy. She saw the circle of his flashlight beam fade away.

Elizabeth tilted her head to one side. "I hear the fire truck."

Victoria, too, heard the heavy thrum of the engine. From where she stood she could see the fog glow as the truck's rotating red lights mimicked the lighthouse above them. Figures trudged up the steps, and she recognized Nelson Minnowfish, his boy Sam, and a third person she didn't know. They were carrying ladders, more rope, and handheld searchlights that threw shadows of the chain-link fence against the bank of fog beyond.

"Evenin', Miz Trumbull," Nelson said. "Where's Hiram?"

Victoria pointed. "He's climbing down to where I saw the person."

"Shoulda waited for us to get here." Nelson aimed his searchlight. "Hiram!" he yelled down. "Can you hear?"

"Nelson?" Hiram's muffled voice came back up the cliff. "We got a problem. Send down the stretcher."

"Somebody down there?" Nelson shouted.

"Yep," Hiram shouted back.

"Man or woman?"

"Man," Hiram said.

"Alive?"

"Can't tell." The words echoed against the cliff.

Everything was a blur to Victoria from then on. Radio, lights, the ambulance, EMTs, shadows of moving people. Ladders lowered down the cliff, ropes, shouts. The aluminum stretcher was handed up and over the fence and set on the ground. EMTs and firefighters crowded around.

Victoria stepped away. She did not want to see the form on the stretcher. The only voices were sharp orders. Except for the foghorn moaning off Paul's Point and the mournful clang of the bell buoy, the only other sounds were mechanical. She heard the throb of the fire engine, the click of the rotating lights on the ambulance, a shout of "All clear!" and the buzz of a defibrillator that might start a heart pumping again.

Finally, the EMTs, the firemen, the police, stood aside, and, one by one, moved away from the stretcher.

A technician Victoria had seen at the hospital passed her, peeling off a surgical glove, his head down.

"Is he dead?" Victoria asked.

The EMT looked up, disoriented.

"What?" He focused suddenly on Victoria.

"Is he dead?" Victoria asked again, louder.

He nodded, peeling off the second surgical glove. "He was gone, ma'am. Nothing we could do."

4

"Do you know who it is?"

He shook his head. "No, ma'am. They thought he was from West Tisbury. I'm not from up-Island, myself. Excuse me." He moved on down the steps to the ambulance.

Elizabeth eased next to her grandmother and put her arms around Victoria's sloping shoulders.

"It's lucky you found him, Grammy."

Victoria looked up at her granddaughter. "They said he's from West Tisbury. Someone we know? If only we hadn't lingered so long at Hiram's. The person was still alive when I first saw him, I'm sure he was."

"They said he'd lost too much blood, Gram. That he was too badly hurt. They said he must have crawled up from the rocks where he fell to where you saw him. They said it was a miracle he could move at all, after the fall. It's almost two hundred feet. There was nothing anyone could do. Nothing at all. That's what they said."

Together, Victoria and Elizabeth walked back to the car. Victoria held her lilac stick tightly, not because she needed it, but because it comforted her.

"It wouldn't have made any difference if we'd left Hiram's earlier," Elizabeth said into her grandmother's silence. "Even if we hadn't stayed to hear his talk about politics and casinos, we couldn't have saved the guy."

"I suppose we'll find out soon enough who he was." Victoria brushed sand off the car seat and sat on the edge, her feet on the ground. "Phew! I didn't realize how long I'd been standing." She faced out into the dark night. "That poor man."

Around them figures passed in front of the fire truck and the ambulance. Victoria heard subdued voices, but couldn't make out what they were saying. Objects strobed in and out of view, illuminated briefly by flashing lights that came from every direction.

Elizabeth turned the key, and the car started up with a rattle. "I wonder how the *Island Enquirer* will report this. The newspaper wants visitors to think Martha's Vineyard is an idyllic retreat, that accidents and deaths and casino plans don't exist."

Victoria lifted her long legs into the car and shut the door.

Elizabeth went on. "According to the paper, we don't have any crime. No arguments. No poor people. No racial tension. No political scummery . . ."

"I'm not sure scummery is a word," Victoria said, stowing the lilac-wood stick behind her.

Elizabeth backed out of the parking spot. When they'd arrived, theirs was the only car. Now the parking area was full of emergency vehicles and villagers who'd heard over the scanner about the man who'd fallen off the cliffs. Elizabeth's car headlights shone on a police officer who had materialized at the pedestrian crossing.

Victoria rolled down her window. "Have you seen Hiram Penny-backer?" she asked the officer.

"He left quite a while ago, Mrs. Trumbull," she answered. "Right after I got here."

On the main road heading toward West Tisbury and home, neither Victoria nor Elizabeth spoke for some time. The curvy road skirted fields and meadows held in with stone fences, hidden now in darkness. Their lights picked up a deer by the side of the road, its eyes bright, tensed to leap. Elizabeth slowed, and the deer turned and bounded back over a stone wall.

"I can't imagine how he could have fallen," Victoria said finally. "Everybody from the Island knows how to get to the bottom of the cliffs safely."

"Maybe he got dizzy or lost his balance," Elizabeth said. She switched on the high beam, and the fog turned into a dazzling white wall. She dimmed the lights again and the wall receded.

"But you don't go straight down the cliffs. Everybody knows that." Victoria opened the window a crack and the sound of the night came in. She lifted her great nose to smell the salt air, the last hay crop, sun-dried and baled in fields they couldn't see, wet wool as they passed sheep grazing on the hill that overlooked the Atlantic.

"The way to the foot of the cliffs is down that gully," Victoria continued. "It's steep, but you wouldn't kill yourself if you fell. You'd slide to the bottom."

"No one's supposed to climb on the cliffs."

"We climbed all over them when we were children," Victoria said. "We'd smear clay on our bodies and pretend we were Indians."

"Native Americans," said Elizabeth.

"We'd bring the clay home," Victoria went on, "and make ashtrays. You had to be clever not to mix up all the different colors into a muddy-looking creation. Everybody had ashtrays then."

As they left Aquinnah, the rugged hills eased into flatter land, the road straightened, and the fog thinned.

"Did Hiram know who the man was?" Victoria asked.

"I couldn't tell. He had a funny look on his face when he came back up the cliff with the stretcher bearers."

Victoria was quiet for a moment. "He was undoubtedly upset about the man being badly hurt."

"It was more than that," said Elizabeth. "He seemed upset about something else. I got the impression that he wasn't surprised at finding that man."

They dipped into the valley that marked the West Tisbury town line, passed the gas station and the old Grange Hall, Town Hall, and the church.

"You remember how Hiram was telling us about the tribe's plans for a casino, Gram?"

Victoria nodded. "Hiram is tedious with his talk about town politics and gambling casinos. I don't want to hear another word about either."

"We're going to hear a lot more before it's over," Elizabeth said. "If the tribe gets approval for a casino, it's going to change the Island forever."

"There's nothing wrong with change."

"Surely you don't approve of a gambling casino at Aquinnah, do you Gram?"

"The Gay Head Indians . . ." Victoria started to say.

Elizabeth winced. "Grammy, it's Aquinnah now, and they're not Indians, they're Native Americans."

"They have a right to use their land any way they see fit. The Gay Head Indians are a sovereign nation and can set their own rules."

"Not for a casino," said Elizabeth. "The town's got zoning regulations."

"If the tribe decides that's what they need, it's their business." Victoria emphasized her words.

7

Elizabeth slowed and turned in between the two granite fence posts that marked Victoria's driveway.

"I can just imagine you at the casino, Gram, playing the slots."

Victoria laughed. "Probably so."

Chapter 2

By the next morning, the fog had vanished, dispelled by bright sunlight. Victoria was eating her breakfast in the cookroom, a small room off the kitchen.

Elizabeth had not yet come downstairs. It seemed such a short time ago, Victoria mused, that her granddaughter had come to stay with her. Temporarily, Elizabeth had said. She'd needed a week or two of peace and quiet. Elizabeth was still here, divorced, and with a full-time job. And now Victoria, who had always cherished her solitude, couldn't imagine life without her lanky, sunny granddaughter.

When the phone rang, the sound startled her.

"This is Hiram, Victoria."

"Where did you disappear to last night?"

"No reason to stay after the body was recovered. Will you be around for a while?"

"I have errands to do. I'm eating breakfast now."

"I'll be there shortly."

"Wait, Hiram. Don't hang up yet. You knew the man who was killed, didn't you?"

"I knew him, all right." She heard him puff on his pipe. "It was that neighbor of yours, the engineer. I was telling you about him yesterday."

"You can't mean Jube Burkhardt?"

"Afraid so."

Victoria pushed her cereal dish aside. "Well," she said into the silence. "That makes a difference, doesn't it."

"I need to talk to you right away."

"I don't have much time, Hiram," said Victoria, thinking of his seamless monologues.

"This won't take long."

Victoria sighed and set the phone back in its cradle. Just then Elizabeth appeared, rubbing sleep out of her eyes.

"Did you know Jube Burkhardt?" Victoria asked, after she'd greeted her granddaughter.

"Just by sight," Elizabeth said. "Why?"

"He was the man on the cliffs last night."

"That's weird. Hiram was talking about him last night. I wasn't paying attention, to tell the truth. Was Jube a friend of yours?"

Victoria shook her head. "Not really. He was a bit of a recluse. I knew his mother quite well, though. As children, we liked to play in the barn loft where his grandfather stored hay." Victoria carried her breakfast dishes to the sink. "Hiram is coming by in a few minutes."

"Would you like me to make blueberry muffins?"

"Good idea. Keep his mouth full."

Elizabeth laughed. While she mixed batter and poured it into muffin tins, she and her grandmother talked about Jube.

"He lived right on the pond, didn't he?" Elizabeth asked.

Victoria nodded. "In the old Mitchell place, his family house."

The muffins were still baking when Hiram drove up. He parked his van under the maple tree, and Victoria could see him knocking ashes out of his pipe on the sole of his boot.

He paused at the kitchen door and sniffed. "Morning, Victoria, Elizabeth. Something smells good."

Victoria led the way into the cookroom and waited until Hiram had seated himself. "What did you need to see me about, Hiram, Jube Burkhardt's death?"

Hiram nodded. "That, but something else as well."

"It's hard to believe Jube could have fallen from the top of the cliffs and then crawled all the way back up to where I saw him."

"I agree." Hiram clasped his hands on the table and studied them. "I told you, didn't I, that Jube attended the tribal council meeting the day before yesterday?"

"To report on his soil tests, you said."

"Tests for a septic system, actually. Four members of the tribe and Burkhardt were at the meeting."

Elizabeth brought in mugs of coffee and a basket of hot muffins, and sat across from her grandmother.

Hiram smiled and helped himself. After he'd buttered his muffin and taken a large bite, Victoria asked him about the meeting. "Who was there besides Jube?"

Hiram patted his mouth with his napkin. "Chief Hawkbill, of course. He's only a figurehead now that Patience VanDyke is chairman. She was there and so was that assistant of hers, Peter Little."

"And the fourth person?" asked Victoria.

"Obed VanDyke, the fisherman."

"He's Patience's first cousin," said Victoria.

Hiram nodded. "Dojan Minnowfish would have been there, but he's still in Washington."

"The first time I saw Dojan, he practically scared me to death," said Elizabeth. "He looked like something out of a horror movie."

"It's all an act," said Hiram.

"When is he due back on-Island?" Victoria asked.

"Not before Christmas."

"From everything I hear, he seems to be a capable tribal representative," Victoria said.

"The federal government certainly accepts him." Hiram wiped his mouth. "He fits right in with government insanity."

"I suppose he goes to work barefoot," Elizabeth said, "with that feather stuck in his hair?"

Hiram grunted. "Burkhardt told me that Obed got into a squabble with Patience. She's applying for a federal grant for the tribe to build a casino."

"Here we go again," mumbled Elizabeth.

"I gather Obed doesn't approve of the casino proposal?" Victoria asked.

Elizabeth sighed and glanced at her watch.

"Obed insists that gambling goes against tradition." Hiram patted the pocket where he kept his pipe. "Patience says the tribe lost its traditions years ago."

Victoria passed the muffin basket. "Have another."

"Delicious." Hiram nodded at Elizabeth.

"How come Patience is tribal chairperson?"

"The tribe has always had a woman chairman." When Elizabeth frowned, Hiram added, "That's the official title. *Chairman.* Not chairperson."

"Both her mother and grandmother were tribal chairs," said Victoria. "She's following in their footsteps."

"According to Burkhardt," Hiram continued, "Peter Little and Patience were upset with each other."

"That's odd," Victoria said. "I thought they were like that." She held up two fingers close together.

Hiram shrugged. "Burkhardt didn't say. He had his own agenda. Peter had accused him of taking bribes."

"What for?" asked Elizabeth. "To skew the soil tests? I thought Burkhardt was working for the tribe."

"No, he was working for the town. The town hired him as a consultant."

"So the tribal council wasn't exactly sympathetic?"

"Decidedly not," said Hiram.

"What kind of tests were they?" Elizabeth asked.

"Perc tests. To see if the site would percolate enough for a septic system. But the tests were never done."

"A casino would mean a huge influx of people," Elizabeth said. "And a huge septic system."

"Right." Hiram felt for his pipe again. "A casino would need a fair-sized sewage treatment plant, not a septic system. At one point during the meeting Jube lost his temper—"

Victoria interrupted. "He's not the first person on this Island to lose his temper over an issue."

"No, but he evidently touched raw nerves."

"In what way?" asked Victoria.

"Before stalking out of the meeting, he said the entire tribe was a pack of mongrels."

Elizabeth set her coffee mug down. "That's what he said? That they were *mongrels*?"

"We're all mongrels," said Victoria.

"It's not exactly sensitive to call a minority group 'mongrels,'" said Elizabeth. "Do you think Jube Burkhardt really *was* taking bribes?"

"Probably. He wasn't known for integrity."

"And he refused to recommend a waiver for *any* septic system?" Elizabeth asked. "Or sewage plant?"

Hiram nodded. "That's what he told me. Burkhardt could have delayed things for a long, long time." Hiram crumpled up his napkin, dropped it beside his plate, and sat back. "Patience is claiming tribal sovereignty. She says the tribe doesn't need Burkhardt's tests or the town's approval. Or to concern itself with state regulations."

"Whew!" said Elizabeth. "Why did Burkhardt tell you all this?"

"I'm on the town's health board. He wanted me to certify that the planned casino sites had failed the perc tests."

"Did they fail?" Elizabeth asked.

"As I said, he never ran any tests."

"Did you sign the papers?"

Hiram was silent.

Elizabeth stared at him.

Hiram changed the subject. "I promised I wouldn't take up much of your time."

Victoria waited.

"Burkhardt had come to see me on personal business." Hiram seemed to be working something out in his mind. "He was supposed to meet someone on the beach below the cliffs the following night, and asked me to go with him."

"Last night," Victoria said. "The night he was killed."

"Right."

Victoria thought for a moment. "Did he say who the person was? Or why Jube wanted you to go with him?"

"I got the impression he wanted a witness."

"Did you meet with him?"

Hiram shook his head. "I walked a quarter mile or so along the beach to the foot of the cliffs, but I never saw him. Or anyone else. The fog had come in, thick. I waited until six, then left. I figured Burkhardt got held up for some reason, and would get in touch if he needed me."

"That must have been about two hours before I saw him on the cliff," said Victoria.

"About that. You brought the chair by before supper."

"And we stayed an hour or so. We were at your house roughly from six-thirty to seven-thirty."

Hiram started to say something, then stopped. He began again. "We're so focused on that damned casino, you'd think nothing else was happening in the world."

Victoria watched him, her eyes half-closed.

"I must tell you something, get it off my chest."

"Of course."

Elizabeth got up. "I'll make my bed," she said.

Hiram clasped his hands on the table again. "I have a friend, Victoria, a close friend, Tad Nordstrom. A banker, lives in Omaha. Married, nice home, two teenage kids." Hiram shifted in his seat. "He's greatly respected in his community. A fine human being."

"I gather you and he are more than friends?"

Hiram nodded.

"How did you meet?"

"We were both stranded in the Chicago airport for two days during a snowstorm six years ago. We've kept in touch."

"Everyone who knows you, certainly, understands you're, um, not the marrying type," said Victoria. "So I assume it's your friend who has the problem, not you?"

Hiram glanced out the window. "He visits me every year. Tells the family he's going on retreat."

"I suppose that's close to the truth," said Victoria.

"His wife thinks she's to blame for the disintegration of their relationship. He feels guilty and angry."

"Why doesn't he simply come out and tell her he's gay and suggest a divorce?"

"Money, kids, church, family, position in the community. He lives in Nebraska, not Martha's Vineyard."

"This is the twenty-first century," said Victoria. "People recognize that so-called lifestyles are not a matter of choice."

"Not where he lives."

"Wherever he lives, he'd better do something soon, while his wife can still make a new life for herself."

"We've talked about that—"

Victoria interrupted. "I have no patience with a man whose priorities are money and position in the community."

"Children . . ." Hiram began.

"Does he think he's helping his children by pretending he's something he's not?" Victoria started to get up.

"Wait, Victoria. I haven't told you the problem."

"The problem is that your friend is a hypocrite," said Victoria, "and you're not helping his family by covering for him."

"Please, sit down and listen to me."

"I've heard more than I want," Victoria said, but sat again. "I take it Jube figures in this in some way?"

"When Burkhardt came to see me the other night with the faked soil tests, I said I couldn't sign them. At that, he brought out an undated copy of a letter he had written."

"About your friend Tad?"

Hiram nodded. "To Tad's bank, with copies to the local paper. And to his wife."

"I hope you told Jube what he could do with it?"

"I signed the certificate."

Victoria pushed her chair away from the table and stood up again. "Hiram, I'm ashamed of you." She leaned on the table. "I never expected *you* to give in to blackmail."

"Victoria, listen to me—"

"I've listened to you and told you what I think."

"There's more." Hiram swallowed hard. "Burkhardt and I were lovers before I met Tad."

Victoria turned and looked down at him. When she saw his expression, she sat down abruptly and took a deep breath. "Hiram," she said, "you didn't kill Jube Burkhardt, did you?"

CHAPTER 3

Hiram sat up abruptly. "Of course I didn't kill Burkhardt!"

"When the police learn that you were to meet him on the beach *below* the cliffs around the time he died," Victoria said, "they're going to wonder how he could have fallen to his death from the *top* of the cliffs."

"That's right." Hiram tugged at his short beard. "However, the police are calling his death an accident. A fall from the cliffs. They're about to close the case."

Victoria studied her fingernails, short and ridged with a line of gardening dirt she hadn't been able to scrub clean. "That decision must be a relief to you. You'd be a likely suspect otherwise."

"No, it's not a relief at all. Burkhardt's death was no accident. Someone killed him. Who? And why?"

Victoria looked up. "Then explain that to the police."

"So the police can arrest me? Even *you* think I might have killed him."

They were both so quiet, Victoria could hear the town clock ring in the church steeple. She looked at her watch. "Ten o'clock. I have to be somewhere at eleven."

Hiram sighed. "Victoria, I'm worried. The killer must have known Burkhardt expected me to go with him."

"What makes you say that?"

Hiram lifted his empty mug, then put it down. "After you left last night, I listened to my answering machine. Burkhardt had left a message saying he'd been delayed and would meet me an hour later. Same place." Hiram toyed with his mug. "The killer may have overheard Burkhardt. Or perhaps Burkhardt told him I'd be there?"

"If Jube was so suspicious of the person he was meeting that he asked you to accompany him, why would he then go alone with him when you didn't show up?"

"I don't know what went through Burkhardt's mind, Victoria. My first thought when he asked me to go with him was that it involved the blackmail letter. But that didn't make sense. Why not simply meet at my house?" Hiram paused.

Outside the window, a blue jay tried to land on a small perch of the bird feeder and flew off with a flutter of wings and a squawk. The feeder swung back and forth, dropping seeds into the browning iris leaves.

"And who, on the Island, anyway, would care about Tad's and my relationship? Then I thought the meeting might have to do with one of Burkhardt's nieces. He'd been having some problems with one or both of them, you know."

"Or they with him," said Victoria.

"I imagined other scenarios. Burkhardt meeting with a motorcyclist. Talking to someone about casino plans, taxes, septic permits, the tribe. But nothing made sense. Why would anyone need to meet him on the beach?" Hiram ran both hands through his crew cut. "I believe now that the killer planned to lure Burkhardt to a secluded place to kill him."

"Did Jube suspect the meeting was a trap?"

"Burkhardt was uneasy about the meeting, but I doubt if it occurred to him that anyone would have the temerity to attack him."

"Where is your friend Tad now? Did he know that Jube was blackmailing you on his account?"

"Tad knew," said Hiram, gazing out the window. "Tad has been visiting me for the past two weeks."

"Is it possible that Tad was meeting with Jube?"

"Tad?" Hiram stared at her. "Good heavens, no."

"Where is Tad now?" Victoria asked.

"On his way back to Omaha."

"Is he driving?"

"Tad's not a killer, Victoria."

Victoria checked her hands again, tried to wedge dirt out from under her thumbnail with a fingernail. "Under the right circumstances we can all be killers."

Hiram looked at her in surprise.

"If someone threatened my family? Yes."

Hiram stared at her.

She continued. "Suppose Tad contacted Jube, offered to buy the letter, asked to meet him somewhere private."

"No, Victoria. No."

Victoria looked up. "Jube, of course, contacted you to join them. When Tad realized you'd agreed, he put the meeting off an hour. That fits with the facts we have."

"I spoke with Tad after he left yesterday morning. He was on the ferry, just about to dock in Woods Hole."

"He called on a cell phone, didn't he?"

Hiram groaned and tilted his chair backward.

"Don't lean back in the chair," said Victoria.

Hiram set the chair down.

Victoria said, "Do you have any idea what happened to the letter Jube wrote?"

"Once I signed the faked test results, he put the letter back in an inside pocket in his windbreaker. Last night when I reached Burkhardt on the cliff, he was still wearing the same jacket. I searched his pockets."

"Did you find the letter?"

Hiram shook his head. "No."

Victoria scowled. "If Tad will discuss his situation honestly with his wife, that letter will be toothless."

"That won't happen, Victoria. You don't understand."

Victoria's face flushed. "Yes, I do. Perhaps the killer took the letter."

Elizabeth returned from upstairs, running a comb through her damp hair. "Okay to come back?"

Hiram nodded, and Elizabeth joined them again at the table. "Are you still talking casinos?"

"Not exactly," said Victoria.

Hiram reached for his pipe absentmindedly. "Patience claims a casino will bring in jobs for Aquinnah."

"Go outside if you need to smoke," said Elizabeth.

"I don't *need* to," said Hiram, stiffly.

"Once they build a casino, Aquinnah will sell liquor, and the town won't be dry any longer," Elizabeth said.

"Some members of the tribe think that would be a benefit," said Hiram.

Elizabeth looked from her grandmother to Hiram. "What were you two discussing, anyway? Jube Burkhardt? You both seem really upset."

Victoria looked out the window.

Hiram picked up his empty mug. "No one was quite sure where Burkhardt stood. If the tribe loses its case for sovereign immunity and can't get permits in time, they'll probably turn to private investors who've already shown interest in funding a tribal casino."

"Could Jube have held up the application for six months? And would that have been long enough to give a private investor an opening?" Elizabeth asked.

"Absolutely."

"I've heard you saying at some point, Hiram, that he was upset about motorcycles. Was it the noise?"

Victoria turned back to the table. "His house is more than a mile from the main road."

"It wasn't just the bikers," said Hiram. "He was upset about his taxes going for a casino. The taxes on his property were more than he earned, he said."

"He could hardly sell his family's house," Victoria said. "It would be like selling your child."

"Did he have children?" Elizabeth asked.

"He had no family except for his nieces. At one time he planned to give his property to his younger niece, but night before last he seemed unsure."

"The younger niece?" Victoria was surprised. "I would have thought he'd give his property to both equally."

"The elder niece is fooling around with a biker."

"Ah," said Elizabeth. "So that's it."

"He figured he could get out of paying taxes," Hiram said, "by giving the younger niece the property now, with a life tenancy for himself."

"Does she have money to pay taxes?" asked Elizabeth.

"Burkhardt figured that was her problem, not his."

Elizabeth made a face. "Nice guy."

"During the tribal meeting, he thought about his taxes going to a casino, he told me. What right would a foreign nation have to fund a casino with U.S. taxpayers' money?"

"Probably be an advantage to be a foreign nation," said Victoria.

"A Native American tribal entity is hardly a foreign nation," said Elizabeth. "Sovereign nation is different." She got up, refilled Hiram's coffee mug, and held the pot toward her grandmother.

"No, thank you," Victoria said. "Jube's house has a nice view. Right on Tisbury Great Pond, surrounded on three sides by water. You can see the ocean from there."

"An expensive piece of property." Hiram stirred milk and sugar into his coffee.

"What do you think it's worth?" Elizabeth asked.

Hiram shrugged. "If you still have the taxpayers' listing from the *Enquirer*, I can tell you."

Victoria lifted herself out of the chair and went into the dining room, where she sorted through a heap of papers and magazines piled on the piano bench and on the floor next to it until she found the issue Hiram wanted.

Hiram paged through the tax supplement. "Burkhardt." He scanned the columns. "Here it is. Burkhardt, Jubal. How does eighteen million dollars sound to you?"

"You must be joking." Victoria was aghast. "It couldn't possibly be worth that much."

"He's got thirty-two acres and waterfront." Hiram peered at Victoria over the top of his glasses. "The real estate people would describe it as a charming, historic eighteenth-century Vineyard estate with water frontage."

"I can't believe it. The old Mitchell place? They must have misplaced a decimal point. If it were eighteen thousand dollars, I'd be surprised."

"He was paying taxes on eighteen million."

"No wonder he took bribes," Elizabeth said.

Victoria looked at her watch. "I don't know what you want of me,

Hiram. You don't intend to go to the police, which is what I advise you to do. You don't like my suspects."

"I need your help, Victoria. Before I go to the police, we have to find the killer. It's neither of your two suspects, believe me."

"That's the second time you've used the word *we*," said Victoria.

"You're the obvious person. You know everybody on this Island and who they're related to. You know more history than anyone. In fact, you've lived much of it. And, you've gotten yourself a reputation as a sleuth."

Victoria looked down at her hands.

"You know that Gram is a deputy police officer, don't you?" Elizabeth asked.

Hiram smiled. "Everybody on the Island knows."

"I can't imagine what I can contribute this time." Victoria studied him. "You're holding something back, aren't you, Hiram." She waited.

Hiram sighed again. "When Elizabeth came to get me last night, I had a hunch that the person on the cliff was Burkhardt. When I got to him, he was still alive. He mumbled a few words I couldn't make out. Then he said clearly, 'Sibyl,' before he went unconscious."

Victoria was silent.

Hiram repeated himself. "Just that one word, 'Sibyl.'"

"Do you know anyone named Sibyl?" Victoria asked.

"I don't. Do you?"

Victoria shook her head. "It's not a common name. That was what the ancient Romans and Greeks called their oracles—Sibyl. Go to the police, Hiram."

"I'll go to the police when we find something concrete that will clear me."

Victoria felt a presence behind her and turned to look out the window. A dark form skirted around the side of the house. "We've got a caller," she said.

Hiram, too, looked. The visitor, dressed entirely in black, had ducked into the entry. Hiram stood abruptly. "I've got to go. I'll call you around five this afternoon. I have something else I have to tell you." He slipped out through the rarely used east door rather than the usual entry door to the west.

"What's his problem?" Elizabeth muttered.

There was a rap on the door that Hiram hadn't used, the door opened, and a figure stepped inside.

Victoria leaned forward and saw a tall man wearing a black muscle shirt and black jeans. He had a huge black beard and a wild mop of curly hair with a bent osprey feather protruding from it as if from an untidy nest. His eyes were dark irises floating in red-rimmed white seas. His feet were bare and dirty.

Victoria got up from her chair with a broad smile.

He greeted her, his right hand lifted.

"Dojan!" Victoria went toward him. "You're back!"

CHAPTER 4

While Dojan and Victoria were standing in the doorway discussing the torments of his life in the nation's capital, Joe Hanover, the plumber, was making a U-turn in front of Alley's store. He parked his pickup truck under the dying elm across the road. It was almost lunchtime.

"Stay here, Taffy. Good girl." Joe ruffled the hair of his golden retriever and slammed the door shut. Taffy rested her head on the window frame, her mouth open. Joe waited for an old red Volvo to pass, and crossed to the store.

The gang was on the front porch under the overhanging roof. Donald Schwartz sat on the bench next to Sarah Germaine. Lincoln Sibert leaned against the storefront, moving his shoulders back and forth, scratching his back.

"What's up, Sarah?" Joe shifted the wad of Red Man in his mouth, and spit discreetly off to one side, where customers usually didn't step.

Donald sat with his hands on the knees of jeans that were blotched with fiberglass resin from the boatyard. "She wasn't going to tell us until you got here."

Joe lifted his once-tan baseball cap, scratched his head, and settled the cap back again. Printed across the front was DRAINS R US.

Sarah wrinkled her nose. She had a part-time job at Tribal Headquarters and was still dressed in her working clothes—black slacks and bright blue T-shirt imprinted with a portrait of a chieftain wearing a feathered bonnet.

"That ain't no Wampanoag." Joe pointed his thumb at Sarah's chest.

Sarah looked down.

Lincoln moved his shoulders against the storefront. "It's not polite to point at a girl's boobies," he said.

"Woman's," Sarah corrected automatically.

"Okay, okay, don't keep us in suspense." Donald turned his head so he could look at Sarah's Indian chief.

"They voted for the casino?" Joe asked.

"Nope." Sarah shook her head.

"They found Jube Burkhardt's car," said Lincoln.

"Nope." Sarah smirked.

"I'm gettin' me a cuppa coffee." Joe reached for the handle on the screen door. "This shit is making me thirsty. Anyone else?"

"Dojan's back," Sarah said abruptly, and folded her arms over the Indian's jutting chin. The feathered headdress lifted with her breathing.

"No shit!" Joe dropped his hand from the screen door, stepped back, and turned toward her.

"I thought they buried him in some Indian agency in D.C.," said Lincoln. "Rumor was he killed some guy."

Joe laughed. "Island rumors are as good as gospel."

A motorcycle went past the store followed by a second and a third.

"All *right!*" said Joe. "Some fancy bikes."

"We're gonna have to put up with that for the next week." Donald indicated the passing motorcycles.

Sarah put her hands over her ears. The bikes roared by. The first, a bright metallic purplish-blue, was driven by a biker wearing a sleeveless T-shirt with a grinning skull on the back. The two following bikes were black with shiny exhaust pipes that ran almost their entire lengths.

"Can't hear yourself think." Donald shook his head as if to clear the noise out of his ears.

"You know what those bikes were?" Lincoln's voice had a touch of awe.

"Harley-Davidson," said Joe. "Can't miss 'em."

"The first was a Harley. The other two were Indian Chiefs. Antiques, probably '47 or '48."

"Yeah?" Joe squinted at the receding bikes. "When's the rally begin?"

"Not until this weekend, but a bunch of them arrived early." Lincoln moved back against the shingles.

"The rally's giving a lot of money to Island charities." Sarah looked around at the other three.

"I'll believe it when I see it." Donald shifted in his seat and crossed his legs. "Where are they staying at?"

"All over the place," Lincoln said. "Place I caretake, they already have half a dozen tents set up in the field."

"How come Dojan's back?" Lincoln asked Sarah.

"Peter Little called him in Washington, had him drop everything to fly here."

"What was the hurry?" Joe put his hands in his pockets, bent his knees, thrust his pelvis forward, and rocked back and forth from his toes to his heels.

Sarah shrugged. "Who knows?"

"Peter sent for him?" Donald asked.

"Chief Hawkbill told Peter to call Dojan," Sarah said.

"What did what's-her-name say about all that?" Joe rocked up and down, toes to heels.

"Patience VanDyke? What could she say? She's not about to go against the chief."

"If I was her, I wouldn't trust that slime," Joe said.

"You mean Peter Little?" asked Lincoln.

"He's after her job, believe you me," Joe said.

"Well, I wouldn't trust *her*, neither," Donald said. "All she cares about is money, money, money." He rubbed his thumb and third finger together. " 'Poor, indigent tribe!' she says, 'poor me, all I can afford is this old pickup truck,' and all the time she's buying another half-million-dollar property."

"What's she got now, three parcels?" Joe asked.

Sarah nodded.

"All up-Island?"

Sarah nodded again.

"When did Dojan get here?" Lincoln asked.

"Yesterday. He hitchhiked from the MV airport."

Joe grinned. "They didn't send a limo for him?"

"He land on-Island before that engineer got himself killed?" Donald asked.

Sarah nodded.

"Wasn't no accident. Someone gave him a shove." Joe looked from Lincoln to Donald to Sarah. "So Dojan the killer flies in from D.C. and—bingo—the tribe gets rid of a little bitty nuisance. Pretty convenient timing, I'd say."

"How long will you be here, Dojan?" Victoria asked the tall, shaggy man. Dojan and she were still standing in the doorway between the kitchen and the cookroom.

He shrugged, and the broken feather bobbed up and down.

"I understand you're doing a good job," said Victoria.

"Come on in, Dojan," Elizabeth said. "My grandmother's tired of standing up."

"Ah!" said Dojan.

Elizabeth led them back to the cookroom, and Victoria sat in her usual chair.

"I wear shoes," said Dojan, when he'd seated himself. "And a suit."

Victoria looked thoughtfully at the Wampanoag. "You won't have to stay there much longer. Another two years?"

"I should be setting lobster traps now." He grinned suddenly. "With your help, my friend."

Victoria smiled. "I'll be ready. Two years will go quickly. I hear you're living on a boat on the Potomac River?"

"A plastic houseboat," Dojan said with disgust. "At a yacht club. On the Washington Channel, a backwater."

Elizabeth laughed. "You mean, it's not saltwater."

"That's better than living in a high-rise apartment building with an elevator," said Victoria.

"Are you here because of all the casino talk?" Elizabeth asked.

"Chief Hawkbill told me to come."

"Did you get back before that man was killed?"

"Killed?" said Dojan.

"They say he fell from the top of the cliffs," said Elizabeth.

"Who was it?"

"Jube Burkhardt," said Victoria. "Did you know him?"

Dojan opened his eyes wide, and his dark irises seemed to float in bloodshot white.

Victoria changed the subject. "Are you staying on your own boat while you're here?"

Dojan nodded, and without another word, got up from the table, walked silently to the door, and slipped out.

"He's weird," said Elizabeth, after he'd left.

"Don't underestimate Dojan. He's different, but he's not stupid." Victoria looked at her watch. "We'd better get going, if we hope to do our errands."

"I feel sorry for him," Victoria said, after they'd put the top down on the convertible and were on their way to Vineyard Haven.

"I suppose the tribe is paying his yacht club fees and dockage?" Elizabeth said. "Not bad."

Victoria frowned. "Washington is Chief Hawkbill's idea of punishment."

"Did Dojan really kill that man?"

Victoria nodded.

"That's why he was so prickly when I mentioned Jube Burkhardt getting himself killed. I guess if it weren't for the chief, Dojan would be in prison?"

"If it weren't for Chief Hawkbill, Dojan wouldn't have been punished at all," said Victoria.

"Because of the tribe's sovereign nation immunity?"

"Exactly."

Elizabeth steered around the sharp turn by the cemetery, and the yellow ribbons on Victoria's straw hat fluttered around her face.

"Dojan looks awfully pale," said Elizabeth. They were on the straight road that went past the new Ag Hall.

Victoria smiled. "Now we can read the inscriptions on his tattoos."

They stopped in North Tisbury and bought sandwiches and clam chowder. Victoria held the paper bag in her lap while Elizabeth drove through the late summer traffic, down the hill into Vineyard Haven, where they came to a standstill at the end of a line of cars.

"Hey, Mrs. Trumbull!" A teenager crossed the street between Elizabeth's convertible and the car in front, his baseball cap on backward, his jeans drooping around his feet, the braces on his teeth sparkling in the sunlight. He slapped the hood. "Pretty sporty car."

"Hello, Jed," Victoria said. "Looks as if you'll get there before we do, wherever you're going."

"It's August." Jed dodged among the shoppers who were ambling along Main Street and disappeared up Center Street.

On the outskirts of town, four or five blocks and ten minutes later, they turned down the steep hill to Owen Park, and carried their lunch to a bench overlooking the harbor.

Below them the ferry from Woods Hole rounded the jetty, entered the harbor, and moved into its slip. Partway around the harbor, just this side of Packer's wharf, was a high-tech vessel shaped like a gargantuan grapefruit seed.

"Look at the way that deck slopes," said Elizabeth. "No one can possibly stand on it."

Two broad stripes ran from bow to stern, the lower one turquoise, the one above it lime green.

Victoria studied the vessel. "It must be speedy."

"Fifty knots." Elizabeth shaded her eyes with her hand. "Who wants to go that fast in a boat?"

The vessel's name, *Pequot*, was spelled out in three-foot-high letters that slanted backward to add to the illusion of speed.

Victoria opened her container of chowder and spooned it up as she spoke. "Do you know who owns the boat?"

"That casino in Connecticut."

"*Pequot* was an Indian word for 'destroyer.'"

"Destroyer as vessel, or as wrecking people's lives," Elizabeth said. "I wonder if they know how apt that is?"

"A bit of gambling can be fun," Victoria said. "I wouldn't mind taking a ride to Connecticut at fifty knots, visiting the casino, and winning some money."

Elizabeth shook her head.

The captain of the casino ferry, wearing a dazzling white uniform, greeted passengers. Gold stripes on his shoulder boards glittered in the noon sunlight.

"Isn't that Patience VanDyke?" Victoria pointed to a large woman in a purple muumuu who was walking sedately up the gangplank.

"It's hard to tell from here." Elizabeth studied the passengers. "The man behind her looks like Chief Hawkbill."

"And Peter Little," said Victoria, tugging down the brim of her hat to shade her eyes from the glare off the water. "Practically the entire tribal council."

"Is that Hiram behind the rest?"

Victoria tilted her head. "I don't think so. Hiram didn't mention anything this morning about a boat ride. In fact, he said he'd call me around five." She looked at her watch. "I want to be sure to be home by then."

"I suppose the tribal council is checking out the casino," said Elizabeth. "What's Hiram calling about?"

"He started to say something before he left suddenly."

"When Dojan showed up. What's Hiram got against Dojan?"

"I have no idea," said Victoria.

The woman in purple reappeared and moved back down the gangplank. "There's Patience again," said Elizabeth. "With Peter Little right behind her. Guess those two aren't going after all."

As they finished lunch, the *Pequot* slid away from the dock, slowly rounded the jetty, then lifted partway out of the water on what looked like skis.

In the harbor, children buzzed around in an outboard motorboat, trailing a long wake. A boy dived off the dock in front of them and swam out to an anchored sailboat. The *Pequot* rounded West Chop and disappeared from sight.

As they were leaving their picnic spot, a stream of cars debarked from the three-thirty ferry. Elizabeth took the back road past the waterworks to avoid traffic. They crossed the town line into West Tisbury.

Victoria looked at her watch.

Elizabeth checked the rearview mirror and passed a line of mopeds. "We'll be in plenty of time for your phone call, Gram. He's not supposed to call for another hour."

They drove past West Tisbury's tiny gray-shingled police station and turned in between the gateposts of Victoria's driveway.

Elizabeth carried in the groceries, and Victoria followed.

"Message on the answering machine," Elizabeth called out. "Want to hear?"

Victoria went into the dining room and leaned her forearms on the buffet where the dial phone and the new answering machine were connected by a maze of wires.

"Victoria, this is Hiram. It's half-past three now. I'm at Burkhardt's place." He gave the number. "I've got to talk to you. It's urgent. Call me back. Right away."

CHAPTER 5

"That's a strange message. Jube Burkhardt's number?" Victoria dialed. The phone rang and rang.

"Ten rings." Victoria looked at her watch. "It's not five o'clock yet." She thumbed through the phone book. "I'll try Hiram's, see if he's returned home."

Elizabeth stood by silently.

Victoria counted the number of rings, and the answering machine picked up after five. She hung up and looked at her watch. "He called from Jube Burkhardt's at three-thirty. That was almost an hour ago."

"Do you want to drive to Jube's? Or to Hiram's in Aquinnah?" Elizabeth asked.

"I'm not sure what to do. Jube's house is only a mile or so from here. Perhaps we should go there first."

Victoria taped a note to the kitchen door saying where they'd gone in case Hiram stopped by. She unhooked her hat from the entry where she'd left it. Elizabeth was already at the car, brushing fallen leaves off the seat.

"You might hurry, Elizabeth. I'm uneasy about Hiram."

Elizabeth turned left onto the main road, then left again onto New Lane, past Doane's tidy hay field and Victoria's unkempt pasture.

After a half mile the paved road ended and Elizabeth slowed. "I don't know my way from here, Gram. You'll have to navigate."

Victoria directed her onto a rutted road that followed the shore of Tisbury Great Pond. At one point they lost their way in the maze of branching roads, and Elizabeth had to backtrack.

On the road to Burkhardt's they saw only two vehicles. A red pickup truck turned off onto a side road before they reached it. A Jeep pulled aside onto the brushy edge so they could pass. Victoria waved thanks.

The road became a mere track, overgrown in the middle with grass and brush. The brush scraped along the underside of the car; grass swished past. Elizabeth slowed for tree roots that extended across the ruts. They wound through scrub oak and huckleberry brush. They could hear towhees rustling in the undergrowth calling, "Che-wink? Che-wink?"

The track stopped abruptly at an open grassy area.

An old gray-shingled house, much like the main part of Victoria's house, stood in the center of the clearing. The front door faced the ocean. A visitor would arrive at the back door, which meant going through the added-on kitchen. No one used the front door of Vineyard houses. Burkhardt's front door was probably swollen shut and unusable. Grass had grown up knee-high by the step, and bayberry bushes encroached on what might once have been the front lawn.

The curled weathered shingles of Burkhardt's house were streaked with black. A line of gulls perched on the peak of the roof, which was stained with their droppings. When Elizabeth stopped the car with a rattle and a clank, the gulls lifted into the air, crying. Around the frame of each window, the paint, once green or blue, was peeling, showing bare wood that had weathered to an unhealthy brownish-black.

The house was on a small promontory, surrounded on three sides by the main body of the pond. To the left, a barrier bar separated Tisbury Great Pond from the ocean. Breakers crested on the other side. Victoria could feel the steady rumble of pounding surf.

She opened the car door and stepped onto the crisp dry grass. "I don't see Hiram's car."

"It doesn't look as though anyone's home." Elizabeth knocked on the back door. No answer. She knocked again.

"Can you see through the windows?" Victoria asked.

Elizabeth went around the house, cupping her hands against the glass to cut the reflection.

"There's an awful lot of stuff in there," she said.

"We might as well try the door." Victoria stepped up onto the large granite stone by the kitchen door and lifted the latch. The door opened with a squeal onto a small entry. A calico cat darted out of the house and tore off into the huckleberry undergrowth beyond the grassy area.

"I hope it's all right to let her out." Victoria looked in the direction the cat had disappeared.

"Hallo!" Elizabeth called. "Anybody home?"

No answer.

The entry was hung with coats and yellow slickers, a denim carpenter's apron, a couple of baseball caps. Three or four fishing rods, a kayak paddle, and a pair of oars were propped against the inner door, and a collection of lures, most of them old looking, lined a shelf. Spiderwebs festooned the ceiling, wedded the sleeve of one coat to another, strung the lines of the fishing rods together. The splintery wood floor, partially covered with a worn piece of linoleum, had a collection of hip boots, waders, and worn leather boots, their rusty eyelets laced with rawhide thongs, green with mold.

"Whew!" said Elizabeth. "Men!"

Victoria entered the kitchen, and stopped abruptly.

The sink was full of dirty dishes from days' worth of meals. The kitchen table was covered with old-fashioned oilcloth cracked in places so that brown cloth backing showed through. The oilcloth itself was almost hidden by newspapers, coffee mugs, dishes from which someone must once have eaten eggs, a blackened aluminum coffeepot, and a day-old half-grapefruit.

Victoria was aware of the hum of the refrigerator, off to one side of the kitchen. It may once have been white, but now it was a pale coffee color, a greasy sheen that was thicker on its curved top. A layer of bacon fat in a black iron skillet on the stove showed tracks and tooth marks and droppings of last night's mice.

"Well," said Victoria, looking around without touching anything. "Let's see what's in the living room."

A path, only wide enough for one person, wandered through waist-high stacks of newspapers and magazines and books and unopened mail and catalogs. Pieces of clothing, cardboard boxes, a broken lamp, seeded the stacks.

Victoria followed the path to a cul-de-sac where there was an overstuffed easy chair with a reading lamp next to it and an end table covered with papers. A wastepaper basket on the floor over-flowed with clipped newspapers and orange peels and plastic wrappers. A coffee mug with a half inch of moldy coffee sat on the floor. The chair and table were surrounded by the indescribable wall of stuff.

"I've only read about people like this," Elizabeth said after they'd surveyed the hopeless sea of junk.

Victoria sighed. "I'm sympathetic. He wanted to read all those newspapers and clip out items of interest. Those old curtains were probably too good to throw out. That bucket looks like something he picked up on the beach. Who knows when you might need something like that?"

"Don't talk like that, Gram, it's scary!"

Victoria looked around. "Hiram called from here."

"A pile of stuff probably fell on him, and he's buried underneath it."

"That's not amusing." Victoria frowned. "You probably never heard of the Collyer brothers in New York. That's how they died. Buried under stacks of newspapers that toppled over on them."

"Let's see if we can find the telephone." Elizabeth moved down a side path. "It's probably near his chair. Is there a table anywhere under all this?"

Victoria stood amid the heaps of stuff, scanning the walls, the ceiling, the windows she could see above the piles, the floor, where she could see it.

"A wire comes in through that window. If we can follow it under all this . . ." Victoria stopped. "Here's the phone. On a desk as you move toward the front of the house."

"How could he do any work at all? It's choked."

"He probably knew where everything was." Victoria gazed at the mess.

They stood in the small opening where the drop-leaf desk was piled with papers, and studied the mess around them. To one side of the desk was a computer, its fan humming. The lighted screen read FATAL ERROR, in white print on a blue screen.

Victoria stopped. "Something is spilled on the floor. Recently, I would guess." She pointed to a reddish-brown stain, still wet looking, which covered part of an unfolded newspaper and ran over onto a thin once-green carpet.

"Blood?" Elizabeth whispered.

"I don't know what it could be."

"You don't suppose . . ."

Victoria stood up straight. "We've got to get Casey here, right away."

CHAPTER 6

Police Chief Casey O'Neill was scooping corn out of a large galvanized trash can and flinging it to the ducks, geese, and swans that gathered around her when Victoria and Elizabeth pulled into the oyster-shell parking area in front of the police station. The geese hissed and nipped at one another and at the chief.

"Hey, Deputy, what's up?" Casey dropped the scoop back into the trash can and put the lid back on. "I'm about to go home for supper. Remember how I said those ducks made my police station look unprofessional?" She swept her arm around. "Well, they do, and now I figure to hell with it."

"I remember you also resolved to get the selectmen to install a lock on the station-house door."

"Can you imagine a twenty-four-hour, walk-in, unlocked police station anywhere else on earth?" Casey looked closely at Victoria. "What is it now, Victoria?"

"I think you need to see what we found."

"What did you find?"

"We've just come back from Jube Burkhardt's house."

"What were you doing there?"

"Looking for Hiram Pennybacker."

"I will never understand you Islanders," said Casey, shaking her head. "You walk into people's unlocked houses any old time, day or night." Casey, who came from off-Island, had been hired as police chief after Ben Norton, chief for thirty years, retired. "Let me make sure the station-house door is at least latched so ducks don't wander in. Get in the Bronco, Victoria. I'll be right with you."

"If you don't need me, I'm going home," Elizabeth said.

Victoria lifted her hand in acknowledgment. She took her blue baseball cap from her cloth bag, lifted herself into the passenger seat, and set the cap on her chair. She pulled down the sun visor to expose a small mirror. The cap was the one Casey had given her. Stitched on it in gold letters were the words WEST TISBURY POLICE, DEPUTY.

"I heard on the scanner how you found Jube Burkhardt's body, Victoria," Casey said as she climbed into the driver's seat. "What a shame, an accident like that."

"It was no accident. It couldn't have been."

"The Aquinnah police have no reason to suspect anything else."

"There's plenty of reason," Victoria insisted. "Jube knew his way down the cliffs. He wouldn't have fallen by accident." She paused. "Hiram got to him before he died. His last word was 'Sibyl.'"

"Who's Sibyl?" Casey backed out of the small parking lot and headed toward New Lane.

"I don't have any idea who Sibyl is. So far they're not taking Jube's death seriously."

"They certainly are. They're checking the fence to make sure it's secure."

"That's what I mean. He didn't fall from there. Now Hiram's missing. He called me from the old Mitchell place around three-thirty, almost three hours ago."

"What was he doing there?"

"I have no idea."

Casey slowed to let a flock of guinea fowl cross the New Lane in front of her.

"Is Sibyl one of his nieces?" she asked while they waited for the guineas to fluff their polka-dotted feathers, stretch their necks, cackle a series of metallic cries, and stare at the vehicle. Casey tapped the horn and the birds scurried to the side of the road.

"His older niece is Harriet and the younger is Linda. I don't know their middle names," Victoria said.

"Let's hope this is a wild goose chase." Casey made a wry face. "I think you may be oversensitive after finding Burkhardt's body."

To their left, every tall weed and shrub in Victoria's overgrown meadow glowed with golden light from the afternoon sun. Casey slowed to make a tight turn down the hill.

"Over the past week Burkhardt must have called me a dozen

times to complain about the motorcycle rally this weekend." At the bottom of the hill Casey made a sharp turn. "You'll have to help me find his place."

"How many motorcycles will there be altogether?"

"About five hundred. It's a combined Harley-Davidson/Indian rally. They hope to raise around twenty-thousand dollars for charity this weekend."

"They've been driving past my house for the past three or four days. I can't hear myself think. Isn't there some way they can make less noise and still have a good time?"

"The noise is part of the shtick," Casey said. "The town's noise ordinance is almost impossible to enforce. First you have to catch the offending biker."

"They'll ruin their ears," said Victoria. "Turn right here." She indicated a road that skirted the cove. "Why was Jube so upset about the motorcycles?"

"Noise. Bad guy image."

"Can't the selectmen do anything?"

"The selectmen support the bikers."

"That leaves you in an awkward spot, doesn't it?"

"If someone complains about noise, I'll have to track down the motorcycle, test it, and issue a citation."

"Do I call you to complain?"

"Maybe I should set you up in a folding chair by the side of the road with a clipboard and a decibel meter."

"I'll do it," Victoria said. "Turn left here."

"I don't know, Victoria. Twenty-thousand bucks for the hospital and the teen club will make a difference in their budgets. Burkhardt's feeling stems from personal matters. His older niece lives with one."

"Right," said Victoria, pointing.

"He told the gang at Alley's that his niece had gotten herself tattooed, a large rose on her shoulder, a clump of ivy twining around her ankle."

"Nose rings?" Victoria asked.

"What was Hiram doing here, anyway?" Casey asked, shifting down to steer around roots in the track.

"I don't know. If he was looking for something, you'll see why it might be difficult to find."

"Oh?" Casey had reached the open area. The sun was behind the house now and threw a long shadow across the dry grass. It was difficult to see more than the looming bulk of the house. Each blade of grass, each weed, each stone, was magnified by its own shadow, until the shadows were the reality.

"This is a setting for a spook movie." Casey slid out of the Bronco and surveyed the desolate-looking place. The house perched in the middle of the open flat, surrounded by dried grass, dead weeds, and low bushes.

Casey knocked on the door and entered. Victoria followed.

"Lord!"

"I know. It makes me feel tidy by comparison," Victoria said. "Keep going, bear right through the mess to get to his desk where the telephone is."

They edged their way between the stacks of paper.

"This is the stain I was telling you about." Victoria stopped and knelt down next to it, bracing herself against an unstable stack of papers and an old television set.

"Watch it!" said Casey, holding her hand out to keep the stack from toppling over onto Victoria.

The stain had turned from reddish-brown to brown. A half-dozen blue flies buzzed around it.

"I don't know how you do it, Victoria," Casey said, half-admiringly, getting to her feet. She held out her hand to help Victoria up. "We don't have a body, so we don't call the state cops. It doesn't look like cranberry juice or ketchup, and it smells a lot like blood."

"Where do you suppose Hiram is?" Victoria asked.

"I'll radio the police chief in Aquinnah. Hiram's probably at home. In the meantime, I'll contact Junior, have him check out this place. Don't touch anything, of course, that sort of thing." Casey made her way back through the shadowy house. Victoria followed closely. "I hate to think of the person who has to go through all this stuff. It'll take weeks."

"That computer is eerie with its 'Fatal Error' message," Victoria said. "Should we get Howland Atherton to check it out?"

"The drug-enforcement agent? He knows computers?"

Victoria nodded.

"I don't know, Victoria. I think it's premature to poke around in Burkhardt's computer."

"We need to find a killer," Victoria said.

"Nobody's been killed yet, as far as the police are concerned."

"But . . ." said Victoria, and snapped her mouth shut.

They returned to the Bronco and sat with both doors open while Casey radioed the Aquinnah police and her sergeant, Junior Norton.

While they'd been in the house, the sun had sunk lower. The sky was pink at the horizon and shaded up into darker and darker blue until it was deep purple above them. With the growing dusk, mosquitoes started to hum around them. Victoria swatted at her forehead, where one had landed.

"Have to be careful what I say over the radio." Casey unhooked the mike from her dashboard. "Everyone on the Island has a scanner, and they're all listening. Ouch!" She slapped at her upper arm.

"Jube probably didn't imagine his life was in danger, or he wouldn't have met the person where he did."

"What are you talking about?" Casey turned to Victoria. "Met who? Do you know something more you're not telling me?"

"There's a mosquito on your neck," Victoria said.

"You're suggesting someone pushed him, right?"

"He didn't fall from the cliffs."

"You think he was killed on the beach?"

Victoria said nothing.

Mosquitoes whined.

"Let the police worry about this, okay?" Casey was visibly upset. "Just because you're my deputy doesn't mean you can try to solve crimes all by yourself."

Victoria folded her arms across her chest, her mouth set. While they waited for Junior to arrive, she examined the outside of the darkening house, the sweep of bare grass. The shadow of a goldenrod spear stretched from the house to the barn across the open area. The barn door was ajar.

"What is it, Victoria?"

"There are no cars here. As I mentioned earlier."

"You wouldn't expect to see one. Hiram probably came and went, and Burkhardt must have taken his car to Aquinnah. Look in the glove compartment, Victoria. See if I have any bug spray in there."

"His car wasn't at the parking lot near the cliffs."

"You have to push the button hard," Casey said. "Maybe he met somebody and they went together. They'll find his car someplace obvious."

Victoria found the spray can and squirted some on her hands, rubbed her arms and neck, and passed the can to Casey. "No one would drive away and leave Jube without transportation."

"Jube's death was accidental, Victoria. Believe me. Those cliffs are treacherous."

Victoria glanced at Casey. "Not for a person who knows the Island."

"Okay, okay," said Casey.

"And where is Hiram?"

"We'll find Hiram at home or shopping or something."

Victoria pointed to long indentations in the grass, picked out by the low sun. "Someone wheeled a motorcycle into the barn."

"You're imagining things."

Victoria shook her head. "I'll look in the barn while you wait for Junior."

"Okay," said Casey, getting out of the vehicle and opening the door on Victoria's side.

Casey held her flashlight in one hand and swung the beam around. The line where the dry grass was mashed down in front of the barn showed clearly in Casey's flashlight beam. She opened the door. The hinges squealed. A barn swallow flew out and soared away, pointed wings and forked tail silhouetted against the sky.

The interior of the barn was inky black and smelled of ancient hay and long-gone horses. When the door was fully opened, twilight washed across the dusty wooden floor. The flashlight beam made a circle of brightness that blotted out everything else.

"Look there." Victoria pointed.

In the dust, showing clearly, was the track of a large motorcycle and a small splotch of oil.

CHAPTER 7

"Dojan." Chief Hawkbill reached up and put his hand on the tall man's shoulder. It was the morning after Dojan had called on Victoria. "Some good may come of your being sent to Washington."

Before he'd left Washington at the chief's command, Dojan had shed his silky city suit as if it were an old skin, and was now wearing his black mesh shirt and black jeans. He had tied his black scarf, printed with white skulls, around his neck. The frayed ends whipped in the brisk wind rising up the cliffs.

"You knew he would be killed," Dojan said.

The tribal chief watched the flock of eider ducks drifting on the rollers near the foot of the cliffs, far below. The surf crashed on the rocks. He could see the current eddying around Devil's Bridge, and hear, far below, the bell buoy that warned vessels to stay away.

"No," the chief said finally. "No. That possibility didn't enter my mind."

"But I came, and he was killed."

The chief turned from watching the water below them and looked up into Dojan's eyes.

"No one suspects you of killing him, Dojan. The police have called it an accident."

"Someone killed him."

The chief shrugged.

"Peter Little called me. He knew why I was sent to Washington. I flew here. And then Burkhardt was killed."

"I asked Peter to call you, Dojan, because we need to involve the federal government. Jubal Burkhardt's death has changed things, but only somewhat. He was threatening to hold up permits at the state level. I need you to push through environmental permits at the federal level."

"For the casino. You support a casino."

The chief held up his hand. "I am impartial, Dojan, I must be. You must be impartial, too."

Dojan shook his head, and his bone necklace rattled.

"This must be judged on the basis of what the majority of the tribe wants, Dojan, not on what you and Obed and I think is right for them."

Dojan shook his head.

"There are good reasons on both sides," the chief continued. "We must not allow a personal bias to prevent the tribe from making its decision. Mr. Burkhardt was trying to suborn the process for personal reasons. That was why I called you, even before he was found dead. We must apply for permits as if we planned to build a casino. We can say no later."

Dojan walked to the chain-link fence and peered over the edge. "Patience says the tribe doesn't need permits."

"Patience's claim of sovereign immunity is being tested in the courts. We can't predict what the court will decide." The chief stood next to Dojan and put his hands on the railing. "Perhaps the police have a point, Dojan. They say he fell by accident to his death."

"He didn't fall by accident," Dojan said.

"You don't think so?"

"Look down." Dojan pointed past the rosebush that marked the top of the sharp drop. "How many feet down?"

"A hundred fifty?" the chief said. "Two hundred?"

"A careless step, a fall." Dojan waved his arms, as if he, himself, were falling. "A killing height. He would tumble down the cliff. Broken bones. Scrapes. Bruises. Torn clothing. His body would rattle like ice in a plastic bag. Yet he could crawl up the cliff?"

"Perhaps a freak landing. A stone broke his fall."

"Was his body bruised? Was his clothing torn?"

"No, it was not," said the chief thoughtfully. "And Mr. Burkhardt was not a careless man."

"He wasn't pushed off the cliffs." Dojan turned his eyes on the chief.

The chief looked away from Dojan and gazed at the thin line of the Elizabeth Islands on the horizon. "You don't think someone pushed him from here?"

"Would he go near the edge of the cliff with someone he didn't trust?" Dojan shook his head.

"No. He wouldn't."

"A killer would be foolish to kill here. A fall is almost certain death. But a fall would not guarantee death."

"Let's go back to the tribal building so we can talk."

Dojan shook his head again. "I am going down to the beach at the foot of the cliffs. He was killed there." Below them, lacy scallops of foam washed high onto the shore, melted into the sand, and the next set of breakers washed up another scalloped line. "He was killed on the beach."

While Dojan was conferring with Chief Hawkbill, Casey and Victoria were sitting in the Bronco, which was parked in front of the West Tisbury police station.

"Aquinnah's not my territory." Casey glowered at Victoria's eagle-beak profile set in a mass of stubborn wrinkles. "The Aquinnah police chief stopped by Hiram's place. Doors unlocked, of course. This Island is a cop's nightmare. Anyway, he went inside, nothing seemed wrong. Nothing seemed out of place. The cat wasn't upset; it has a big bowl of cat chow and plenty of water."

"Was his van there?" Victoria asked. Her blue cap was perched on her head.

"No, which doesn't mean anything, one way or the other," Casey said. "He's down-Island, shopping. Or he's visiting a buddy in Vineyard Haven. Or he's gone to the bookstore in Edgartown. Maybe he's at Bert's getting a haircut. He's gone to the liquor store in Oak Bluffs."

"He doesn't drink."

"I can't do it, Victoria. If Hiram lived in West Tisbury, I could bend a rule or two, but I'm not taking you to Aquinnah, and that's final."

"All right." Victoria reached into the backseat of the Bronco for her stick. She opened the passenger door and slid off the seat onto the oyster-shell paving. Her back was rail-straight. She took off her cap and thrust it into her cloth bag, which she slid partway up her arm.

"Where are you going, Victoria? I'll drive you home." Casey leaned out the window of the Bronco.

"No thank you. I'm taking myself to Gay Head or Aquinnah or whatever they're calling it now." She marched around the back of the Bronco, over the oyster shells, past the ducks that had settled in the shade of the police vehicle, stopped at the side of the road, and stuck out her thumb.

Casey dropped her head on her arms. Her coppery hair fell over the steering wheel. "When is she going to start acting her age?" she muttered. She wrenched open the driver's door and got out in time to see a green pickup truck pull off the road with a squeal of brakes. The driver got out, took off his cap to Victoria, who was smiling up at him. He reached into the back of the truck and lifted out a black milk crate, helped Victoria step up onto the crate and into the passenger seat, and drove off in a cloud of dust.

"Lord," said Casey, as the truck geared up and sped past the millpond. "I ought to give him a speeding ticket just because."

"You sure you don't want me to wait, Mrs. Trumbull?" The driver set down the milk crate and helped Victoria out. He had stopped by the side of the road where tour buses parked for visitors to view the cliffs.

"I'll be fine. Thank you for the ride, Ira. Give my regards to your father."

It had been Asa Bodman's son Ira who had picked up Victoria by the police station. He was going as far as Seven Gates, he told her, but when she said she wanted to go to Gay Head, he had detoured the thirteen miles to take her there.

Ira moved off slowly, and Victoria watched him drive around the circle to where it rejoined the main road. He returned her wave before he disappeared from sight.

The parking area was utterly different from what it had been two nights before. Today the area was packed with cars and people. The Aquinnah patrolman was holding up traffic for people to cross the road to the short flight of steps that led toward the top of the cliffs. People were every possible age and shape, dressed in everything from flowing long skirts to embarrassingly small bathing suits. Most were wearing sunglasses, including the scads of small children that hung from parents' hands.

Victoria fell in line behind a family, two harried young parents with three small children. One held his father's middle finger with an obviously sticky hand while sucking his thumb, the other dragged a woebegone teddy bear by its ears. The father shook loose the sticky paw long enough to lift a baby stroller up the steps. The sleeping baby's head lolled.

"Would you like a hand, too?" he asked Victoria, good-naturedly.

"No, thank you. You have your hands full." She grasped the iron railing tightly as she went up the concrete steps. At the top there were a dozen or more small shacks selling souvenirs—T-shirts and Indian headdresses and caps and tomahawks and postcards. Beyond the lines of shacks a restaurant overlooked Vineyard Sound to the north, the ocean to the south. She paused in front of the restaurant to catch her breath, and then continued up the hill to the fenced-in place where she and Elizabeth had stood in the fog two nights before.

By day, in bright sunlight with children in gay colors shouting and laughing, Victoria had a difficult time imagining anything had ever seemed sinister. What was she doing here? she wondered. She felt as though she'd been foolishly stubborn, rather than bravely determined, in telling Casey she was going alone to Aquinnah.

To her right, the Gay Head light sent its red and white rays far above her, pallid in the strong sunlight. She stood next to a five- or six-year-old boy with short hair and thick glasses who was standing on tiptoe beside the chain-link fence.

"Do you see anything?" Victoria asked him, bending down so she could match his height.

"Yeth," he said. "Boath."

He was right. The sound was speckled with white sails. Powerboats streamed rooster tails of spray behind them, fishing boats headed toward Georges Bank to set their nets, windsurfers and jet skis dodged each other. Victoria looked up and saw, high in the sky, a man or boy in a black bikini hanging from a parasail. She traced the line from the boy in the sky down to a small boat.

She scanned the slope below that led to the top of the sheer cliff. She could see the rosebush, an undistinguished plant that clung to the edge of the cliff. From here, in daylight, she could see that the ground around the bush was scratched up. That was where Jube Burkhardt had stopped in his death throes. That was where Hiram and the stretcher-bearers from the fire department had disturbed the thin soil on top of the clay.

"Mrs. Trumbull, ma'am."

Victoria turned to see a uniformed policeman standing behind her. His shoulder patch read AQUINNAH POLICE DEPARTMENT.

"I suppose Chief O'Neill sent you?" Victoria said with some asperity.

"No, ma'am. My chief did. Chief O'Neill called him. Asked us to extend whatever reciprocal privileges we could to her deputy. That's you."

Victoria nodded and looked in her bag to make sure her baseball cap was still there.

"Patrolman VanDyke, at your service, ma'am."

The small boy at the fence stared at the patrolman, his beaky nose, dark skin, straight back. The boy's eyes were huge behind his glasses. "Are you a real Indian?"

"Yes, sir." Officer VanDyke saluted the boy, who saluted back with a cupped hand and a grin that showed missing teeth.

"Are you Patience's younger brother?" Victoria looked up into his gray eyes.

"Her first cousin, Obed's brother. How can I help?"

"I want to go to the base of the cliffs. I thought I could climb down, but it's higher than I remembered."

"No problem," said the patrolman. "We'll drive down my grandmother's road onto the beach."

He offered his arm and she took it. Together they walked through the crowd of gaping tourists that parted to let them pass. The patrol car was at the foot of the steps, and Officer VanDyke opened the passenger door for Victoria, waited for her to get in, slammed the door shut, and went around to his side. He nodded at the policeman who was directing pedestrians, waited until everyone had crossed, then drove slowly around the circle. Instead of turning onto South Road, he turned off onto Lighthouse Road.

The day was sparkling bright with high puffy clouds. The sun reflected off masses of poison ivy that festooned the telephone poles, and glinted on bayberry and wild rose leaves. Gemlike crystals in the sand along the roadside glittered as they passed.

"I suppose I'm being foolish," Victoria said.

"Not at all, ma'am. My chief said all of us could learn a thing or two from you."

Victoria sat back, a faint smile wrinkling her face. She reached into her bag, brought out her blue cap, and set it on her head again.

They had turned off onto a sandy road that curved around low bluffs and dunes. The Gay Head light swung around over their heads, red, white, red, white. The cliffs rose up on either side. Gulls soared above them. The surf boomed louder, echoing against the cliff walls. VanDyke turned left, and suddenly they were on the beach. Victoria could see the Elizabeth Islands in the distance. The individual sailboats she had viewed from the high cliffs now seemed an almost solid line of white.

"You want to go to the base of the cliffs, ma'am? I can drive along the beach."

"Let's stop about a quarter mile short of the overlook and walk from there. That is, if you don't mind." She looked at him. How handsome he and his fisherman brother were, she thought. The patrolman was staring straight ahead. His nose, not quite as large as hers, was lifted slightly.

"No, ma'am. Don't mind at all."

The two walked slowly along the base of the cliffs. Victoria zigzagged from the water to the cliffs, turning over clumps of seaweed, flipping stones, prying up pieces of driftwood with her lilac-wood stick. The patrolman walked slowly in a straight line, hands behind his back.

Occasionally she bent down, picked something up, and put it in her cloth bag.

"Look here," she said to the patrolman. He strode over to her. "Footprints. Bare feet."

"Yes, ma'am. A lot of people come here to swim."

"This is different from somebody coming for a dip or to sunbathe." She pointed with her stick. "The footprints go from the cliffs to the water, then disappear. Look ahead, you can see them again where they haven't been washed away."

"Yes, ma'am. A big man. Feet my size or larger."

Victoria scanned the cliffs. "It looks as though he came down that gully. That's where the prints start."

The patrolman put both hands on his belt, and walked next to Victoria.

They had almost reached the base of the overlook, the place where Burkhardt must have started his climb. The footprints continued ahead of them.

"I wonder where he can be?" Victoria could see no one.

"Could be a tribal member. We can be hard to see if we want." He grinned and Victoria smiled back.

She heard the rattle of falling stones, and stepped back quickly. A shower of baseball-size cobbles hit the sand and fanned out in front of them. Officer VanDyke stepped between Victoria and the cliff, put his hand on his belt, and looked up. Victoria shaded her eyes to search for the source of the rocks. The rocks seemed to have come from partway up the cliff.

Someone laughed, and the laughter echoed against the steep cliff face.

CHAPTER 8

The echo of the laugh died out, and Dojan, camouflaged by the brown and orange and red clay of the cliff, leaped from a shadowy recess onto the sand.

He greeted Victoria with a gap-toothed grin. "My friend!"

Victoria frowned. "You didn't need to frighten us."

"Whaddaya say, Dojan!" The patrolman held up his hand.

"Not much, Malachi!" Dojan replied, slapping his hand against VanDyke's.

"Thought you were in Washington," the patrolman said.

Dojan turned his head and peered at the line of islands to the northwest.

VanDyke laughed. "Hear you're living on a yacht on the Potomac River. The first Indian member of the exclusive Washington Yacht Club. I hear they're accepting women members, too. What's the world coming to?"

Dojan growled.

VanDyke laughed again.

"Why don't you sit over there on that flat rock," Victoria ordered the patrolman. "Dojan and I need to talk."

The surf crested and broke onto the rocks, no longer a steady rumble, but a distinct roar, crash, and swish.

Dojan said, when they were out of the patrolman's hearing, "Somebody killed him."

"Of course someone killed him."

"You think somebody pushed him off the cliff?"

"What do you think?" Victoria asked.

Dojan shook his head, and the string of bones around his neck rattled. "He was killed down here."

Victoria nodded. "We need to find a weapon. A rock, I suppose." She looked around the beach, which was paved with cobbles. "A rock big enough to bash in his skull, but small enough so someone could hold it in one hand."

"Maybe he threw the rock into the ocean," Dojan said. "Maybe the tide came in and washed it clean."

"Maybe, but who knows. We may find something." They walked slowly away from the patrolman, who sat on the rock where Victoria had told him to sit. Dojan walked with his hands behind him, his back bent. Victoria continued her back-and-forth search, occasionally looking up the side of the cliff.

"See, Dojan, this is where he began his climb."

Dojan came over to her and looked up the gully in the steep cliff. They could see marks in the naturally eroded clay, marks of fingers clutching for rough spots to pull a person up. A long smooth stretch that might have been caused by a stomach sliding up the cliff. They could see an occasional splotch of dark color that contrasted with the clay. As they looked higher, they could see where tufts of grass had apparently been grabbed for a handhold, flattened places where a foot must have rested.

Starting from the base of the cliffs above the high tide mark, they combed the beach in a widening semicircle.

"Here, Dojan. This would be about the right size." Victoria pointed with her stick to a rounded cobble about the size and shape of a baseball.

"No." Dojan shook his head. "Must be bigger. Rougher."

"I'm taking it with us." She picked it up, and set down her cloth bag so she could take notes. They circled, collecting stones. Dojan took the cloth bag, which had become quite heavy. They found a dozen likely cobbles before they went back to where Patrolman VanDyke sat, piling sand into a castle. He had set small stones around the castle's turrets, a flag of Irish moss on a tower. A wave crashed. The swash raced toward his castle and filled the moat with foam and hopping sand fleas.

His radio crackled, and VanDyke unsnapped it from his belt and answered. After he signed off, he asked, "Where's your van, Dojan?"

"Tribal Headquarters."

"Okay if I take you and Mrs. Trumbull there and leave you? I got to respond to a call. Can you get her home?"

Dojan held up his hand, palm out. "I will drive my friend home after we report to Chief Hawkbill."

Malachi dropped them off at headquarters, and the two went inside to the chief's office. The chief was dozing at his desk, his hands clasped in front of him, his head nodding. Behind him Victoria could see the sweep of the Atlantic Ocean, an unbroken steel blue.

The chief sat up with a jerk, smacked his lips together, and smiled sheepishly. "This paperwork is an ideal excuse for a nap," he said. He stood up and held out both hands to Victoria, who took them in hers. "I thought you had run away, Dojan. Gone to the beach with your girlfriend?" The chief smiled. "The police have closed the case, you know."

"It was no accident," Dojan said.

"Yes. Yes, certainly. We agree." The chief shrugged.

"Suppose we were to find a weapon," Victoria asked. "Would the police reopen the investigation?"

Chief Hawkbill looked from Victoria to Dojan and back to Victoria. "Let us see your weapon. Please sit, Victoria Trumbull. And you, Dojan Minnowfish."

Dojan hefted Victoria's cloth bag onto the chief's desk with a thunk of rock against varnished wood.

Victoria pulled her chair close to the desk.

"What have we here?" the chief asked.

"We don't want to scratch the finish on your desk," said Victoria.

The chief pointed. "Dojan, please hand me that copy of the *Enquirer*." He moved what he'd been working on from his desk to a table behind him and spread the newspaper out.

Victoria pulled out one rock after another until they covered the desk. "One of these may have been the murder weapon," she said.

The chief looked over the top of his thick glasses. "So the three of us will look them over carefully for hair and blood," he said. "If we identify any such thing, we will call the Aquinnah police."

Victoria's eyes were bright and she nodded.

"Not at all likely," the chief said. "Have you identified them in some way?"

Victoria showed him her notebook with its sketch maps. Chief Hawkbill picked up one of the rocks and turned it over, scattering damp sand on the newspaper. "Not likely, Mrs. Trumbull," he repeated.

Victoria could hear the distant sound of breakers on the South Shore, the cry of a hawk, the mewling of gulls.

The chief glanced out the window. "The wind is dying down. It's going to be hot this afternoon." He opened his desk drawer and gave Victoria a large magnifying glass.

"What's this!" Victoria had found some hairlike stuff clinging to the seventh or eighth rock she examined.

"Seaweed," Dojan said. "Algae."

She set the rock aside and continued her search.

"Ah!" She handed another rock to the chief, pointing to a brown stain on it.

The chief looked it over carefully. "That is an iron stain. That rust-red color is common on the Aquinnah beach and cliffs." He shook his head. "You have gone to a great deal of effort in vain. It is most unlikely that two amateurs—wise and clever amateurs, it's true," he looked over his glasses at them—"would find a rock that happens to show evidence of murder. We don't know for a certainty that Mr. Burkhardt was killed on the beach. Nor do we know it was a rock that killed him." He sighed. "The police, even believing his death to be an accident, have been over that beach with the same thought, looking for anything he might have fallen onto that would have killed him."

"It's worth looking," Victoria said, stubbornly.

"Yes, it is worth looking. But the tide has been in, the tide has been out, four or five times in the two days since Mr. Burkhardt was killed. You will only find evidence remaining on a weapon if it was left above the high tide line." The chief peered at them. "A murder that may not be a murder, on a beach that may not have been the site, with a weapon that may or may not have been left at the scene. Why wouldn't the killer use the simple expedient of tossing the weapon into the ocean? Surely he wouldn't drop it where you, Victoria Trumbull, and you, Dojan Minnowfish, would find it?"

They continued to look at the rocks, but found nothing more than hairlike seaweed and bloodlike iron stains.

The chief sat back when they had finished. "If I were planning a killing, I would not take a chance on finding a deadly beach cobble. Unless, of course, this was a spur-of-the-moment killing."

"It wasn't." Victoria put the stones back in her cloth bag. "Jube planned to meet someone on the beach."

"In that case, if it were me," the chief spread his chunky hand on his chest, "I would probably carry something with me, a tire iron comes to mind, or a handheld sledgehammer, something small with considerable weight."

"Wouldn't it be obvious to Jube that the person was carrying something suspicious?" Victoria asked.

"Not necessarily. The loose clothing we affect today conceals everything. Excess weight, for example." He patted his own gut, cloaked in a brilliantly flowered Hawaiian shirt. "Dojan, can you take a small boat off the beach?"

"On a calm day."

"The wind has shifted," Victoria said, looking out the window at the tall cedars that were no longer swaying.

"Will you be able to see bottom?" asked the chief.

Dojan shrugged. "It is shallow as far as a man could throw a hammer, not even a fathom. The water is clear."

"Who has a dinghy we can use?" Victoria turned from Dojan to the chief.

Dojan stood. "Obed has an inflatable."

The chief lifted the phone and dialed. When he finished speaking, he set the phone down again and turned to Dojan. "Cell phones are a modern miracle. Obed is out on his boat now. He will bring his dinghy ashore and meet you near his grandmother's house."

Dojan grunted.

"And you, Victoria Trumbull, are you willing to stay onshore to keep Dojan in a straight line?"

Victoria nodded.

Twenty minutes later Dojan parked his van at the edge of Trudy

VanDyke's property, and they waited for Obed, who rowed ashore in his dinghy from his anchored fishing boat.

"I got nothing better to do," Obed said. "The fish aren't biting. Almost a slick calm out there now."

The waves now lapped on the shore, gentle swishes that hissed softly. A sandpiper scurried along the edge of the swash, dipping its long beak into the sand.

After Dojan showed Victoria where to stand, Obed shoved the rubber inflatable off the beach and took the oars. Victoria leaned on her stick and watched for signals. Dojan peered down into the water. Obed rowed out, fifty feet, Victoria guessed. Then they turned toward her. Each time they came in close to the beach, Dojan signaled Victoria, who moved three paces down the line. Her back ached from standing and shuffling along. When she reached a large rock, she was glad to sit. The water was so calm she could hear every word Dojan said to Obed. "Go left." "Stop." "Keep going."

The afternoon wore on. Three times Dojan dived to retrieve some object he'd seen. He was still wearing his mesh shirt and black jeans. Each time, the object turned out to be a false lead. The sun settled to Victoria's left. She realized she hadn't had lunch, and reached into her cloth bag for the candy bar she'd bought at Alley's when she'd cashed a ten-dollar check this morning.

"Stop," Dojan ordered for the fourth time.

Victoria looked up.

"My friend," he called out to her. "We have found something this time."

Victoria crumpled up the candy wrapper and put it in her bag, then drew out her notebook and pen.

Dojan again catapulted himself out of the dinghy with a splash. He stood, chest-high in the water, and wiped his hand across his face. Then he bent over in a surface dive, head and shoulders underwater, feet in the air, and resurfaced seconds later brandishing a tool. The tool had a foot-long handle that ended in a thick curved iron rod with a flat spadelike head.

Victoria shaded her eyes against the glare coming off the water. "That's a weeding hook," she called out. "Looks like a new one. I have a weeder just like that."

"Want to keep looking?" Obed said to Dojan.

Dojan shook his head, spraying water from his wet hair like a black dog. He hefted the heavy tool from one hand to the other as he waded toward shore, his clothes dripping water.

"Don't get your fingerprints on it!" Victoria called.

Dojan grunted, and held the tool by the leather thong that threaded through the handle.

"You could do some serious damage with that thing," Obed said to Victoria.

"It's certainly death on weeds," said Victoria.

CHAPTER 9

Chief Hawkbill had already closed his office door and was heading for the parking lot when Victoria and Dojan arrived.

Victoria held up the weeding hook by its rawhide thong.

"What have we here, Victoria Trumbull?" The chief reopened his door, turned on the lights, offered Victoria a chair, and took his own seat behind his desk. Dojan stood, water still trickling from his clothes and hair, and dripping onto the rug.

"I don't suppose there'll be any fingerprints?" Victoria handed him the lethal-looking weapon. The chief took a clean handkerchief out of his pocket and held the tool gingerly.

"The forensic scientists can do miracles with microscopic evidence," he said. "Yes, this should go to the police." He peered over his glasses at Dojan, then at Victoria, whose face was pinkly sunburned. "I will recommend to the Aquinnah police that they keep this as possible evidence."

"It's more than possible evidence," Victoria said. "There's no reason for a nice shiny garden tool to end up in Vineyard Sound. I'm sure they can match Jube Burkhardt's injuries with the curve of the hook."

Chief Hawkbill nodded. "Although the police have closed the case, their minds are sometimes open."

The following afternoon, Victoria was writing at the cookroom table, glancing out the window occasionally. Chief Hawkbill had called earlier to say he had given the weeding hook to the Aquinnah police, and would call when he had information.

In the meantime, Victoria wondered, where was Hiram? And where was his friend Tad? Had Tad killed Jube and then run off with Hiram? She was sure the stain on Jube's floor was blood, but whose?

A person's? Hiram's? It was too fresh for Jube's. And where was Jube Burkhardt's car?

The hazy afternoon light touched the goldenrod and Queen Anne's lace, the tall grass, the lacy yellow fern of the asparagus bed. Everything shimmered with a dusting of soft gold. She could see the old Agricultural Society Hall next to the church, and the new library this side of it.

Jube Burkhardt had met his killer on the beach below the cliffs. Of that, she was sure. If she had planned to kill someone, she thought, she'd have suggested they first meet someplace convenient to both of them, then go together in one car. In that way, she wouldn't need to worry about two cars being at the scene of the crime. But where would she leave a car if she were the killer? Somewhere between Jube's house and Gay Head. Victoria had trouble calling Aquinnah any name other than the one she'd known all her life, Gay Head, named for the brightly colored clay of the headland.

She continued to stare out at the golden rooftops. The trees had grown, of course. Maley's Gallery was new, only forty years old or thereabouts, but his house was old. Next to Maley's were three or four other houses, hidden, now, by trees.

Where would Jube have met his killer? A place where both would get into one car to drive up to Gay Head. The Ag Hall parking area would be too public, if the killer expected Burkhardt's car to be left behind. The hiding place would have to be where a car could remain for a week or two weeks or even a month without anyone paying much attention to it. Someplace the police were not likely to check regularly. A place that wouldn't make Jube Burkhardt suspicious if the killer were to suggest meeting there.

From where she sat, Victoria could see the roof of the garage across from the Ag Hall. Eighty years ago, the garage had been a blacksmith shop. She used to go there with her grandfather to have their horse Dolly shod.

The garage.

She got to her feet, holding the arms of her chair.

"Elizabeth," she called to her granddaughter, who was putting books away in the living room.

"Yes, Gram?"

"I know where Jube Burkhardt's car is."

Elizabeth set the books she was holding onto the coffee table. "Where?"

"At the old blacksmith shop. Tiasquam Repairs. There's that area in back where people leave cars to be worked on, or summer people store them until they return from vacation."

"But why would Burkhardt leave his car there?"

"I imagine the killer told Jube he needed to leave his own car for some work, an oil change, something simple like that. He'd have said, 'No point in taking two cars all the way to Aquinnah, besides my car needs some work.' After he killed Jube, he drove Jube's car to the lot and picked up his own."

"His or her," Elizabeth said. "Okay, Gram, let's go. Do you know what kind of car Burkhardt drove?"

Victoria had already started out the door. "He drove a red Volvo 1985." She gathered up her walking stick from the entry, marched down the steps ahead of Elizabeth, and got into the car.

They drove past the police station and the millpond, and slowed on Brandy Brow. Joe and the usual gang were sitting on the porch of Alley's store. Taffy barked from the driver's seat of Joe's truck as they passed. Sarah waved.

"Don't those guys ever work?" asked Elizabeth.

Victoria looked at her watch. "It's after five."

They turned in at the gas station and went down a bumpy dirt road to the garage, which was closed for the day. Behind the garage, a field of stored cars waited for owners to claim them. "There must be two dozen red Volvos here," Elizabeth said in dismay. "We'll never be able to single his car out, even if it is here."

"We can eliminate any that have grass growing up around their tires. Also, any that have out-of-state license plates."

After they had paced up and down the weedy aisles between cars, Elizabeth said, "We're down to three red Volvos."

"This one seems promising," Victoria said. "Cardboard cartons, a couple of milk crates full of papers, and a couple of bags full of soda cans." She moved to another car. "This one has a soccer ball, a child's soccer shirt, candy wrappers, a copy of *Mad Magazine*, a doll." Victoria crossed it off her list.

"Not this one either," Elizabeth said.

Victoria cupped her hands against the windshield to look in. She set in motion a plastic grass-skirted hula dancer stuck to the dashboard with a suction cup. Next to the dancer were wadded-up tissues with lipstick smears.

"Back to the first of the three." Victoria strode through the long grass to the car, opened the passenger door, and sat on the stained and worn seat.

"Should we be doing this?" Elizabeth looked around behind them, as if she expected someone to stop them.

Victoria opened the glove compartment. "Of course we should." She lifted out a handful of papers, paper napkins, plastic ketchup containers, and white plastic spoons. She sorted through them and put everything back except an envelope from the Vineyard Insurance Agency. She opened the envelope and examined the policy. "It's made out to Jubal M. Burkhardt."

"Can we leave now?" Elizabeth asked.

Victoria nodded. "We'll stop at the police station and report to Casey."

Casey was coming down the steps as they parked in front of the station. She walked over to the passenger side, and Victoria rolled down the window.

"Good job, Deputy," Casey said after Victoria told her about finding Jube's car. "I'll notify his nieces and the Aquinnah police."

Elizabeth started to say something, but Victoria put her hand on her granddaughter's knees. Elizabeth looked at her, surprised. Victoria had arranged her face into a warning, and Elizabeth stopped in midsentence.

As they pulled away from the police station, Elizabeth said, "Why did you stop me, Gram? I wanted to tell the chief that Dojan and you found the weapon."

"She'll know soon enough. Before they declare Jube's house a crime scene, we need to look around again. We're missing something."

"You can't do that, Gram. It's trespassing or tampering with evidence or something."

"It's not tampering with evidence," Victoria said. "The police have closed the case. Accidental death. Will you drive me there, or shall I walk?"

"I'll drive you," Elizabeth muttered. She backed out of the parking spot, oyster shells crunching beneath her tires, and retraced the route to Burkhardt's house.

"We've got to find Hiram," Victoria said. "And the key to finding him is in that house."

The haze thickened as they drove toward Burkhardt's place. They reached the open grassy area, where his house stood, desolate in the tall grass, and pulled up next to the barn.

A clammy fog was sifting in from the ocean, bringing with it the sulfurous smell of tidal flats and the iodine smell of seaweed. The windshield was beaded with droplets of mist. Elizabeth put the top back up on her convertible while Victoria walked over to the barn. The door was ajar, the way it had been when she had first seen the motorcycle tracks the day before. She pushed the door open. The hinges shrieked.

A seagull on the roof of the house raised its wings, opened its bill, and echoed the sound of the door, a long drawn-out mournful cry followed by a series of short calls. It lifted off the roof, followed by six other gulls, ghostly forms that dissolved along with their cries into the thin fog.

The surf rumbled on the other side of the barrier bar. A fish splashed in the pond. When she opened the barn door, something rushed by her head noiselessly. She had disturbed a barn owl. There were not many places left on the Island where barn owls could nest.

She looked down at the floor. There, in the dust, was a second set of motorcycle tracks, scuffed over by at least two, possibly three, sets of boot prints.

"What do you make of that?" Victoria said to Elizabeth, who had come up behind her. "These marks were made sometime after Casey and I were here yesterday afternoon."

"Maybe Junior Norton made the prints when he came to check out the stain on the floor?"

Victoria shook her head. "He came in the police car."

"Maybe Burkhardt's niece and her biker friend?"

"I don't know." Victoria left the barn door ajar so the owl could return. "Let's go through the house again. There must be a clue as to Hiram's whereabouts somewhere in there."

As they walked across the dry grass, there was an explosive *qwawk* and a rush of wings. A large blue-gray bird materialized out of the mist and flew low over them toward the pond.

Elizabeth let out a startled cry.

"Night heron," Victoria said.

"This place is bad enough in bright sun."

"Wait out here if you want while I go inside."

"I'm sticking with you." Elizabeth trailed after her grandmother, who had opened the entry door and was already inside Burkhardt's house.

Elizabeth sniffed. "Stinks in here. How could he stand it?"

"It's the humidity," Victoria said. "It brings out mildew."

Something swished past them with small clicking sounds, almost touching Elizabeth's hair. She screamed.

Victoria looked around in alarm, then laughed. "A bat. That accounts for the smell. Let's start at his computer and work back toward the entry." They threaded their way down the narrow aisle between stacks of Burkhardt's keepsakes to his desk and table, piled with papers and books. The stain, now dark brown, had a chalk mark around it.

"I guess Junior took a sample?" Elizabeth said.

Victoria stopped abruptly and Elizabeth bumped into her. "Something isn't right."

"Nothing is right," Elizabeth said. "It's getting dark. Let's get Casey. We won't find Hiram this way."

"It's the computer," Victoria said. "When we were last here, it read 'Fatal Error' in white letters on a blue background. I remember because it seemed so macabre. Now it's blank."

"No wonder. The CPU is gone."

"CPU?" Victoria turned to her granddaughter.

"The central processing unit, the box the monitor sits on. It has the hard drive in it. It's gone."

CHAPTER 10

"What are you talking about?" asked Victoria.

"The guts of the computer. The hard drive contains everything."

"Perhaps Howland Atherton took it away. I asked Casey to have him look at the computer, but she didn't."

"Maybe she changed her mind," said Elizabeth.

"If Howland were to take just that box, he wouldn't need the monitor or keyboard, would he?"

"He wouldn't need these particular ones," said Elizabeth, pointing to the blank screen and the keyboard. "He could borrow someone else's to read the files."

"I'm sure he'd have said something to me if he'd taken it." Victoria studied the desk where the base had been. "Could the unit be carried on a motorcycle?"

Elizabeth lifted her shoulders. "I guess so, although it would be awkward. Maybe Junior Norton took it?"

"Casey's sergeant wouldn't have taken something without informing her. And Casey would have told me." Victoria shook her head. "We'd better get busy. We don't have much time before dark."

She started a systematic search, for what, she wasn't sure. Any clue to Hiram's whereabouts. Had he left something here? She looked in places where she herself might have left something, next to the telephone book, by the dictionary, beside a picture. Before it became any darker, she would need to go down the aisles of Jube's collections, see if she could find any trace of Hiram. She didn't want to go upstairs to the second floor, and she certainly didn't want to draw attention by turning on lights.

"He has a cordless phone," Elizabeth said, lifting the instrument out of its cradle. "*Phew!* The smell is really getting to me." She fanned her hand in front of her face. "I bet he programmed numbers into the phone." She slid a panel on the back of the instrument and found a list of names.

Victoria stopped her search briefly to look.

"The first two are the governor's office and the Environmental Protection Agency," said Elizabeth. "A couple of other numbers like MIT and Wampanoag headquarters."

Victoria continued her search, moving away from the computer table, examining items that larded the stacks.

"One is for Harley. Any idea who that might be?" asked Elizabeth.

"Perhaps the elder niece, Harriet. The one who lives with the motorcyclist."

"I suppose he rides a Harley. Cute." Elizabeth made a face. "The next one is Linda. The other niece?"

"The younger." Victoria stood with arms crossed.

"Here's one for Bugs."

"I have no idea what that would be." Victoria scanned the piles on either side of her, then retraced her steps down one of the side passages.

"I'm going to call." Elizabeth pressed a number.

Victoria started to tell her not to, when someone answered. She could hear, even across the room, a man's raspy voice, "Bugs here."

Elizabeth hung up quickly.

"That was *not* a good idea," Victoria said. "What did you hope to learn from that?"

"I don't know. He sounded like something out of a 1940s gangster movie."

The phone rang. They looked at each other.

"Don't answer," said Victoria, but Elizabeth had already picked up the phone. Before she answered, the voice on the other end said, loud enough for Victoria to hear, "What do you want, Burkhardt? Better be important."

"I'm sorry," Elizabeth said in a small voice. "I must have dialed the wrong number."

"Wait a minute, lady. I dialed star sixty-nine, and it rang Burkhardt's number. You want to explain?"

"I'm sorry," she murmured, and hung up.

"Well," said Victoria. "Well, well. That was odd."

"That was stupid of me." Elizabeth blotted her forehead with a paper towel she'd taken from her pocket.

Victoria moved down the side passage. She brushed against a tall stack and it toppled over, knocking her down.

"Gram, are you okay?"

"Yes. Help me out of this mess."

Elizabeth moved an old typewriter case off Victoria's legs. A flattened cardboard box. Used gift-wrapping paper, card still attached. Burned-out lightbulbs, seed packets.

She moved a wire basket and a flyswatter and a mousetrap with a mummified mouse and copies of the town report for 1975 and an ancient Sears Roebuck catalog.

Victoria lifted her arm. "Give me your hand so I can stand up without anything else falling onto me." Elizabeth helped her to her feet.

The telephone rang. They looked at each other.

Victoria frowned. "This time, don't answer."

The phone continued to ring. Neither Victoria nor Elizabeth moved until it stopped after a dozen rings.

Somewhere in the house something shifted, and there was the sound of a heavy object falling.

"What was that?" Elizabeth stood still. "Let's get out of here. Now." She started back down the narrow aisle between the stacks of junk. "You didn't get hurt when that stuff fell on you?"

"Of course not. I'm fine. But I'd like to know what made that noise."

"We've got to get out of here before it gets darker."

The diffuse light coming through the dusty windows gave the shadows an undefined quality. The stacks of rubbish and papers began to blend together. Even to Victoria it was as if they were morphing into a gray dough.

The bat circled again, swished low, swooped high, making its eerie clicking noise.

Once they were outside, Victoria looked back at the house. The mist gave the low sun a sickly green hue. Dusk had reduced colors to shades of gray. The cedar trees across the cove were a dark gray-green. The grasses, dripping with condensation, were a grayish tan. The house itself was almost black. It must have been a lonely place for a man living by himself with nothing but his computer and piles of stuff that he might find a use for someday.

"Where do you suppose the computer is?" Victoria turned toward the house. "I've got to go back and make one more attempt to find it." She started toward the kitchen door.

Elizabeth caught her grandmother's sleeve. "No way!"

As Victoria turned to reply, she saw flashing blue lights jouncing along the track that led through the woods. The police Bronco pulled up next to Elizabeth's car.

"I might have known." Casey leaned out her window.

Victoria walked over to the passenger side. "What are you doing here?"

"I got an anonymous call from a guy who said there was an intruder at Burkhardt's place. What are *you* doing here?"

"Did he have a raspy voice?" Elizabeth asked.

Casey stepped out of the Bronco, and shifted her belt with gun, radio, and handcuffs to a more comfortable position.

"Yes, he had a raspy voice. You're trespassing, you know that."

"Nonsense. The door wasn't locked."

"Get in the Bronco, Victoria."

"I'll meet you back at the house," Elizabeth said.

The road through the woods was dark now. The Bronco's headlights magnified every rock and root and pothole.

Casey listened while Victoria told her about the missing computer and the phone call.

"You simply must not handle evidence that way," Casey said when Victoria finished.

"There was no reason to think I was handling any evidence," Victoria replied. "You police are calling his death an accident."

"Not anymore, Victoria. The Aquinnah police chief called me. That wicked hook you guys found matches the wound on Burkhardt's skull. They've reopened the case." Casey steered around a large pothole. "The state police are now treating Burkhardt's death as murder."

CHAPTER 11

Victoria walked to the police station the next morning to hear Casey's explanation of why the Aquinnah police had changed their minds about Jube Burkhardt's death. When she arrived, Casey was on the radio with Junior Norton.

"Mrs. Summerville, Chief," said Junior. "She's complaining about motorcyclists camping in her pasture."

"I'll check on Mrs. S., Junior. Where are you now?"

"Behind Maley's. Got more bikers camping out here. I'll make sure they've got sanitary facilities and water."

"Roger." Casey hung up the mike. "I'll be glad when this rally is over. The bikers aren't as bad as they want us to think, but there are five hundred of them. That's an awful lot for the Island to absorb."

"You know where Mrs. Summerville lives, don't you?" Victoria asked.

"Somewhere near that split oak in North Tisbury?"

"On the road branching off to the left. I'll show you."

"Let's go, then."

Victoria climbed into her seat in the Bronco, and Casey took off toward North Tisbury. She had slowed to negotiate the sharp curve by the cemetery, when a string of seven motorcycles roared up behind them and passed, cutting across the solid line in the middle of the road. Casey swerved onto the grass to their right as a car approached from the other direction. The bikers cut sharply in front of the police vehicle as the driver of the oncoming car went off the road with a squeal of brakes.

"You all right, sir?" Casey shouted to the driver of the car, a white-haired man with a young boy next to him.

He nodded. "Go after 'em!" He made a fist and shook it.

"Hold on, Victoria." Casey swung away from the verge and switched on her siren and lights. "Seat belt?"

Victoria settled her cap firmly on her head, and fastened her seat belt.

When they reached the straightaway beyond the cemetery, Casey sped up. The siren wailed. Ahead of them, beyond Whiting's fields, past Scotchman's Lane, in front of the New Ag Hall, they could see the motorcycles, two in front, two in the middle, and three bringing up the rear. The bikes took up the entire right lane.

"Let me have the mike, will you, Victoria."

Victoria handed it to her.

"I need help," Casey told the dispatcher. "I'm almost at the intersection of North and State Road, and we may have a problem with some motorcycles."

Casey passed the mike back to Victoria, who hung it up. "That's a bad intersection," Victoria said. "I hope they slow down before they get there."

Casey pushed down on the accelerator, and the distance between them and the bikers decreased. One of the bikers turned in his seat and, with a grin, lifted a middle finger.

"I hope I can stop them before the bridge."

The motorcycles were pulling farther ahead, and Casey accelerated until she was right behind them again. She held out her hand for the mike. "The bikers are almost at Mill Brook," she said after she'd identified herself. "Where are you, Tango 9?"

"At the dump road."

"That was Tisbury," Casey said to Victoria over the sound of the siren. "Where are you, Charlie?"

"This is Charlie 2, passing Seven Gates."

"Chilmark. We'll stop them, Victoria." Casey gave the mike to Victoria, who hung it up again. "I just hope they don't run into some kid on a bicycle first."

The motorcycles started a kind of dance, weaving from the right side of the road to the center line, crossing in front of one another, each tilting at a sharp angle. One of the bikers dragged his gloved left hand along the pavement.

"They think they're playing dodger car in an amusement park."

Casey's voice was sharp. "They won't stop until they kill someone." The road dipped into a small valley and crossed the brook.

Victoria, hoping to ease the tension, spoke up over the siren. "That used to be a ford, where the bridge is," she said. "Our horse would step through the water daintily, lifting each foot, pulling the wagon behind her."

Casey stared through the windshield, her back straight.

"In spring, water would sometimes come up to the wheel hubs," Victoria continued. "Dolly would always stop to drink on the way home from Vineyard Haven."

"What did you say, Victoria?" Casey glanced at her.

"Nothing," Victoria said, settling back in her seat and tugging her cap as far over her ears as she could.

In the second it took to cross the narrow bridge, Victoria smelled the cool lushness of ferns and moss. Then they were across, still behind the bikers, the noise of motorcycle engines almost drowning out the siren.

They reached the Y in the road where North Road joined State Road. Victoria saw a half-dozen cars parked near the bakery. The bikers sped up as they took the curve at the intersection, bodies leaning with their bikes.

"Lord, don't look, Victoria!" Casey shouted.

Victoria heard a long drawn-out squeal of tires skidding and the crunch of metal. A car horn blared and continued to blare. Someone screamed. A cloud of dust rose up in front of the bakery. Casey halted the Bronco in the middle of the road, almost blocking it, and the siren wound down to a whimper, then died. Rotating lights flashed across tree trunks to one side.

"Man the radio, Victoria." The chief raced to where a knot of bakery customers was gathering. The car horn continued to blare.

One of the motorcycles had rammed into a red Volvo that was pulling out of the bakeshop parking area. The biker was lying in the road, his motorcycle on top of him, its front wheel twisted and spinning eccentrically. His leg was pinned under the machine, and he seemed to be unconscious. His bare shoulders were sanded down to raw flesh. His helmet had been flung to the side of the road. From where she sat, Victoria saw that he was not young, probably mid-fifties, with thick silvery hair cut nicely. Blood seeped out of his nose and the corner of his mouth, staining his mustache and what looked like a two-day growth of beard.

Casey cupped her hands around her mouth and yelled to Victoria, "Get on the radio and call for the ambulance." She turned to the silent crowd. "Someone cut off that car horn!"

Victoria went carefully through the list of radio procedures and called the dispatcher.

"We'll be there in five minutes," the dispatcher said. "Stand by the radio, Mrs. Trumbull, in case we need you."

The Tisbury police cruiser arrived at the scene, herding the four lead motorcycles it had turned back. Shortly after, the Chilmark cruiser pulled to the side of North Road with its blue lights flashing.

Casey knelt next to the biker and listened for his breathing. His companions were still astride their motorcycles. "You!" Casey pointed to them. "Lift the bike off of him. Hurry up." As they rushed to obey, Casey said, "Gently. Watch how you lift. His leg may be caught."

The Tri-Town Ambulance came up behind the Bronco, passed around it, and stopped near the bakery. Within another five minutes, the EMTs had strapped the biker onto a stretcher, and the ambulance took off.

When it was all over and Casey had seen the injured man hustled off to the hospital, had ticketed the bikers, and had collected statements from witnesses, she checked the damage to the red Volvo— surprisingly not much. She rejoined Victoria and together they filled out paperwork.

"What are they thinking when they hot-shot like that?" Casey muttered. "Fortunately, that biker wasn't killed, but he could have been. Or he could have killed a kid or an old lady or someone's dog."

"Maybe they learned a lesson."

"I doubt it." Casey started up the Bronco, turned around in the intersection, and headed toward Mrs. Summerville's to take care of her complaint about bikers camping in her back pasture.

"How long will you be on-Island, Dojan?" Obed VanDyke was loading lobster pots onto his boat, which was tied up at the commercial dock in Menemsha. Dojan was helping him.

"Not long enough," Dojan replied, shaking his head so the broken end of the osprey feather bobbed in his hair.

"What are you telling them in Washington about the casino?" Obed took a trap Dojan handed down to him and stacked it with the ones already on his boat. The wooden slats of the lobster pots cast striped shadows on the deck.

"An obscenity!" Dojan stopped lifting. "What would our grandmothers think? Are we a noble people so we can suck money from the weak the way leeches suck blood?"

"The chief brought you back to get federal help with the permits." Obed stood in the cockpit of his boat in his yellow oilskin trousers, his rubber boots, and a white undershirt. He set his fists on his hips.

"I have no choice." Dojan held out his hands, palms up.

"The chief says we're supposed to keep our minds open," Obed said, getting back to his pots.

"Gambling is a sickness. The devils who build gambling casinos cause sickness."

"I agree." Obed reached up. "Hand me down another one."

"I can play Burkhardt's trick." Dojan swung a pot down to Obed. "Go by the rules. One permit every six months."

"And get yourself killed like Burkhardt?" Obed lined up the lobster pot Dojan had handed him with the others, a cargo of a dozen traps.

"What bait you using?" Dojan asked.

"Fish heads." Obed took the lid off a barrel on deck, and the aroma wafted up to Dojan.

"Good, good." Dojan sniffed appreciatively. "Ripe."

"You know Hiram's missing, don't you?" Obed replaced the lid of the bait barrel.

"Saw him day before yesterday at Mrs. Trumbull's."

"He's disappeared. His van's gone."

Dojan shrugged and rolled his eyes.

"You knew he was first to reach Burkhardt, didn't you?"

"I heard." Dojan swung down another pot.

"Hiram was the first to reach him. But your friend, the old lady, found him. Burkhardt was still alive, she says." Obed stopped, put both hands on his back, and stood up straight. "Patience is right.

71

How many more years can I do this? I'm not yet thirty, and already I'm an old man."

"You go to Washington, old man, and I'll fish your lobster traps." Dojan grinned his gap-toothed grin. "Look at me." He held out his arms. "Pale."

Obed examined them. "Yeah." He squinted. "I can see now it says, 'I Love Mindy.'"

Dojan twisted his neck to look at the tattoo on his left shoulder. "That is an eagle with a serpent." He slung another pot down to Obed who caught it and stacked it.

"Excuse me, sir." A middle-aged woman with a little-girl voice had stopped on the dock and was addressing Dojan. "Are you a Native American?"

"Yes, ma'am!" Obed shouted up from his boat. "He surely is, ma'am. He don't speak no English."

Dojan stared at Obed.

"Will he let me take his picture?" the woman asked Obed, bringing out a disposable camera from a large plastic bag she was holding.

Dojan started to say something. Obed interrupted quickly. "He says, ma'am, if you take his picture, you will steal his soul. However, a small offering, say ten dollars, ma'am, will assuage his gods."

"Oh!" said the woman. "May I give the money to you?"

"Yes, ma'am." Obed held out his hand. Dojan glared at both of them. The woman snapped his picture. Dojan growled. The woman turned quickly and scurried down the dock, winding the film as she went.

"I'll split it with you." Obed held up the ten-dollar bill. "We got a gold mine here, Dojan, you and me."

Obed caught the pot before it hit the deck.

"You planning on coming out with me today to set traps?" Obed said conversationally.

Dojan threw another pot.

"We can talk about casino plans."

"You stink as bad as the rest," Dojan said, and leaped from the dock onto the boat deck.

———

Patience was in her office at Tribal Headquarters when her assistant Peter Little came in and, without invitation, sat in the canvas director's chair in front of her desk. He leaned forward and snapped his fingers at the metal nameplate inscribed PATIENCE VANDYKE, TRIBAL CHAIRMAN.

"What is it now, Peter? I can't be disturbed. I've got to get this application out immediately." She tapped her pen on her desk. One wall of her office had framed crayon drawings of Aquinnah scenes by children of the tribe. One wall was a window that looked out on the fields of russet grass and low bushes behind the tribal building. One wall had a huge photograph of the Gay Head cliffs, and beside the photograph was the door. The fourth wall was covered with framed diplomas and certificates of appreciation and photographs of Patience posing with dignitaries, a state senator, the tribe's storyteller.

"With Burkhardt dead, you have some breathing space." Peter smoothed his hair and slumped in the chair. He crossed his legs and gazed at the diplomas on her wall.

"Quite the contrary," said Patience. "With Burkhardt dead, I must act quickly."

"It's obvious someone killed him, isn't it?" Peter smiled, a one-sided, thin-lipped smile.

"No, it's not obvious. I need to get back to work, Peter." Patience looked down at the papers in front of her and thumbed through them. "Whoever the governor appoints might be worse than Burkhardt. We have only a few days to get these out."

"Certificate of appreciation from the senior center," Peter murmured, looking at the framed documents on the wall. "What on earth did you do to earn that, Patience? Help Mrs. Trumbull cross the road?"

She flushed. "Peter, I'm running out of time."

"Back to the killing, because someone did kill him." Peter slumped still farther in the chair until his neck rested on the canvas back. "Why is Dojan exiled to Washington? Because he's a killer, that's why. Exiled because the tribe has sovereign nation status, and the U.S. law can't touch him. Washington's his punishment. Chief Hawkbill sends for Dojan. Dojan arrives. Burkhardt is killed." Peter lifted his shoulders and raised his eyebrows. "Voilà! One problem taken care of neatly." He smiled again. "And traditionally, I might add. Clobbered on the head by a crazed Indian. Nice touch would have been to scalp him."

Patience stood. "Get out of my office, Peter. I don't like your talk. I need those grant applications. Right away. Bring them to me in the next hour. Filled out." She pointed toward the door. "Get out. And shut the door behind you."

CHAPTER 12

It was still early afternoon when Victoria answered the knock on her kitchen door. A girl with a mass of curly blond hair stood there. She was several inches shorter than Victoria, and was wearing ironed jeans and a bright blue shirt the color of her eyes.

"Are you Mrs. Trumbull?" She held out a slim hand with rings on each finger. "I'm Linda, Jube Burkhardt's niece."

The girl's voice was soft and high.

"Please come in," Victoria said. "I'm so sorry about your uncle. Let me fix you a cup of tea."

"Thank you."

As she shut the door behind the girl, Victoria caught a strong whiff of patchouli. She didn't like perfume, especially patchouli, which made her think someone was covering up the smell of marijuana. She sneezed.

"Bless you," said Linda.

"Thank you." Victoria wrinkled her nose for the next sneeze. She tore a paper towel from the roll over the sink.

Linda looked around the kitchen with interest while Victoria filled the teakettle and put it on the stove.

"I just love your house, Mrs. Trumbull," she said.

Victoria started to pick up the tray with the teacups, but felt another sneeze coming on.

"I hope you're not catching cold?" Linda asked.

Victoria shook her head and sneezed again. "I'm afraid it's your perfume."

"I'm so sorry! I'll keep my distance." Linda backed up a step. "May I carry that into the other room?"

"Thank you." Once they were seated in the cookroom, Victoria said, "Your uncle's death must be a shock to you. His only relatives, as I recall, are your mother and you two girls." She poured tea and passed a cup and saucer to Linda.

"I wasn't really close to him."

"Sugar?"

"No thanks, no sugar."

"Your mother was younger than your uncle, wasn't she?"

"More than ten years," said Linda. "Uncle Jube was in his late fifties. My mother was only forty-five when she died two years ago."

Victoria waited for the girl to continue.

Linda cleared her throat and looked down into her cup. "You must wonder what I'm doing here, Mrs. Trumbull."

"I assume it has to do with your uncle."

Linda nodded. "My sister and I have to settle Uncle Jube's affairs. She's on-Island for the motorcycle rally, but I don't know where to reach her."

"Oh?" Victoria was noncommittal.

"I thought of staying at Uncle Jube's house."

Victoria said "Oh" again.

"I guess you've seen it?"

Victoria nodded.

"I don't understand how he could have lived that way."

"It was his own mess. That makes a difference. Where do you plan to stay?"

"The police sergeant, Junior Norton?"

"Yes?" said Victoria.

"He said you sometimes rent rooms?"

"Occasionally."

"Would you consider renting one to me for a week or two? I can pay. I simply can't stay in my uncle's house."

Victoria shifted in her chair and thought of patchouli permeating the pillows in her spare room. Then she thought of Jube Burkhardt's house and smiled at the girl. "I'd be glad to rent you a room for as long as you need it."

"Thank you so much." Linda looked up and smiled. "I won't wear perfume, Mrs. Trumbull, honest. Okay if I bring my things in?"

"As long as you're not like your uncle," Victoria said, and then felt bad about her small unfunny joke. But the girl laughed before she became serious again.

"I guess someone has to clean up that place. That means me, unless we can find Harley?"

"You can pay a cleaning company to take care of it, I'm sure. They know what to keep and what to throw out. If it were me, I'd be tempted to read everything, all those magazines and newspapers."

"I'm not sure it's worth cleaning up. The house smells awful and it's in terrible condition." The girl got up from the table and carried the cups and saucers to the sink.

"It's a lovely old house," said Victoria, defending it. "Once it's cleaned up and painted you'll be pleasantly surprised. You can rent it during the summer to pay for repairs and taxes."

Linda shrugged and went out to her car, a blue Ford. When she returned, Victoria showed her into the downstairs bedroom, the room Victoria herself preferred in winter, when the west wind made her unheated upstairs bedroom too chilly.

"This is neat," Linda said. "I've never seen so many doors in a house. Where does this go?"

"Into the library," said Victoria. "Your uncle's house is like mine. Each room has at least two doors. For ventilation and in case of fire."

Linda hung up her garment bag in the small closet next to the fireplace and set her suitcase on the floor.

"I'll get towels," Victoria said. "The bathroom is off the cookroom, the door on the left."

Linda followed Victoria to the kitchen door. "I suppose the police will locate my sister?"

"I believe they've already contacted the man who organized the rally."

"Harley's going to love that. She and the police don't get along real well."

"I hear she didn't get along with your uncle, either."

"Nobody got along with my uncle."

"He apparently thought highly of you." Victoria didn't want to pry, but she was curious to know what was going to happen to Jube Burkhardt's eighteen-million-dollar property.

"Harley was his pet until she got into motorcycles, you know? He hated them. I think she did it just to spite him."

"Why did your uncle feel that way?"

Linda lifted her shoulders in a shrug. "I heard it was something from when he was a kid."

While Victoria was getting towels from the linen closet, Elizabeth came home. She was still wearing her harbor uniform, tan shorts and a white short-sleeved shirt.

"What a day!" She held out her hand to Linda, who was standing beside the refrigerator. "I'm Elizabeth."

Linda introduced herself.

"I'm sorry about your uncle."

"Thanks. I guess I've got a lot of work ahead of me."

"If there's anything we can do . . . ," Elizabeth said.

Victoria appeared with towels and soap. "Linda's going to stay with us until she gets things sorted out."

Elizabeth rolled her eyes. "That might take a while. At least this house is tidier than your uncle's."

Linda smiled. "That's for sure."

Victoria gave Linda the towels. "Your uncle had a reputation for being difficult."

Linda shrugged. "He held grudges forever. Harley and I had to be careful around him." Linda spoke rapidly and her face was flushed. "Uncle Jube always bragged that he'd get even with whoever, no matter how long it took."

Elizabeth narrowed her eyes. "Nice guy," she said.

Dojan had returned from the morning of setting lobster pots with Obed. His forehead, nose, and arms were sunburned bright red. He carried a bucket of lobsters into the chief's office at Tribal Headquarters and plunked it down next to the desk. The chief looked up from his paperwork.

"Is this a bad time?" Dojan asked.

"If those lobsters are for me, it's not a bad time."

Dojan nodded.

"I'm filling out forms for a federal grant, Dojan. I'm glad to be interrupted." The chief pushed the papers to one side of his desk, and indicated the chair next to him. "Sit." He looked into the bucket. In it were four lobsters partially covered with seaweed, claws held together with yellow rubber bands.

"You support a casino." Dojan stared at the old man. "You want our people to gamble." He leaned over the chief's desk. "A white man's sickness." He slapped the desk and the chief's pen bounced and rolled off onto the floor. The chief leaned over and picked it up.

"No, Dojan. I am not promoting a casino. Gambling is poison. Our people have always gambled, and it has always been poison."

"Why, then?" Dojan jabbed a dirty finger with its raggedly gnawed nail at the application forms on the desk.

"Because our tribe must decide for itself. I visited a casino the other day, I went on the *Pequot*, that boat that takes people directly to the gambling. It takes them cheaply and quickly, so they can throw money at the gaming machines happily. The casino has good food, cheap. Pretty Native American girls, handsome Native American boys, run the games and the machines. The pretty girls and handsome boys make it seem like good clean fun. The young people smile at the foolish old people who want something for nothing. Perhaps it is all right. A nice cruise, good cheap food, a day's entertainment. All they have lost is money. The casino? It looks like a forest with plastic bears, deer, and beaver. You hear falling water. It's all a chimera."

"Why, then, why?" Dojan asked, slapping the desk.

"Who am I to dictate right and wrong to the tribe?"

"You are the chief, our leader."

"Tribal members are not looking beyond money or glitter. Patience says, 'a casino means jobs for our young people,' Peter says, 'money for education and housing.'"

"Gambling money is dirty!"

The chief lifted his shoulders. "Sit, Dojan. Sit." He leaned forward at his desk, his hands clasped, and peered at Dojan through his thick glasses. "Dojan, these are the facts of life. Sit. And listen to me."

Dojan glowered at him, and when the chief continued to stare back, he dropped his gaze and sat where the chief had told him to sit.

"A casino means more money than any of us has ever dreamed

about." The chief held up a hand. "Don't interrupt. Hear me, Dojan. Patience wants a casino on the Island. Peter wants a casino ship. He is working behind her back. Patience wants to think he is working with her. He's not."

Dojan shifted impatiently.

"Listen to everything I have to say, Dojan. I need you to work with me, but you must do it my way."

Dojan focused his eyes on the chief.

"Peter wants a casino ship. Gamblers will go out to it by launch, some from the Island, some from the mainland. Peter is politically astute. A ship will not be the threat to Islanders that a six-story building would be. Patience does not agree with him, and she is the boss."

Dojan started to say something.

The chief spread his hand on his chest. "I'm not the boss, Dojan. My position is ceremonial, like the queen of England's. I carry no weight except for my years. And ..." He patted his stomach. "My years have given me wisdom and a craftiness that Patience and Peter do not suspect."

Dojan stared out of the chief's window. While Patience's office was at the back of the building with no ocean view, the chief's was in a front corner where he had a constantly changing vista of sea, sky, and cliffs.

"Concentrate on what I say, Dojan. Patience hopes to get government funding, so that any resulting casino would be controlled by the tribe. She's right. Should a casino be built, we do not want private interests as partners, which is what will happen if private money is involved."

"What private money?" Dojan asked.

"Ah, Dojan, you would not believe how much money is out there in the hands of people who do not care about the tribe. Peter accused Mr. Burkhardt of taking bribes. Perhaps he was. Was he killed by private money? I don't know. Was he killed by a member of the tribe?" The chief shrugged. "He was not a popular man. Had he ruffled the feathers of the motorcycle people, unrelated to the casino? A possibility. Was there a family feud of some kind? Who knows."

"What do you want of me?"

"I want you to be careful, first." The chief waited until Dojan settled back in the chair. "Peter is telling Patience you killed Mr. Burkhardt."

Dojan pushed himself out of his chair. "I did not!"

"Of course you did not. I sent you to Washington as penance for killing that man. You won't kill again. You are not a killer. Washington will cool that blood of yours. You will stay there until I tell you to come home."

Dojan gave the chief a desolate look.

"It's better than prison, Dojan. Believe me." The chief turned slightly so he could look out at the Atlantic Ocean, spread before him as far as anyone could see.

"Mrs. Trumbull was right to bring you to me. The white men wanted to cover up your killing. They wanted to blame it on another man. But you would be in agony if there was no punishment. Victoria Trumbull understands this. You will do good works for the tribe in Washington."

Dojan put his head in his hands.

"Be patient, Dojan." The chief continued to gaze out at the view. "I want you to examine the place Mr. Burkhardt died. Did he bury something? Did he try to uncover something? No one must see you on that cliff. The police have determined that someone unknown killed Mr. Burkhardt. They are calling where he was found a crime scene, and keeping sightseers away. However, you must go there, somehow. Take Mrs. Trumbull with you, if she is willing."

Dojan sat silently.

The chief said, "I cannot believe a tribal member killed Mr. Burkhardt, but I may be wrong."

"We've located the other niece," Casey said. She and Victoria were following up on a report of a missing car. "Harley and her biker boyfriend were in that group of seven yesterday. They went to the hospital with the guy who got hurt. She didn't know about her uncle's death."

"Now what?" Victoria held on to the armrest as they passed around a slow-moving front loader.

"The state police are in charge now. I imagine they'll go through Burkhardt's house." Casey made a face. "Then the nieces have to decide about funeral arrangements. No one seems to know whether there was a will or not. If not, the property is likely to be tied up in probate for a time."

"Jube told Hiram he was leaving the house to Linda, his younger niece."

"Someone has to find a will, then," Casey said. "That's an expensive piece of property."

"Maybe the will is in his house."

Casey slowed as they turned onto Scotchman's.

"Any idea yet where Hiram is?" Victoria asked.

"None whatsoever," Casey replied. "We haven't found his van. We can't do anything until we find it."

"Or his body," said Victoria.

"I keep hoping he'll show up alive, but it seems less likely as time goes by."

"Have you tried to reach his friend, Tad Nordstrom? Perhaps Hiram went with him."

"Could be."

Victoria shifted to a more comfortable position. "Who's taking care of Hiram's cat?"

"The neighbors are feeding it. If Hiram doesn't show up soon, they're taking it to the animal shelter."

Victoria thought for a moment. "I could take the cat in temporarily."

"What about McCavity?" Casey said, with a smirk.

"McCavity will get used to it. If Hiram doesn't come back, McCavity's house would be better than the shelter."

"The Island's shelter is like the Ritz-Carlton for stray animals. Burkhardt had a cat, too. Want two strays?" She looked sideways at Victoria, who changed the subject.

"Is Harley camped out somewhere?"

"With a bunch of bikers behind Maley's," said Casey.

"I wonder what's going to happen when Harley and her sister Linda finally meet up? There seems to be something amiss between them."

"Eighteen million dollars, maybe?" said Casey.

CHAPTER 13

It was late that evening, well after dark, before Victoria and Elizabeth sat down for supper. Once Linda had settled her things into the guest room, she told Victoria she was going to the movies and wouldn't be back until late.

Elizabeth set a fluffy golden soufflé on the table, a soufflé that rose two inches above the sides of the blue oven dish that Victoria's great-granddaughter Fiona had given her, when they heard the siren in the firehouse a half mile down the road. Within a few minutes, the first fire truck went past the house, lights flashing. The truck turned left onto New Lane. Victoria put her fork down and got up from the table. A second fire engine followed the first. Victoria was still standing at the window when, less than a minute later, Casey pounded on the door. The Bronco was in the drive, its engine running, blue lights circling round and round.

"It's Burkhardt's house," Casey shouted at Elizabeth, when she opened the door. "If your grandmother's ready to go, I'll take her with me."

"I'm ready." Victoria grabbed a sweater and her cloth bag, and was out of the house and into her seat in the Bronco before Casey climbed back into the driver's seat.

"Junior saw the flames from his shack on the other side of the Great Pond," Casey said as she turned on her siren and accelerated out of Victoria's drive.

"On the Island, we don't call a shack a shack. We call it a camp," said Victoria.

Casey grinned. "How many years is it going to take me to become an Islander? Fifty?" She turned to Victoria, who was looking straight ahead. "Anyway, Junior radioed in the first call and then rowed across in his dinghy."

The Bronco jounced and swayed from one side to the other along the track that led to Burkhardt's. Victoria barely caught her breath before she was tossed again as far as her seat belt would stretch. In the rear-view mirror she could see the blue and red lights of emergency vehicles bouncing behind them. The sky ahead of them was brilliant orange near the treetops, pink higher up. They raced around the last bend in the road and reached the open area surrounding Burkhardt's house.

The house was an inferno, a halo of fire against the dark sky, its windows bright with flame.

Casey stopped behind the West Tisbury pumper and went over to the firefighters, who were unreeling hoses.

"Have you seen Junior Norton?" she shouted.

"Over there." One of the firefighters pointed to the other side of the house.

Victoria got out too, and stood beside the Bronco.

It was clearly too late to save the house. Flames poured upward out of every window. Sparks streamed out of the chimney. Burning wood crackled, timbers crashed within the shell of the house, men shouted, the pumper throbbed. Water hissed into steam as it hit the stone foundation of the house. A beam fell. A section of the roof caved in with a wrenching crash. Glass shattered.

Firefighters, in yellow slickers, boots, and helmets, hosed down the dry grass around the house. Casey finally located Junior, and they stood upwind of the fire.

One outer wall had come down, and the inside of the house showed up in cross section. The second floor, like the first, was heaped with junk. As Victoria watched, the floor collapsed into the center of the building. Piles of burning stuff slid along the sloping floor and fell with a rumble onto the floor below.

In two hours, the house was gone. All that remained was smoldering timbers, the standing chimney, beams leaning at an angle like a giant hearth fire, flames licking along them gently. The fire was still bright enough so Victoria could see among the ruins piles of papers that seemed almost intact. She could make out the blackened refrigerator and the stove, leaning at crazy angles. She could see, where the entry had been, a charred kayak paddle leaning against an empty blackened door frame.

Casey returned with Junior to the Bronco. Victoria was back in her seat.

"The fire department is leaving a truck and two men to keep an eye on things," Casey said. "Junior is staying here all night. Do you have a sleeping bag?" she asked him.

Junior nodded. His eyes turned down at the outer corners; his mouth turned up. To Victoria, he looked exceedingly young.

"Was the fire set by someone?" Victoria asked him.

"Seems likely," Junior agreed.

"I'll call the arson squad on the mainland," Casey said. "We'll come back in the morning when it's light and the ashes have cooled. I'll take you home now, Victoria."

Home again, Victoria described the fire to Elizabeth as they ate the cold and fallen soufflé.

"I'll make a fresh omelet," Elizabeth said.

"Pretend it's supposed to look like this," said Victoria. "Put parsley around it, and we'll have a new culinary treat."

Elizabeth grunted.

"Linda's not home yet?" Victoria asked.

Elizabeth looked at her watch. "She should be back by now, if she made the early movie."

"I don't look forward to breaking the news about the fire to her," said Victoria.

"She may be relieved. Think of all the papers and junk she won't have to look at."

They waited up until after midnight for Linda. Finally a car pulled into the drive, and Linda came into the kitchen, wearing black slacks and a flowered blouse.

Victoria and Elizabeth were in the kitchen. "Bad news, I'm afraid," Victoria said. "You might want to sit down."

"Oh?" said Linda.

"I'll get you a glass of sherry," said Elizabeth.

"Scotch," said Victoria.

Linda looked from one to the other. "What happened?"

"Your uncle's place burned down tonight."

Linda sat with a plop in the big captain's chair in the kitchen. "I guess I could use a drink." She waited until Elizabeth handed her the glass. "Did it burn to the ground?"

"There's not much left," Victoria said.

"Well, that takes care of the problem of cleaning up," said Linda, holding up her glass. "Here's to Uncle Jube."

"Where was the fire last night?" Sarah was sitting on the bench at Alley's. She looked from Joe, who had lifted up his cap and was scratching his head, to Donald, who was picking at fiberglass resin on his jeans.

Joe leaned against the post that held up the porch roof. "I didn't know there was a fire."

"Chilmark and West Tisbury both responded," Sarah said. "I had my scanner on, but I couldn't hear what they were saying." She stirred her coffee with a plastic straw and sucked on the end of it before she tossed it toward the trash can. "Somewhere on the Great Pond, I gathered."

"Here comes Lincoln," Donald said as a truck with rakes and a lawn mower in back pulled up behind Joe's pickup.

"Whaddya know?" Lincoln greeted the three on the porch.

"Where was the fire last night?" Sarah asked.

Lincoln pushed his hair out of his eyes. "Wanna guess?"

"I've got to go to work in a couple of minutes." Sarah looked at her watch and smoothed her bright red T-shirt, a map of Martha's Vineyard with a glittery arrow aimed at the western end of the Island. "Where was the fire, Lincoln?"

"Jube Burkhardt's place. Burnt to the ground. Junior saw it from his camp. By the time they got there it was too late. Funny it picked now to burn."

"Wouldn't put it past either of the nieces to set it," Joe said, stirring his coffee. He took a gulp. "The one who hangs out with the biker is some weird, let me tell you."

"Just because she's tattooed." Sarah stretched out her own arm with its tattooed bracelet of leaves. "Grandmothers are getting tattooed these days. It's the 'in' thing."

"The younger one, the too, too sweet one," Joe rolled his eyes and wriggled his hips, "she makes my dentures ache." He showed his horsy yellow teeth in a grin.

"They say Burkhardt left his place to her." Donald leaned forward, elbows on his knees.

"Far as I know, nobody's talked about a will." Lincoln moved to his usual place, his back to the shingled front of the store.

"I wonder who does inherit his place," said Sarah.

Lincoln shrugged. "Eighteen million dollars."

"Eighteen million," Sarah mused. "That's a pretty good motive for killing one's uncle."

At the police station, Casey looked at her watch. "The arson team was on the eight o'clock boat. They'll be here any minute."

"What about Junior?" said Victoria.

"He'll stay at the place until I relieve him." Casey straightened papers on her desk. "I've got to finish a couple of things before they get here. Here's the motorcycle accident report. Look it over, will you? See if it makes sense to you."

The morning was clear and cool, almost fall-like. Victoria wore a sage green turtleneck under her blue fleece jacket. She read Casey's report, made a couple of minor corrections, and handed the papers back to the chief, just as the off-Island team pulled up in a white van.

Without waiting for introductions, Casey and Victoria got into the Bronco and led the way to Burkhardt's. The arson van bumped along behind them.

In the bright sunlight, the remains of Burkhardt's house seemed pathetically small. Smoke was still rising from the ruin. The chimney stood tall, untouched by the fire. Half-charred beams and boards, sills, flooring, and uprights stuck out at odd angles like jackstraws.

Victoria walked around the remains. In places, the grass was scorched where embers had fallen and started small fires. The air smelled of stale cigars, burned tar paper, burned plastic, burned metal, burned meat, paper, trash, garbage, rubber.

She was amazed to see piles of unburned newspapers and magazines in the midst of the rubble, odd things she thought would have burned, and metal things, twisted and molten, she thought would have survived.

Casey introduced Victoria to the arson team, two men and a woman, all three wearing boots and white jumpsuits that covered them completely. Victoria watched them move through the still-smoldering ashes, talking quietly, measuring, taking notes.

"Shit!" one of the men said. "Come here—Hank! Beth!"

The two hurried over to him, picking their way carefully through the ashes.

"Was someone in the house?" he called out to Casey.

"Not that I know of," said Casey.

"We've found what looks like human remains."

Victoria's skin prickled.

Casey walked over to where the team stood.

"Any idea who could have been in the building?" the woman, Beth, asked Casey, who shook her head. "The owner?"

"Not the owner. He's dead." Casey stood at the edge of the ruin, her polished boots dusted with ash.

"A relative?"

Casey turned to Victoria. "What about Linda?"

Victoria felt as though she were somewhere else watching. "She came home last night, later than I did."

Casey unsnapped her radio. "I'll ask one of the guys to check on Harley. She was camping out last I knew."

Victoria focused on Casey. "Hiram." She said it softly, and when Casey looked over at her, she repeated it. "Hiram," she said. "He called me from here three days ago. We found blood on the floor. It must have been his. That smell . . ."

Beth indicated the shapeless charred mound in the rubble. "All we can go by now are dental records." Victoria looked away. "It's going to help, having some idea who the victim might have been."

Victoria walked to the edge of the grass clearing and looked up at the crystal blue sky. A gull soared overhead. The gull might have been the same bird she remembered from nearly a century ago. She heard the surf, pounding as it had pounded before her great-great-grandmother was born, and would continue to pound when her own many times great-grandchildren were older than she. Nothing would change that soaring gull or that beating surf. The sea would eat up the Island and disgorge it as sandbanks to snare mariners three thousand years from now.

She took a deep breath and let it out. She walked back toward Casey, who looked at her with concern.

"Are you okay, Victoria?"

Victoria stood up straight, stretching to her full height, which was still tall.

"Certainly." Victoria strode back to the ruins, her nose held high. "How can I help?" she asked.

While Victoria had turned her back to the site, the arson team had zipped the remains into a plastic body bag and had carried it to the van.

Beth pulled down the mask that covered her mouth and nose. "Tell us if any of these objects we put off to one side mean anything to you."

The team lifted up bundles of half-burned paper, a mattress that was nothing but springs, a lamp with a skeleton shade.

"Here's the base of a computer," said the man called Hank, his voice muffled by his face mask.

Victoria stared at it. "The CPU?" she asked.

"Right. I'll set it next to the other things." He pulled his face mask down. "These masks are a pain."

"Where was the computer, can you tell?"

"Judging from what was underneath the unit when we found it, I would say it was on the second floor, probably in a room at the front of the house." Hank stretched. "Back to work. If you think of anything, holler."

Victoria moved an upended bucket close to the computer and sat down to examine it. The metal box was about a foot wide, almost two feet long, and about six inches high. The unit was charred and blistered on three of the five sides she could see. The two unburned sides had once been tan, but were now smoked to an ugly greenish gray. On what must have been the front, one of the unburned sides, there were two slots. On the opposite side were holes where wires might once have gone. Except for the slots and the back side, the box was featureless. Victoria examined it more closely. She eased herself onto her knees and studied the unit. She could make out what must have been a decal on the front that read, "digita . . ." and she couldn't read the rest of the letters. She examined the smoky unburned side. It looked as though there might have been another decal. She wet her finger and rubbed the smoke off. She could barely make out the letters S . . . I . . . B . . . Y. . . . And that was all she could read. It was enough. She had found Sibyl.

CHAPTER 14

Victoria scrambled to her feet.

Casey was squatting near the charred wreckage of the house. She looked up at Victoria, concerned.

"Can you call Howland on your radio?" Victoria asked.

"I can contact the communications center and they'll phone him," Casey said. "What's up, Victoria?"

"I've found Sibyl."

"What?"

"When Jube Burkhardt said 'Sibyl,' the last word he said before he died, he was referring to his computer."

Casey stood, with her notebook still in one hand. "A guy's dying words are about his *computer*?"

"Something important must be on that computer," Victoria insisted. "Important enough for Jube to worry about Sibyl, rather than face the fact that he was dying."

Casey examined the box. "That computer's a wreck."

"Howland Atherton can retrieve something."

"He's not a magician."

Victoria stood tall. "Before the computer was burned, I asked you to have Howland look at it. We still have a chance of finding some clue."

"Okay, okay. I'll try to reach Atherton," said Casey.

"Where's Junior?"

"I sent him home." She nodded to the opposite shore.

Victoria shaded her eyes and could see Junior's dinghy pulled up on the beach in front of his camp. When she turned back, Casey was on the radio, giving the woman at the communications center directions to Burkhardt's place to relay to Howland.

Casey hung up the mike and went back to where the arson team was sifting through the rubble. Their once-white jumpsuits and white boots were black, from feet to thighs, and their once-white gloves were filthy.

Victoria looked around for her bucket seat, found it tossed to one side, upended it and wiped it off with a paper towel from her pocket, then sat where she could watch both the arson team and the road.

She was composing a complicated poem on the back of an envelope, a sestina on the relativity of time, when about three-quarters of an hour later, she heard Howland's car, an ancient white Renault wheeze into the grassy opening and stop with a shudder.

Howland unwound himself from behind the wheel, slammed the door, turned and examined the ruin. "What a mess."

Victoria arose from her bucket seat. "They found Hiram."

"He was in the house?"

"Someone was," said Victoria. "There's not much left to identify."

Howland thrust his hands in his pockets and scowled. "Not a pleasant way to die."

"I'm sure he was already dead," said Victoria.

Howland looked at her thoughtfully. "I got a garbled message from the communications center about someone called Sibyl, a burned computer, and instructions to get here as quickly as I could." He lifted his eyebrows at Victoria. "Communications said the message was from you."

"Jube was still alive when Hiram reached him. He mumbled something, then said 'Sibyl' distinctly."

Howland frowned.

Victoria went on. "Two things have puzzled me. One was the identity of Sibyl. Why would Jube call out that name as he was dying? As far as I knew, he had no relatives or friends named Sibyl."

"And the second?" asked Howland.

"When Elizabeth and I came here after Jube's death, his computer was running with a message that read, 'Fatal Error.' When Elizabeth and I returned the next day, the computer screen was blank, and the box, the computer itself, was missing."

"And you've now found it?"

"The arson squad found it," Victoria said. "They thought it might have fallen from the second floor."

"Where does Sibyl come into this?"

Victoria described finding the decal on the side of the unit. "We need to know what's on his computer."

"What do you expect of me, Victoria? It's not likely I can recover anything from a computer that got burned up in a fire, then fell to the ground from the second floor."

"I asked the arson team to set it in the shade."

"Lot of good that'll do," Howland muttered.

Victoria led him to a gnarled apple tree growing beside the barn. Late summer apples were rotting on the ground, where the sweet scent of fermenting fruit had attracted a steady buzz of yellow jackets. The computer leaned against the trunk of the tree.

"Great," said Howland. "I'm allergic to wasps." He stepped back as a yellow jacket flew past his head.

"Casey and I will carry it to your car."

"Oh, Christ," said Howland. "I'll move it. Outta the way, wasps." He stepped gingerly through the fallen apples, carefully brushed aside the yellow jackets that had landed on the computer, and carried the box to the open field near his car. He crouched down and studied the burned case from every angle. "I doubt if I can recover anything, Victoria. This thing is in bad shape."

"If the computer can be fixed, you can do it," Victoria said. She bent over him, her hands on her knees.

"You don't understand." Howland got to his feet and stood up straight, towering above Victoria, who was not short. She looked up at him. She'd always admired his fine patrician nose, almost as large as hers. His turned-down mouth gave him an expression of strong disapproval, which Victoria knew was not the case. His mouth turned down even further when he smiled. He was wearing the gray sweater she remembered from some time ago, the one with the moth hole in the back, the coffee stain on the front. A big toe stuck out through the broken stitching in the front of one of his shoes. The only tidy aspect of Howland was his hair, silver on the sides, dark on top. It curled around his forehead and over his ears in elegant waves. Not a hair was out of place. Victoria suspected Howland had nothing to do with the way his hair placed itself neatly on his head.

"You're not listening, Victoria. You can't expect a computer to go through a fire, get dropped fifteen or twenty feet, and then expect to be able to recover anything at all."

"I'm sure you'll find a way to get something from it," Victoria said, and walked away.

Howland glanced at her, and his mouth turned down. "Okay, I'll get the chief's approval to take it."

After he conferred with Casey, Howland loaded the box named Sibyl into the back of his station wagon and slid it toward the front of the car.

"Be careful of it," Victoria cautioned.

"Yeah, yeah," Howland mumbled as he slammed the back of the car shut. "Where do you want me to take this thing?"

"Can you examine it at my house?"

"Your house is better than mine," said Howland.

"Then leave it on the desk in my library."

"I gather you'd like to watch me work," Howland said. "I suppose if I can find anything at all on the hard drive, I can use Elizabeth's computer to read it." He held up both hands. "Don't expect miracles, Victoria. The insides are undoubtedly fused. At the very least, the data on the hard drive will be affected by heat."

He got back into his car. Victoria watched until he drove around the curve and out of sight.

Casey was at the front of the house, carefully moving rubble out of the wreckage and noting where it had been. Instead of disturbing her, Victoria went to the barn.

The door was ajar, the way it had been earlier. The hinges squealed as she opened it. She heard a rustling inside, a mouse perhaps, or the barn owl. When her eyes adjusted to the dim light, she stared at the floor where the tracks had been. They were gone, as if they had never been. The floor had a thin layer of dust and chaff, as if it had not been disturbed for years. There were no traces of tracks, no grease spots. The floor didn't even seem to have been swept. Victoria knew that she had not imagined the tracks. She, Elizabeth, and Casey had all seen them.

Victoria stepped outside into the sunlight again and beckoned to Casey, who came over immediately.

"What do you think of this?" Victoria showed her the unmarked floor.

"Somebody took a lot of trouble to clean up," Casey said. "I wish I'd taken photos of those tracks."

"There was no reason to," Victoria said. "No one thought a crime had been committed."

"I should have listened to you," said Casey.

CHAPTER 15

"This isn't your office, Dojan." Peter had walked in softly while Dojan was dialing the phone in Chief Hawkbill's office. Dojan looked over his shoulder.

"I have business," he muttered.

"Your business is in Washington. You take orders from Patience and me, not from that old man."

Dojan opened his mouth in a pink O that contrasted with his black beard; he opened his eyes wide so his dark irises were surrounded by bloodshot whites.

"Don't pull that shit on me, Dojan. You don't scare me with your craziness."

"I have business," Dojan repeated, pointing at the floor. "Here."

"What business? Now Hiram's dead . . ." Peter didn't finish. Dojan stepped toward the smaller man and grasped Peter's upper arms.

"Hiram dead? Liar!"

"They found him, Dojan, burnt to a crisp."

Dojan shook him. Peter's straight black hair flopped back and forth into his eyes. He smiled.

"Temper, temper." Peter's smile was a long thin line with no trace of amusement. "I don't know what you think you're doing, Dojan. Let go of me."

Dojan gave Peter a slight push and dropped his hands to his sides. "What happened to Hiram?"

"They found his body where you left him, Dojan. At least, the old lady, Mrs. Trumbull, thinks it's his body. Can't tell until they check dental records." Peter took his comb out of his pocket and slicked his hair back.

"Hiram can't be dead." Dojan's hands hung by his sides.

"They're already saying you killed him."

"No," said Dojan. "I would never kill Hiram."

"That's not what they're saying, Dojan. You didn't get blamed for killing that guy in Oak Bluffs, but we know who killed him, don't we?" Peter smiled his thin smile. "You'd better go back to Washington before it's too late."

"What do you mean, burned?"

"Come off it. You know as well as everybody else on the Island that Burkhardt's house burned down last night."

Dojan shook his head.

"Your old lady friend and the lady cop and the arson team from off-Island have been at the scene all morning. Where were you last night?"

"On my boat."

"In Menemsha?"

Dojan nodded.

"I suppose you were tied up on a town mooring?"

"Anchored."

"Convenient, Dojan. No one to check on you."

"I had nothing to do with a fire."

Peter changed the subject. "And you're doing all you can to get the casino permit at the federal level. Through the Bureau of Indian Affairs, I suppose."

Dojan was silent.

"More white men controlling our lives," Peter said.

Dojan put his hands in his jeans pockets and gazed across the fields and hills that overlooked the ocean.

"The chief may tell you what to do, but you answer to me, too. The tribe is paying your Washington salary, not the chief. Housing, too, right? On a yacht at a yacht club? Ha! If you know what's good for you—and the tribe—you won't push real hard to get that casino permit through."

"You threatening me?" Dojan asked.

"I wouldn't think of threatening you."

Dojan clenched and unclenched his hands.

Peter laughed. "You and I know the uproar there'll be if the tribe builds a casino on the Island. It's not worth the fight there's sure to be." Peter paced to the window, where he stopped to watch a hawk soar over the field.

Dojan was silent.

"The only plan that makes sense is a floating casino," Peter said. "Privately funded. Patience doesn't see that. She has an agenda of her own. Where is she getting the money for the land she's bought, tell me that, Dojan."

Dojan said nothing.

"Where's her money coming from?" Peter said again. "The owners have been selling land to her at cut-rate. Why? If a casino is built on tribal lands, her property values will soar. Is that conflict of interest, or what?"

Dojan turned toward the desk. "I must call."

"Go ahead." Peter leaned against the door frame and folded his arms.

"In private." Dojan set his bare feet apart and folded his arms over his chest.

"There's a pay phone in the hall."

Dojan unfolded his arms and stepped toward Peter. "Get out." He took another step.

Peter backed out of the office. "I hope you heard what I was telling you, Dojan."

"Shut the door behind you." Dojan pointed.

While Dojan and Peter conferred with each other in Chief Hawkbill's office, Elizabeth and Victoria were eating lunch by the fishpond to the east of the house. Sunlight filtered through the leaves of the old maple and scattered sparkling sun coins onto the water. Two small frogs perched motionless on lily pads, one submerged except for its eyes.

The six goldfish Victoria had acquired two years ago were now eight inches long and had produced dozens of bright offspring. Victoria tossed crumbs from her sandwich into the pond, and the fish converged in a frenzy.

"Did Hiram have any family?" Elizabeth asked.

"Cousins, but no children. He never married." Victoria tossed more crumbs. Victoria's face was partly shaded and entirely somber.

"What a horrible way to go." Elizabeth flicked an insect off the table with her fingernail.

"He was already dead, I'm sure. Someone must have killed him right after he left me that message."

Elizabeth studied her grandmother's solemn face. "There's nothing you could have done to prevent it, Gram. Don't feel bad. I mean, about preventing anything."

The sunlight had shifted so it shone in Elizabeth's face, and she moved slightly so she was shaded again. "Do you suppose he found something at Jube's house?"

"Found something or suspected something." Victoria sipped her glass of iced tea.

"Why would anyone want to kill Hiram?"

"I don't believe he had an enemy on the Island." Victoria set her glass down. "Hiram told me in confidence when he was here the other day about a close friend of his who spends two weeks with him every year."

"A gay friend?"

Victoria nodded. "Married, pillar of the community, two children, church deacon."

"Still in the closet, I suppose?"

Victoria nodded.

"Where does the friend live?"

"Nebraska."

"Oh," said Elizabeth. "Where is the friend now?"

"I don't know," said Victoria. "Hiram told me he was here on the Island up until the night Jube was killed. Tad, that was Hiram's friend, called him from the ferry."

"Cell phone?"

Victoria nodded.

"He could have been anywhere."

"Hiram also told me that before he met Tad, he and Jube had been lovers."

"Ouch," said Elizabeth. "Did Tad know?"

"Hiram didn't say."

"I can imagine this repressed gay guy, pillar of the community, *dah de dah*, living out each repressed year just waiting for his two weeks of freedom. Then he finds out about Burkhardt and Hiram, and Wham!" Elizabeth slapped her hands together, "he explodes. Maybe he killed both Burkhardt and Hiram, who betrayed him." Elizabeth shaded her eyes with a hand. "Have you told the police?"

Victoria shook her head.

"Hadn't you better?"

"I need to think about this," said Victoria. "Somehow, I can't see Tad as the killer."

"Have you met him?"

"No," Victoria said slowly. "No, I never have. The first time I heard about him was the day Hiram disappeared."

"Maybe they went off together and the body's not Hiram's."

"I dismissed that as not likely," said Victoria.

"Go on, Gram. You were about to say something when I interrupted."

Victoria rubbed her hand across her forehead. "Jube was blackmailing Hiram."

"With what? Everyone knew Hiram was gay. He didn't make a secret of it."

"Jube was threatening to expose Tad. That's why Hiram signed the noncompliance paper for the septic system."

"That's positively antediluvian. No one cares these days. Even spies can be openly gay without worrying about blackmail."

"Apparently Tad was vulnerable, and Hiram cared. I urged him to convince Tad to talk to his wife."

"What did Hiram say?"

"He said I didn't understand."

Elizabeth laughed.

"The key to Jube's and Hiram's death is in that computer, I'm sure of it," said Victoria.

"I almost forgot to tell you. While I was doing some errands this morning, Howland must have brought the computer back. He left you a note saying he'd put it on the library floor behind the couch."

Victoria swept crumbs from the table into her hand and tossed them into the pond. "I told him you might let him use your computer if he recovers something."

"Sure. Of course. I can't imagine that data on the computer would have survived the fire, though."

Victoria's face set stubbornly. "Howland can find something."

Elizabeth shrugged. "Before I went to the dump, we got three phone calls. Each time I answered, the person hung up. Strange."

"Perhaps they were calls for Linda?"

"The caller didn't leave a message, didn't say a word," Elizabeth said. "Not even any heavy breathing."

"Is there some way to know who called?"

"Star 69, but it won't work on your dial phone, Gram."

Victoria stacked the lunch dishes and set the utensils on the top plate. "Where is Linda, by the way?"

"I don't know. She left after you did this morning."

"Did she say where she was going?" Victoria asked.

"I assumed she was going to her uncle's place."

"She didn't show up while I was there."

"There goes the phone again." Elizabeth ran into the house and returned in a few minutes. "It was Dojan. He wants to see you right away."

"Now?" Victoria asked.

"He said he'll be here in a half hour. He said for you to be careful."

"Be careful?" said Victoria. "What am I supposed to be careful about?"

"He didn't say."

CHAPTER 16

Seven four-man tents ringed the edge of the field in back of Maley's Gallery, beyond the dancing statues, not far from the brook, and half-hidden under tall pines and oaks. Behind the tents, the soft earth was bare except for a fallen tree. Beside the fallen tree, a patch of ghostly translucent white plants, about seven or eight in all, had grown through the pine needles. They stood about five inches high and had fleshy stems and waxy flowers. The flowers arched over toward the ground. The flowers and stems were the same deathly color. When the bikers set up the tents, they had avoided the plants. Someone said they were Indian pipes. Someone else said they were corpse plants. Someone picked one of the flowers, and within a few minutes, it turned black. From then on, everybody avoided the patch of Indian pipes.

A half-dozen bikers, all men, had set up folding tables in the shade next to the tents, well away from the Indian pipes, and the women had set out lunch, cold chicken and potato salad. There was laughter and giggling and the snap and hiss of beer cans being opened. Rock music blared from a Cape Cod radio station.

A motorcycle jounced across the field toward the group. A heavy-set man seated in a canvas lounge chair looked up as the driver stopped and turned off the engine.

"What's up, Toby?" The man in the lounge chair held out a can of beer.

Toby lifted his leg over the back of his bike, kicked down the stand, removed his helmet, reached for the beer, popped the top, and held it up. "Thanks, Bugs." Toby was tall and wiry, and wore his hair in long dreadlocks. He was one of the few bikers without a beard. He was also the only black biker in the group.

"Did you get to the hospital, Toby?" A slim woman with bright metallic blond hair asked.

"Yeah, I did."

"How's Jesse?" asked a small man hunched at the table.

"Not bad, considering." Toby sat in a white resin chair someone had purchased at the hardware store. "Broke his leg, two ribs, and his collarbone. He's bruised and scraped, but he'll live. Nothing real serious, no internal injuries."

"That was stupid." Bugs's voice was raspy. "He and the rest of you were hot-dogging it with the local police."

Toby looked down at the beer can in his hands.

"How long before they let him out?" the man at the table asked.

"Another couple of days, he thinks. He hurts bad."

"Tough." Bugs growled. "He's lucky to be alive."

One of the women forked chicken and salad onto a plate and gave it to Toby. He smiled at her, teeth white against his dark skin. "Harley was supposed to get in touch with her sister. Anybody know if she did?"

The people around the table looked at one another and shook their heads.

"Haven't seen her all morning," said another blonde with long tightly curled hair. "She said something about hitching a ride into Oak Bluffs." She waved her hand over the chicken to discourage flies that were buzzing around.

"What was she doing in Oak Bluffs?" Toby looked around.

"She didn't say," the blonde answered.

"You've heard the latest, I trust?" Bugs asked Toby.

"Latest about what?"

"Her uncle's house burned to the ground last night, according to the radio." Bugs shifted in his chair, eyes on Toby. "They found a body."

Toby stopped chewing.

"The police are looking for a biker who was at his place three days running."

Toby swallowed his mouthful of chicken. "Yeah?"

"You and Harley go there?" Bugs asked.

"What's it to you?" Toby pushed himself out of the white chair and tossed his beer can at a plastic trash container.

"Pick it up," Bugs ordered.

Toby picked up the can and dropped it into the container.

"You want to know what's it to me? I'll tell you." Bugs got up from his chair, knocking over a butterfly net that had been leaning against it. The metallic-haired blonde picked up the net. Bugs was huge, six foot six at least, with an enormous stomach, huge muscular thighs, and arms like a weight lifter's. His head was small by comparison. He was bald, with a fringe of hair above his ears and a heavy black beard flecked with white and red. He wore thick, horn-rimmed glasses. "Sit down, brother."

Toby sat again in the white chair.

"We're here to have fun, right?"

Toby looked up at Bugs and nodded.

"We're not here to cause trouble, right?" Bugs growled.

Toby shook his head.

"Right?"

Toby nodded and looked at Bugs.

"We've got a reputation for being bad, right?" Bugs stared at the black biker.

Toby nodded.

"We don't mind being bad. But we're not BAD bad, right?"

Toby nodded.

"So you stupid shits try to outrun the local cops." Bugs pounded a fist into his open hand. "On an Island, for Chrissakes. Where did you think you were going? Round and round in circles until you ran out of gas? Smart, boy, really smart."

Toby said nothing. The rest of the group watched Bugs. The blonde waved her hand over the chicken.

"Lucky for us a biker got hurt, not some toddler."

Toby leaned forward in his chair and looked down.

"We're here to raise money to buy toys, for Chrissakes. We're here to change our image. Bad but decent, right?"

Toby stared up at Bugs, who was now pacing back and forth in front of his chair, his eyes fixed on Toby. He paced from shadow into sunlight. His bald head glistened.

"You know what the cops think now?"

Toby said nothing.

"Do you?" Bugs stopped pacing.

Toby shook his head and closed his eyes.

"The cops believe Uncle Jube was killed. The cops think a biker killed Uncle Jube, right?"

Toby opened his eyes.

Bugs leaned over him. "Am I right?" he rasped.

"I don't know." Toby leaned back, away from Bugs's too-close face.

"Well, I am. I'm right. Uncle Jube was making a big scene about bikers' attitudes and bikers' noise and bikers' mess. The cops are asking, did Uncle Jube make so much fuss that he upset the bikers?"

Toby said nothing.

"It all comes through on the scanner, what the cops think." Bugs gestured to the battery-operated scanner on the picnic table. "You and I know what upset Uncle Jube about the bikers, don't we?" Bugs jabbed a finger at Toby. "It's because some black dude biker is screwing his favorite niece, right?"

Toby said nothing.

"You know what else the cops think?"

Toby shook his head.

"The cops think a biker parked in Uncle Jube's barn and killed somebody in Uncle Jube's house. The cops think a biker came back the next day and maybe stole something from Uncle Jube's house. A will, maybe? Would you happen to know about that, Toby? The cops think a biker came back the day after that and torched Uncle Jube's house to get rid of the body and the evidence, then swept away the bike tracks in the barn. You know what I'm saying?"

"Oh God, no!" Toby stood up suddenly, and his chair tipped over.

"You and your girlfriend are in deep doo-doo." Bugs grabbed the butterfly net and strode out into the field, flourishing it by its frail handle like a sword.

The curly-haired blonde whispered to Toby, "Bugs says there's eighty species of butterflies on Martha's Vineyard."

Casey saw Dojan's van fly past the station house going at least twenty miles an hour over the speed limit. She sighed, heaved herself out of her swivel chair, fastened on her belt, and went after him, blue lights flashing. Dojan turned into Victoria's drive. Casey followed.

She got out of the vehicle and was tugging her belt into a more comfortable position, ready to give Dojan a scolding or a speeding ticket, when she saw his expression.

"What's the matter, Dojan?"

"Victoria." His voice was low.

"What are you talking about?"

"The engineer was murdered. Now Hiram is dead."

"We don't have confirmation yet that it was Hiram." Casey stuck her thumbs in her trouser pockets. Dojan's head was thrown back, and he stared down his nose at Casey. His eyes were wild. He wore his black mesh shirt and black jeans, and his bare feet were dirty. Ragged strips of peeling sunburn hung from his forehead, nose, and upper arms. His tattoos looked as if they were covered with shredded plastic.

"Three people knew something that nobody else knew. Jube Burkhardt, Hiram Pennybacker, and Victoria Trumbull."

"She's not involved in this, Dojan."

"Yes she is. The sewage engineer spoke to Hiram before he died. Hiram spoke to Victoria before he was killed. Hiram told Victoria something. She does not know what she knows. But she is next."

"What do you expect me to do? I can't guard her round the clock just because you're worried about her."

"I don't want your help. Victoria is my friend." He jabbed his thumb at his chest. "I will take care of her."

"Lord!" said Casey.

Victoria appeared at the kitchen door. "I thought I heard you drive up. Elizabeth's made a fresh pot of coffee. Come in and have some."

"No, thanks, Victoria, I've got to get back to my paperwork." Casey turned to Dojan. "Will you please slow down when you drive through *my* town? Next time I'm giving you a ticket." She climbed into the Bronco and drove off.

Dojan wiped his bare feet on the grass mat in the entry, and ducked his head so the new osprey feather in his hair would clear the doorway.

Victoria studied him with concern. "What's wrong, Dojan?"

"Is Hiram dead?"

"The arson squad found human remains. I think it's Hiram, but the forensics people need to go through dental records." She paused. "There wasn't much left to identify."

Dojan shook his head. "That day I came to your house, Hiram left when he saw me. What did he say to you?"

"Not much," Victoria said. "Jube Burkhardt, the engineer . . . ?"

"I know who he was."

"He and Hiram had a long talk at Hiram's house the night before Jube was killed." Victoria moved away from the doorway. "Let's sit down."

Dojan followed her into the cookroom and perched on the edge of his chair.

"Hiram said Jube was keyed up, ranting all over the place," said Victoria. "One minute against the casino, the next minute for it."

"Anything else?" Dojan was shaking one leg impatiently. Only his strange eyes showed he was listening.

"He told me Jube threatened to hold up any septic request the tribe submitted. Jube said he would check every septic tank in Gay Head."

Dojan nodded. "That would hold off action for years."

"After that, he stalked out of the meeting."

"Calling everybody 'mongrels,'" said Elizabeth, who'd brought in the coffeepot and mugs from the kitchen.

"What else?"

"The day Jube was killed, he asked Hiram to meet him at the foot of the cliffs along with someone else."

"The killer." Dojan stopped shaking his leg.

"That was all Jube said to Hiram until the night I saw him on the cliff. Hiram climbed down the cliff. Before he died, Jube said to Hiram, quite clearly, 'Sibyl.'"

"Sibyl?" said Dojan.

Victoria nodded. "The arson squad found Jube's computer this morning. On the side was a partly burned decal that read SIBYL."

"Where is the computer now?" Dojan asked, leaning forward. He hadn't touched the coffee Elizabeth had poured.

"Howland brought it here a couple of hours ago," Elizabeth said. "I wasn't here, so he left a note."

"You know Howland Atherton, don't you?" Victoria asked.

Dojan nodded. "The federal drug agent."

"He's also a computer expert. The computer is badly burned, but he's going to salvage whatever he can. Do you want to see it?"

Dojan nodded. The osprey feather bobbed.

"How did you get the new feather?" asked Elizabeth. "Pluck it out of a bird?"

"Under the osprey nest near my boat." Dojan turned to Victoria. "You must put the computer someplace safe. The police station. It's not safe here."

"The police station door doesn't have a lock, either."

"Better there than here." Dojan padded through the kitchen and dining room into the library.

The library was on its way to becoming like Jube Burkhardt's house. Stacks of books were piled next to the bookcases. The shelves overflowed. When she had time, Victoria intended to sort through the books, give some of them to Mary Jo for the library book sale, but she hadn't gotten around to it yet. The sofa was piled with Christmas decorations and wrapping paper she hadn't taken up to the attic yet, a jigsaw puzzle Elizabeth had completed that was too pretty to break apart. There was a big oak desk, its top covered with papers, chairs with caned bottoms in need of repair, a couple of lamps that were too good to throw out. Victoria could sympathize with Jube Burkhardt. Give her more time and she could fill up her house with things that might be useful someday as completely as he had filled his.

"Where is it?" Dojan looked around.

"Howland's note said behind the couch," Elizabeth answered.

Victoria bent down to look. When she didn't see the computer, she and Dojan shifted the couch to one side.

"Where could he have put it?" Victoria said.

"Someone has stolen it," said Dojan.

"Maybe Howland reconsidered and took it home with him, after all," Victoria said.

"I don't like this," said Dojan. "Get out of this house and stay away until the killer is found."

"Don't be ridiculous, Dojan."

Dojan grasped Victoria's arm. "You don't understand, my friend. The killer thinks you know something."

Victoria scowled. "Well, I don't." She stood up. "I am not leaving this house, Dojan, and that's that." She stalked out of the room.

Elizabeth laughed. "The killer's going to have a tough time with my grandmother."

"This is not funny," said Dojan.

CHAPTER 17

Howland arrived ten minutes later, and he, Victoria, and Elizabeth went into the library where Dojan was seated on the thronelike wooden armchair.

"I put the computer here," said Howland, indicating a space behind the couch. "Are you sure none of you moved it?"

"Certainly not," said Victoria.

Howland lifted the end of the couch and moved it still farther into the room, exposing a roll of dust, several pennies, and a golf ball.

"The computer wouldn't have fit underneath," Victoria said. "The couch is too low."

"I searched under and around all the furniture," said Elizabeth. "Definitely not here."

Howland ran his fingers through his hair. "Who knew you'd found the computer, Victoria?"

"The arson squad, Chief O'Neill, Junior Norton, and the three of you." Victoria sat on the arm of the sofa. "Are you sure you didn't take it home with you, Howland?"

"Of course I'm sure," he said curtly. "There's still a crushed spot on the rug where I put the thing."

Dojan, who'd been silent ever since Howland arrived, uncrossed his leg, put both feet flat on the floor, and gripped the arms of the chair. He looked, Victoria thought, like a pharaoh whose beard and hair had gone awry.

"Who'd want Burkhardt's old computer?" Elizabeth asked.

Howland paced back and forth in front of the fireplace. "The line of takers would stretch from here to Alley's."

"I suppose there's a copy of his will on it." Elizabeth plopped down on the couch, jouncing Victoria, who was still perched on the arm. "A list of his blackmail victims."

Howland nodded. "I wouldn't be surprised."

Victoria smoothed the frayed fabric on the arm of the couch. "Both of his nieces will want to see his will."

Howland stopped pacing. "I have no idea where to begin looking for that computer."

Dojan continued to sit like stone.

Victoria cleared her throat. "If I were worried about what was on that computer and then found it after the fire, I would get rid of it."

"Without finding out what's on it?" asked Elizabeth. "Suppose you thought it might have a copy of his will?"

"Anyone could enter a will on a computer," Victoria said. "It wouldn't be valid."

"It would give someone an advantage to know what was in the will," said Elizabeth.

"We want the computer because we hope it may have information that will lead us to the killer." Victoria shifted on her perch.

"That's exactly why the killer would want to discard it," said Howland.

Elizabeth moved to the side of the couch and patted the cushion next to her. "You can't be comfortable, Gram. Have a seat."

"Thank you," Victoria said.

Howland began to pace again.

"How would you dispose of a computer?" Victoria asked.

"I would take it out on my boat," said Dojan. "Drop it overboard into deep water."

"Not everyone has access to a boat," said Victoria.

"I'd take it to the dump," said Elizabeth. "There's a mountain of discarded computers and television sets. They get trucked off-Island periodically."

"That would be too obvious," Howland said. "Easy to spot a burned computer."

"Then I'd toss it into a container at the dump."

"You're not supposed to discard electronic gadgets and appliances in the Dumpsters," said Victoria.

Elizabeth turned to Howland. "Stop pacing, will you? You're driving me crazy."

Howland stopped and leaned against the mantelpiece, hands in his pockets.

"We need to think," said Victoria. "Someone knew we recovered the computer from the fire, and someone knew that Howland took the computer away. That person would have to have been at the site."

"The only people there were the arson team, Casey, Junior Norton, and you," said Howland. "I showed up later."

"None of the people you named would have any interest in the computer," Victoria said. "Therefore, someone else must have been at Jube's place and overheard us."

"Where, though?" asked Elizabeth.

Victoria thought for a moment. "The barn loft. Of course. I heard what I thought were mice or birds in the barn," she said. "A person could easily have been in the loft. We used to hide up there as children."

"He could hardly have followed me to your house without being seen," said Howland.

"We talked openly about taking the computer to my house," said Victoria. "Everyone knows where I live."

Howland nodded.

"He could park off the road the fishermen use. We'd never have noticed," said Victoria. "Then walk to the barn, go in the side door, brush away footprints behind him with a pine branch, climb up into the loft, and watch from there."

"Creepy," said Elizabeth.

"Were you aware of anyone following you when you left Jube's?" Victoria asked Howland.

"A horse trailer came out of one of the side roads after I passed. I wouldn't have seen anything behind the trailer, even if I were looking. And I wasn't looking."

"Would you have been aware of a motorcycle following behind the trailer?" Victoria asked.

Howland shook his head. "I doubt it."

"He didn't need to follow you," said Victoria. "He kept calling until Elizabeth left, then went into the house, saw your note explaining where you'd put the computer, and took it." Victoria glanced around the room, from Howland to Dojan to Elizabeth. "Then what?"

Howland walked over to the windows that faced the road. A car drove past. The dry leaves of the horse chestnut shivered. "I hope the hell he didn't drop it in Vineyard Sound," said Howland.

"Or take it off-Island," said Elizabeth.

"You don't have a dump sticker, sir," the dumpmaster said when Howland pulled up to the shack a half hour later.

The shack, on a knoll in the middle of the dump, was decorated with found objects. Unmatched chairs were set up around a broken-legged table, which was spread with chipped plates and unmatched glasses set on a frayed tablecloth with an off-center wine stain. The table was shaded with a torn beach umbrella.

The dumpmaster himself was enormously fat and had walked over to Howland's car with great effort. His clothes looked as if they, too, had come from the dump, but they were so huge and tentlike it seemed unlikely that there was another person on the Island discarding clothing that would fit the dump master. His chartreuse-and-brown plaid trousers were belted with rope, his orange and magenta Hawaiian shirt was tucked into the great waist of his pants.

He leaned down to look at the passenger side of the car, peered at Elizabeth, and chuckled. "Not you again. You cleaning out your grandmother's house?"

"We're looking for something to take away from the dump, Mr. Lardner," Elizabeth said.

The dumpmaster spread his arms. "Be my guest." He leaned down to Howland. "You ought to patronize this dump, Mr. Atherton. Better-quality stuff than that dump of yours."

"Anybody throw out a computer today?" Howland asked.

"How'm I supposed to know?" The dumpmaster lifted his flowered shoulders. "Everybody in town's come by today. Some twice," he added, looking significantly at Elizabeth. "If they threw out a computer, it would either be over there with the TVs," he pointed toward the mound of television sets and computer monitors, "or with the appliances," he waved his arm to a mountain of washers, dryers, dishwashers, and microwaves, "or in that Dumpster with metal stuff or the one next to it with construction stuff." He ducked his head in thought. "Or they might have dumped it in with household trash. Never can tell where people are going to dump stuff."

"You go through this every week?" Howland asked as they drove away from the shack.

"It's a social occasion," Elizabeth said. "If you're running for town office, this is where you campaign."

"Let's start with TV Mountain."

A short man with a graying goatee, his hair falling over his forehead, hustled toward them with a sheaf of papers. "Elizabeth! Didn't recognize you in that car. Can I get you to sign this petition?"

"I already did, Les. Get Howland to sign."

Howland pulled on the emergency brake. Les hurried over to his side and thrust the petition and a pen at him. Howland signed with a flourish.

Elizabeth leaned across Howland. "Les, did you see anyone dump a computer this morning?"

"Several people, three or four at least. Do you need one? There's at least one good 386."

"Did anyone bring in a burned CPU?" Howland asked.

"I don't think I'd recognize it as part of a computer without the monitor."

"Where did they leave them?" Howland asked.

"I didn't notice." He held up one of his fingers. "Excuse me. Here comes Mrs. Summerville." He hurried off with his petition.

The mound of television sets was much larger than they had expected. They looked up at it.

"If the computer's here, it would have to be in plain sight," Howland said. "He would hardly have moved stuff to bury it underneath."

They walked around the mound, trying to see under easily shifted objects, and finally moved on.

They tried the appliance heap next, and then the large Dumpster. The dumpmaster waddled down the knoll to where they stood figuring the best approach to searching it.

"Someone threw out an aluminum ladder a couple weeks ago.

Thought it might come in handy." He reached behind the Dumpster and started to haul out a bent ladder.

"Absolutely," said Howland, helping.

The dumpmaster brushed off his hands. Between short gasps he said again, "I knew it would come in handy."

Howland climbed to the rim of the Dumpster, then jumped in. There was the sound of breaking glass. Howland swore.

A flock of seagulls rose from the inside. Elizabeth couldn't see Howland from where she stood, and she waited while she heard him shove things around. The gulls circled. One started to land inside, and squawked and soared away when a chunk of metal that looked like the arm of an aluminum lawn chair flew up at it. The gull opened its beak and let out a long cry and a series of short barks. Elizabeth heard Howland walk around on metallic things that sounded as if they were shifting under his weight. He thumped his hand against the metal side of the Dumpster at one point.

"It's hopeless," she heard him say finally. "Nothing but garbage. I've got to get out of here before I pass out."

When Howland reached the ground again, Elizabeth sniffed. "You stink."

"Thanks."

"I thought it was supposed to be metal, not garbage."

"Someone dumped a plastic bag of fish guts. It's been in the sun all morning."

"Come back to my grandmother's. You can take a shower outdoors and I'll put your clothes in the washer."

Howland sat in his car, the door open. "This dump is *not* better than mine."

CHAPTER 18

As they drove back toward Victoria's, Howland muttered, "I don't know why your grandmother is so convinced we need that computer. It's a lost cause."

"She insists you can recover whatever is on it," said Elizabeth.

Howland grunted. "I can't work magic."

"Maybe they dumped it in the woods somewhere," said Elizabeth.

Howland shook his head. "Someone would find it and make a public furor about improper rubbish disposal."

"Maybe they tossed the unit in a Dumpster someplace. The trash gets shipped off-Island. Nobody would notice an old computer."

Howland slowed at Brandy Brow and waited for a car to pass. "Let's say someone picked up the computer from Victoria's. He'd want to move fast, before your grandmother showed up. He'd put it in the trunk of his car . . ."

"Or on the back of a motorcycle, and it could have been a woman," said Elizabeth.

"Right. Car or motorcycle. She—or he—would take the computer someplace nearby where they could examine it without being disturbed. If she or he knows something about computers, she or he might take it apart, remove the hard drive, and discard the rest." Howland paused. "This 'he or she' stuff is nonsense. If he doesn't know computers, he might think the data were destroyed. Where would he go?"

"Probably not into the village. Everybody would notice a strange car or a motorcycle with a computer strapped on back. They'd have to pass the police station and Alley's."

"So he'd probably head toward Edgartown."

Elizabeth sat up. "The baseball field this side of the firehouse has a trash bin." She wrinkled her nose. "Would you like to take a shower first?"

"Can't waste the time. I don't know how often they empty the Dumpsters."

"I'm not sure I can stand you much longer."

"Likely to get worse, unless *you* intend to crawl around in the next few trash bins." Howland tapped the horn as they passed Victoria's house. Tall tiger lilies in front of the house were an orange blaze in the shade of the horse chestnut tree. "Dump day being a social event, every scanner in West Tisbury will be reporting about Victoria's granddaughter and the fed crawling around in the trash."

"Twenty-first-century party line."

The baseball field was about a quarter mile beyond Victoria's house, behind a thick screen of scrub oak and pine. Howland missed the turnoff and had to back up. He turned left onto a grass road.

"New car tracks," he said.

"Baseball games go on all the time, almost every day."

They parked in the shade of an oak, got out, and looked around.

"Two trash bins," said Howland. "One for the kids playing ball and one by the firehouse."

A steady buzz came from the first Dumpster.

"Goddamn!" said Howland. "Yellow jackets."

"Going after soda cans, I bet."

A cloud of wasps hummed around the candy wrappers, soggy ice cream cones, juice boxes, apple cores, half-eaten oranges, and fermenting grapes.

"Damnation," said Howland.

"Can you see in?" asked Elizabeth.

"You look."

A mass of yellow-and-black bodies squirmed around the sweet trash. The Dumpster reverberated with the buzz of beating wings. Elizabeth moved back.

"It's not exactly a sure thing that the computer is here," she said.

"We have to at least look, if I'm to stay in Victoria's good graces. Better check the one by the firehouse first."

They walked past the feed-grain bag that marked first base and across the field of mown grass, and found the bin almost empty, with only a few oil cans, rags, and papers.

"Back to the baseball field," Elizabeth said. "Insect spray?"

"We'd need gallons."

"Protective clothing? Smoke bomb? That would do it, smoke."

Howland sighed.

Together, they gathered up damp leaves from under the trees, and lit a small fire in a cardboard box from the trunk of Howland's car. When the fire was smoldering, Howland tossed the box into the Dumpster, and then they sat under the trees and waited. Dozens of yellow jackets straggled out. The buzzing lessened and eventually stopped.

Howland got up with another sigh and hoisted himself over the side of the trash bin, which was considerably smaller than the one at the dump. Elizabeth watched as he prodded and poked with a broken baseball bat he'd found.

"Ouch! Goddamn!"

Smoke billowed up.

"I can't see a damned thing." There was a metallic clang, a clatter as something tumbled and shifted, and the sound of breaking glass. Then quiet.

"Are you okay?"

Something stirred, something else fell, and then Howland called out, "Found it!"

Glass crunched under his feet as he hoisted the scorched computer, passed it to Elizabeth, and climbed out.

She turned away, laughing. Howland's eyes peered out whitely from his sooty face, swollen now with wasp stings. His clothes and hands were filthy. The smell of rotten fish was overlaid with the smell of smoke and decaying fruit.

She set the computer on the tailgate of Howland's station wagon, and he shoved it inside the car, covered it with a blanket, and closed the tailgate.

Back at Victoria's, he examined the computer. Some charred paint had chipped off, exposing shiny metal and a sizeable dent in one side. He covered the unit again, and locked the car doors.

Elizabeth escorted him to the outdoor shower. "Toss your clothes out, and I'll bring you some of my grandfather's clothes. You can wear them until I wash yours."

While Elizabeth and Howland were searching for the computer, Victoria gathered up her cloth bag and straw hat.

"Chief Hawkbill ordered me to search the cliffs," Dojan had said. "I need your help."

Victoria climbed up into the passenger seat of his van. "Are the cliffs still cordoned off by the police?"

"The police have gone."

They pulled out of the drive onto the Edgartown Road, passed the police station and the old mill. Dojan shifted into low gear to get his van up the gentle rise of Brandy Brow. Beyond Alley's the van picked up speed. In Chilmark, white, brown, and gray sheep grazed on close-cropped hills that overlooked the Atlantic. Victoria heard them bleat.

Dojan wiped his wrist across his mouth. "I will drop you off at the top of the Gay Head cliffs. My cousins own concessions there. They will watch over you."

"I'll be perfectly safe without their watching me," said Victoria.

"After I drop you off, I will park off Obed's grandmother's road and climb up the cliffs."

"You want me to signal if the police come by?"

Dojan nodded. "Or anybody who seems nosy."

Only a few cars were parked near the steps at this time of day, early afternoon when most people were at the beach. Dojan offered his arm to Victoria and they walked past the small souvenir stands. Wind chimes hung from the eaves of almost every shack, and tinkled in the breeze.

"Yo, Dojan," someone called.

"What's happening, Dojan?"

"You associate with that crazy man, Mrs. Trumbull?" a woman in the next-to-last shack said.

"Buy some beads, Dojan, twenty-four dollars."

Above each shack wind socks and banners, some shaped like fish, some like exotic flowers, fluttered and snapped.

Dojan grinned.

Victoria held on to the brim of her straw hat. The yellow ribbon whipped around her face. As they passed the last sheltering building, the wind hit them with full force, swirling dust and papers high into the air. The Elizabeth Islands across the sound stood out clearly. Victoria could make out buildings and trees on Cuttyhunk. Beyond the islands, she could see the Texas tower in the middle of Buzzards Bay that marked the channel to the Cape Cod Canal. Wind blew her hair back from her face, then eddied around and swished strands back into her eyes, making them water. She held one hand on the crown of her hat.

They had reached the chain-link fence. "Do you have a wristwatch?" Dojan asked.

Victoria lowered her arm to show him, and her hat blew off. Dojan seized it in midair. Victoria thanked him and tied the ribbons under her chin.

"In fifteen minutes I will start the climb up from the beach." Dojan brought a tarnished silver whistle on a leather thong from his pocket. "Whistle if anyone seems too interested. One whistle means someone is close, and I will drop down to the beach. Two whistles mean I have time, and I will climb up." With that, Dojan slipped away.

Far below, people walked on the beach. Victoria watched for a while, then sat on the edge of the concrete slab that had been a gun emplacement during the Second World War. After fifteen long minutes, she lifted herself from her hard seat and went to the fence, casually, as if she had simply decided to look at the view from there. The crowd had thinned. A few people stood around, paying no attention to her, looking at the lighthouse and the view of sea and islands.

She had practiced saying to herself, "Can you tell me if those birds are eider ducks?" in case anyone should look down toward the rosebush where Dojan would be, and then she would point away from him.

Now she could see his head and hands. He was climbing slowly up the gully, the one she would have used to slide down to the beach. He was well camouflaged, and she didn't think anyone else would see him.

Off and on during the past several days, she'd heard motorcycles go by, too fast and too loud. She heard them now from her spot next to the fence. There seemed to be more than one, but she couldn't tell for certain.

She hoped the bikers were not going to come here. She was not sure what she would say to them. She realized she must look conspicuous standing there, a not-so-young woman all by herself.

The last few people had left, a small girl holding her father's hand, teenagers who had no idea she was there. A busload of elderly people had come and gone.

She heard voices, a deep voice that sounded vaguely familiar, a softer deep voice, and a woman's laughter.

She looked over the fence. Dojan was moving slowly, crouching, examining the ground, setting one bare foot on the slippery clay and testing it before he moved again.

She turned. Three people were walking up the slight hill toward her, two men and a woman. One man was tall, bald, bearded, and heavyset. The woman was about the same age as Linda, Jube's niece, and looked quite a bit like her, except her hair was an orangey-purple metallic color and her nose had a gold stud on one side. The third person, a man so dark his skin was blue-black was taller than the girl, but much shorter than the bald man. His skin glistened. He wore his hair in long twists that reached well below his shoulders. All three wore black leather clothing.

"Hello," Victoria said tentatively. "Lovely view."

"Ma'am," the tall man said, nodding his head politely.

The girl said nothing.

The black man said, "Real nice here."

"That island you can see from here is Cuttyhunk." Victoria pointed away from the cliff below them.

"Anybody live there?" the black man asked.

"A few people. Thirty-five or so."

"What do they do in the winter?" the girl asked.

The bald man stood behind the others.

Victoria and the two younger people talked about winters on Cuttyhunk and the view. Victoria pointed to the birds and asked if anyone thought they were eider ducks. At that, the bald man stepped forward and looked intently at the birds in the distance and said, in a raspy voice, that they were. Victoria saw an orange and black butterfly flash by, and another and a third.

"Look at that, how lovely they are!"

"Monarchs," the bald man growled. "They migrate to Mexico this time of year."

"They seem too fragile for such a long trip."

"Bugs is into butterflies." The black man inclined his head toward the bald man. "He teaches at Smith College."

Bugs nodded.

Victoria coughed and her eyes watered. Bugs. The man on Jube Burkhardt's telephone list. The voice she'd heard when Elizabeth had dialed the number on Jube's list.

"You here by yourself?" the black man asked Victoria.

"A friend dropped me off. He'll be by to pick me up. He had to do an errand. He should be back soon." Victoria found herself talking too fast and too much, and felt her face flush. She hoped they hadn't noticed.

"Nice to meet you." The bald man turned away from Victoria. "Come here, Toby." He pointed down the cliff to where Dojan crouched, motionless. He rasped to the girl, "That's where they found your uncle." Bugs looked closely. "Someone's down there."

The others moved next to him, and all three peered toward the figure on the cliff.

"What's he doing there?" said Toby.

"I'm calling 911. This is a crime scene," said Bugs.

"Got your cell phone?" Toby asked.

"On my bike."

The two men strode toward the steps and the parking area. The girl hung back.

"Do you need a ride someplace?" she asked Victoria.

"My friend should be here any minute." Victoria wanted the girl to leave, and soon.

"I'll wait with you, if you'd like," the girl said.

"Thank you, but I'm fine."

"You sure?"

"Yes," said Victoria. "Yes, definitely. Join your friends."

The girl shrugged and wandered away slowly. The sun glinted on her hair. When she was out of sight, Victoria blew twice on the whistle. Dojan looked up and she beckoned him to hurry. He snatched something from the ground and had just climbed over the fence when she heard the police siren.

"We've got to get out of here," Victoria said. "Now."

"To my cousin's shop, quick." Dojan took Victoria's arm and hustled her along faster than she normally walked.

CHAPTER 19

Harley fastened her helmet in place over her purple hair. She slung her leather-trousered leg over the back wheel of the motorcycle and settled herself onto the backseat. "You know who that old lady was, don't you?"

Toby stood beside the bike, helmet in hand. Bugs was talking to a woman tourist, helmet under his arm.

The Aquinnah police had come. They looked over the cliff, saw no one, questioned a few people, took the bikers' names, and left.

"Victoria Trumbull. Unmistakable."

Bugs turned at the mention of the name. "Your sister staying with her?" He strode over to Toby's motorcycle.

"That's what I hear." Harley's voice was sulky.

"I want you to meet with that sister of yours."

"Why?"

"To discuss ownership of some expensive property." Bugs's body shaded Harley's face and shoulders.

"I don't give a damn about the property." She looked up at him, silhouetted against the sun, face hidden.

"Somebody does," Bugs rasped. "Eighteen million bucks? You meet with her, and soon."

"I haven't talked with my sister for ages. My uncle either."

"We know why, don't we?" Bugs set his knuckles on his leather-clad hips. "You've got a right to sleep with anyone you want to, but you don't have a right to do it out of spite. You trying to wreck Toby's life, too? To get even with your uncle? Now he's dead, you plan to discard Toby?"

"Toby loves me."

Bugs glanced at Toby, who was looking down at the ground.

"Funny things are happening around here," Bugs went on, "and we bikers are getting blamed for it."

Victoria watched from the back of Dojan's cousin's shop until the bikers were out of sight, heading down-Island. She and Dojan had ducked into Bernice Minnowfish's small store. Bernice offered Victoria a seat, and then brought out glasses of sun-tea with lemon.

"Thank you. It's nice to sit for a change." Victoria smiled up at the stout woman.

"It's an honor, Mrs. Trumbull." Bernice busied herself, folding and straightening the T-shirts and caps and sweatshirts that were on display. "The rest of them," she indicated the double line of shacks, "the rest of them are envious."

After Bernice had waited on a stream of customers from a tour bus and there was a quiet moment, Victoria said, "How are you related to Charity? Charity Minnowfish was my best friend in grammar school."

"Charity was my husband's grandmother," Bernice said. "What a fine woman. I knew her well."

"She was Dojan's great-grandmother, wasn't she? So you must be Dojan's first cousin once removed."

"That's right. First cousin once removed in-law."

Bernice pointed out relatives in the shops across from them, and they discussed who was related to whom, interrupted occasionally when a tourist stopped to buy something. Dojan stood by the window, watching first the police coming and going, then the motorcyclists leaving.

"We go now, Cousin Bernice," he said abruptly. "Come, my friend." He held out his arm, and Victoria lifted herself out of the canvas chair.

"This has been an honor, Mrs. Trumbull. I have a gift for you." Bernice draped a necklace of small Pacific shells, dyed fluorescent pink and green and blue and yellow, over Victoria's shoulders. "Come back soon."

Victoria, who was not much of a hugger, embraced the broad woman and left, her arm linked around Dojan's, the lilac stick in her free hand, the shell necklace swaying with her movement.

Toby parked his bike in the shade of the Norway maple at the edge of Victoria's drive and turned off the motor. He looked over his shoulder at Harley, who was sitting rigidly in her seat.

"Want me to go in with you, sugar, or would you rather face your sister alone?"

Harley swung her leg over the back wheel, set both feet on the ground, took off her helmet, and put it behind her seat. She ran her fingers through her hair.

"I don't see her car."

Toby waited, still astride the bike.

"I don't want to do this, Toby."

"I know," he said.

"She's a bitch on wheels."

Toby said nothing.

"I don't care about the money, honest I don't. Uncle Jube was a sicko, and she is too."

Toby nodded.

"I'll go check. Even if her car's not here." She started toward Victoria's house, then turned. "Tell me first, Toby. Do you believe Bugs? You know, what he said about me and you?"

"Should I believe him?" Toby asked.

Harley looked down. "Maybe at first, because, you know . . ."

"A black Harley-Davidson biker who wears his hair in dreadlocks, and would probably be tattooed if he thought tattoos would show."

Harley smiled faintly. "Because I knew it would jerk Uncle Jube's chain."

"Why did you want to do that?"

Harley wiped her eyes on the sleeves of her T-shirt.

"Get back on the bike, sugar. We're going to Uncle Jube's place and talk."

When they got there, the open grassy area with the charred ruins looked desolate. The barn stood, unharmed, near the oak woods. The blackened, broken skeleton of a house looked like a giant dead crow. It stank of worrisome things. The chimney in the midst of the ruins looked like a spine. The granite back step led up to a charred door frame, black with a shiny crackled pattern, and the door frame opened to a mess. Stacks of partially burned papers had toppled wherever the fire had dropped them. The ceiling had flopped onto the first floor and was draped, like a shroud, over the kitchen stove. A black cast-iron frying pan rested on the burner of the stove.

They walked away from the ruined house to the point, where they would not have to see the rubble, stepped down off the low grassy bank, and faced the unruffled waters of the Great Pond. They could hear wavelets lapping against the pebbly beach. Beyond their small world, breakers rumbled on the other side of the barrier bar.

They walked, hand in hand, along the beach. Harley bent down occasionally, still holding Toby's hand, to pick up an oyster shell or a pebble.

Toby suddenly let go of her hand and plucked something out of the bank.

"Look what I found, sugar." He held up a perfect quartz arrow-head, a tiny bird point. Its facets glistened as if it had been chipped out of a beach stone only hours before.

He held it out to her on the pale palm of his hand. "Whatever happens between us, sugar, this is for you to keep. To remember me."

She took the tiny arrowhead and closed her fingers around it. He held out his arms, and she went into them, nestled her head against his chest and closed her eyes.

"My uncle kept trying to play me against my sister," she whispered into his chest. "I was his favorite, he said. My sister was a tramp, he said. He was leaving the family place to me, he said, not to both of us." She looked up at Toby, his dark face shiny with reflections of sunlight off the water. He relaxed his hold around her.

"I loved this place. We used to come here summers, my mother, my sister, and me. It was before Uncle Jube, you know, filled the house with junk."

They walked along the beach until they came to a log that had washed up on shore, and sat on it.

Directly across from them they could see three or four cabins on the opposite shore of the pond, a half mile or more away, partially hidden by scrub oak. The buildings were weathered to a soft gray that blended into the gray background of oaks and lichens and mosses and stones.

To their left, spray occasionally flew over the long slender bar at the south end of the pond, making shimmering rainbows. A fish jumped. Circular ripples spread out on the calm surface until the circles became so wide they faded away. A slight breeze riffled the water into a cat's-paw that died out as quickly as it had appeared.

"My sister had a room on the second floor next to Uncle Jube's." Harley spoke so softly Toby had to bend his head to hear. "I slept in a little room in the attic. It had a sloping ceiling and funny little angular closets tucked under the eaves. All night long I could hear the ocean. It was like a heartbeat, so steady and regular. Sometimes it was loud and frightening, sometimes soft and gentle, but always steady. In the morning, I could look out my window and see the ocean."

A gull flew over, its wings beating steadily. The air smelled of salt and sun-released pine resin.

Toby put his arm around her.

"If I tell you something, you won't laugh at me?"

He shook his head. His dreadlocks swayed back and forth across his shoulders with a clicking sound of beads.

"When I was a little girl, I used to dream about my prince riding up to my uncle's house on a white charger."

Toby nodded.

"I used to pretend he would toss the reins over the horse's back so it wouldn't step on them, you know?"

Toby nodded.

"He'd slide off the horse, and I'd run to him. I was always wearing a gauzy white dress and flowers in my hair. Then we would walk on the beach, this beach, looking for lucky stones. His horse would crop the grass around the house. You know the sound?" She looked up into his black face, and he nodded. "This place hasn't changed a bit since I was a little girl. Except the house is gone. That's so sad."

"Now the white charger is a purple Harley, and your prince is black." Toby held his arm around her more firmly.

Harley put her hand on his thigh.

"Mother and Uncle Jube had an awful fight about ten years ago. It had to do with my sister, who was twelve or thirteen at the time. She was much prettier than me. We never came back after the fight. My mother died two years ago. I never found out what the fight was about."

"But you can guess," Toby said.

"I can guess. I never talked to my sister about Uncle Jube and the fight with our mother."

Toby gazed across the pond, but his eyes were focused far beyond the opposite shore.

"What happened between Uncle Jube and you?" he asked after they'd been silent for a long time.

"He always had a scheme going, some way to make money or get at somebody for something they did to him. He was always like that. But he was beginning to get too friendly with me, you know what I mean?"

Toby nodded.

"I didn't want to get too cozy with him. He kept telling me I was his heir, that I would own the house and land when he was gone. It was getting to me, you know?"

"So you took up with the most unacceptable person you could find to get Uncle Jube off your back."

"I got to be honest with you, Toby. It started that way. It's not that way now."

"Bugs has a point, sugar. You said it right when you told him Toby loves you. I do. But where will it lead? Would you want to spend your life with me? Would you want to have my kids? Some white— with purple hair." He mussed her hair gently. "Some black as me. Some in between?"

"How many kids we talking about?" Harley smiled for the first time.

"Dozens," Toby said.

"Let's shake on it." Harley held out her hand, and Toby lifted it to his wide lips.

"We got to think about it, sugar. You go to the grocery store with one of our black babies in the cart, and all the nosy ladies peer at our baby and peer at you, and they don't say anything, but you know what they're thinking."

"I can handle it."

"Where do we live, in some white suburb where people stare at me when I go past to my white-collar job? Or in some black ghetto where people stare at you and think, what's he doing with that honky? Ain't there a black girl good enough for him?"

"The world is changing. It won't be like that."

"It's not changed that much, sugar. Suppose we have a fight over you spending too much money, or over me being out too late at night, or whatever. You going to throw in my face that you should've married one of your kind? Am I going to remember Jamesina Thompson, who was black as me, and wish I'd never tangled with some white chick?"

"It won't happen."

"Yes, it will, sugar, believe you me." He gazed over the quiet surface of the Great Pond. "You see how peaceful this is? What's it like in the winter? What's it like underneath? Animals under that water are eating each other up. Even the oysters are sucking in little animals and digesting them. You hear that nice gentle ocean? You better not get caught in a rip current."

"Stop talking." Harley put her finger against his lips. He took her hand away.

"If we're going to survive, you and me, we have to talk to each other. Don't you ever hush me up. Don't ever let me hush you up, you hear me, sugar?"

"I love you, Toby."

Chapter 20

As the tribal chairman walked past the closed door of Peter's office that same afternoon, she heard his voice raised at the visitor. She couldn't make out what the visitor said back, his voice was too low, but she could hear Peter distinctly.

"That butterfly," she heard Peter say, "that butterfly was supposed to stop any consideration of the property."

She stood in front of Peter's closed door, wondering whether she should interrupt this or listen. Or move on and let them talk in private.

She had seen the man come in, a big heavy bald man with a black beard. Peter had shut his door behind the man, and the two had been closeted for more than an hour.

If it is tribal business, Patience thought, Peter should not be transacting it without me, the tribal chairman. She stood for a moment longer, undecided.

"All the more reason to scratch that last property from consideration," Peter said.

Patience made her decision. She knocked on the door and opened it without being invited in. The bald man turned his head, and Peter, whose pale face was unusually flushed, stopped in what was obviously midsentence.

"I beg your pardon," Patience said with a polite smile. "I would like to see you in my office when you're free, Peter." She turned to the visitor, who stood up, a great tall hulk of a man, and held out her hand. "I'm Patience VanDyke, Peter's boss. And you are?"

The visitor bowed slightly. "Michael Jandrowicz at your service." His voice was gruff.

"*Dr.* Jandrowicz," Peter said. "He's a professor at Smith College."

"Delighted," Patience said politely. Bugs took her hand in his great paw. "Are you here on tribal business, Dr. Jandrowicz?"

Before Bugs could answer, Peter said, "He's here to see me, Patience."

"On tribal business?" Patience said again.

"Regarding the casino sites. Yes," Bugs said in his raspy voice.

"Then I will join you." Patience moved one of Peter's chairs to the side of his desk, where she could establish her right to authority.

"Please sit," she said to Bugs. "Would you care to fill me in, Peter? Or shall I ask Dr. Jandrowicz."

"This is none of your business, Patience." Peter had to turn to look at her.

"I think it is my business." Patience smiled and turned to Bugs. "You undoubtedly have heard that the Wampanoag Tribe of Gay Head, Aquinnah, is exploring the possibility of building a casino here on tribal lands."

Bugs nodded.

"It is important that discussions not be carried on outside the tribe. I'm sure you can understand why."

Peter swiveled in his chair suddenly and looked out the window. An antique Indian Chief Blackhawk motorcycle was next to Chief Hawkbill's Cadillac in the parking lot.

"Why don't you tell me about it, Dr. Jandrowicz. I'm sure Peter would prefer that you do the talking." Patience crossed one leg over the other and smoothed her skirt.

Peter kept his back to them.

"Jube Burkhardt, a consulting engineer for the governor's office, contacted me." Bugs stopped and looked questioningly at Patience, who nodded. "I had published an article in a popular science magazine on the butterflies of Martha's Vineyard, which Mr. Burkhardt had read."

Peter swiveled his chair until he faced them. "We don't have to go through all this again."

"I think we do," said Patience, and turned back to Bugs. "Go on, please, Dr. Jandrowicz."

"Mr. Burkhardt was quite knowledgeable about butterflies, for a layman. He asked me questions about endangered species found on the Island. He wanted to know if my students or I had made an inventory of butterflies in Aquinnah. I told him we had not, but my students had made a superficial survey of Island butterflies, covering every month of the year."

"Winter, too?" Patience was interested, even though she was not sure where this was leading. "You don't mean to say you found butterflies during the cold months?"

"Every month except January," Bugs said.

Peter sighed loudly and looked at his watch.

Patience glanced at Peter, then at Bugs. "Why was Mr. Burkhardt interested in endangered butterflies? I think I can guess, but I'd like to hear what you have to say, Dr. Jandrowicz."

"He asked me if we had found any Compton tortoiseshells in Aquinnah. I told him it was unlikely. The habitat is not suitable. Then he asked if the habitat was suitable for variegated fritillaries. I told him it was, however, we had not found any in Aquinnah. They are quite rare throughout Massachusetts." Bugs stopped and looked at Peter. "Do you want me to continue?" he asked.

Patience answered. "Yes, please. *I* would like you to continue." She smoothed her wide skirt over her lap.

"Mr. Burkhardt e-mailed me last month to say he had found two variegated fritillaries on a twenty-five-acre site south of State Road." Bugs looked at Patience. "You understand that would be a significant find."

"Enough to take that property out of consideration as a casino site, I gather," Patience said.

Peter stood. "This conversation is going nowhere." He looked at his watch. "I've got another appointment."

"I think not," said Patience. "I suggest you call to cancel your appointment. We'll wait, Dr. Jandrowicz and I, while you do so." She folded her arms over her ample bosom and Peter sat again.

"Quite definitely," Bugs said. "Finding an endangered species stops development until the state makes a survey."

"Did you follow up on the two butterflies?"

"That's one reason I'm here. Burkhardt's alleged finding of the two fritillaries happened to coincide with a motorcycle rally here on the Island that I wanted to attend, a joint Indian and Harley-Davidson get-together."

"And you met with Mr. Burkhardt?" Patience asked.

"He escorted me to the location and showed me two specimens of fritillaries on the ground, dead, obviously preserved, and obviously from someone's collection."

"And what did you do?" Patience leaned forward.

"I told him they were planted specimens, and left."

"Did Mr. Burkhardt tell you who had hired him to search that particular site?"

"He said nothing to me."

Patience turned to Peter, who was doodling circles within circles on his desk calendar. "Did Mr. Burkhardt come to you, Peter, before that last tribal meeting?"

Peter looked up defiantly. "Yes. He said he had found an endangered species on the property that seemed to be the only suitable site for the casino, and suggested we talk about it. We never got a chance to."

"Had he told you what kind of endangered animal or plant he'd found?" Patience asked.

"Butterflies," Peter answered sullenly.

"Mr. Burkhardt knew you were lobbying for a floating casino, didn't he?"

Peter nodded.

"Had Mr. Burkhardt proposed that money change hands if he was able to hold up or stop consideration of a site on tribal lands?" Patience asked.

"I can't answer that," Peter said.

"Can't or won't?"

Bugs answered for him. "Mr. Burkhardt offered me a considerable sum of money, enough to fund a survey of the area, to verify that he had found the two specimens on the site. I refused."

Patience raised her eyebrows and looked from Peter to Bugs. "Where did Mr. Burkhardt get enough money to throw around in such a way?"

Peter turned and stared out at the parking lot and the Indian parked by the white Cadillac. A ray of sunlight reflected off the Indian's bright pipes and shone on Peter's high cheekbones.

"It's a beautiful bike," Peter said.

" 'Other companies build motorcycles,' " Bugs quoted. " 'We manufacture dreams.' That was the Indian Motocycle Company's motto."

Victoria stood next to the dining room table, her back straight. "I am staying in my own house, Howland, and that's final."

Late afternoon sun glistened in the imperfections and bubbles of the old glass panes of the west windows. Dust motes danced and sparkled in a beam of light that angled across the floor, spotlighting a worn place in the carpet.

At her insistence, Dojan had taken Victoria home and was standing behind her, holding her cloth bag.

"You've got to stay away for a couple of nights, at least." Howland thrust his hands into his pockets.

"You're being ridiculous. The computer isn't here—where is it, by the way?"

"Locked in the back of my car with a blanket over it."

Victoria nodded. "And there's nothing I know that everybody else on the Island doesn't know."

"There's a killer loose, Victoria. We don't know who it is or why Burkhardt and Hiram were killed. Until we have some answers, you're not safe."

"That's absurd." The wrinkles of Victoria's face set stubbornly. She pulled out one of the side chairs at the table and sat. She smoothed the tablecloth absently.

"Listen to me." Howland's eyes glittered. "The state police are on the case. They came in late and have to catch up. They haven't identified the body from the fire yet."

"It was Hiram."

"You and I believe it was Hiram, but the police have to go through procedures. In the meantime—"

Victoria interrupted. "Where's Linda? I haven't seen her all day. She hasn't heard about our finding Hiram."

"Victoria . . ."

"I will not leave my house, and that's that." Victoria turned to Dojan and pointed imperiously to the cookroom. "Put my bag on the cookroom table, please, Dojan."

Dojan slipped past Howland and padded through the kitchen.

"I don't know where the hell Linda is, and I don't care," Howland snapped.

"Would you like a glass of sherry?" Victoria asked. "It's been a trying day. If you'll reach into that door in the buffet, you'll find a decanter and—"

"No, thank you." Howland's cheekbones had a flush of red across them. He marched out of the dining room into the kitchen and stood by the entry door until Dojan joined him.

"I'll talk to you outside," he barked at Dojan.

Victoria had risen from her chair. "Don't think you're going to guard me, Howland, you and Dojan. I'm quite capable of calling 911, and the police station is right down the road. Besides, Elizabeth is here."

Howland glanced through the dining room into the front hall, then turned toward the cookroom. "Where is she?"

"She's out. She has a dinner date."

"Kee-rist!" said Howland.

A blue car pulled into the driveway. "Here's Linda now," Victoria said. "She'll be here. You may leave now."

Linda stepped out of her car, a blue cardigan slung over her shoulders. "Hello, Mrs. Trumbull," she called out. She looked curiously at the two tall men who had walked past her without a word.

Victoria turned and gestured to Howland, who was seated in his station wagon—part wave, part dismissal, and part a regal acknowledgment that she was in command.

Linda came into the house with both arms full of shopping bags and pulled the entry door shut with her foot. "Who are those strange men?"

"Are they still there?" Victoria filled the teakettle and set it on the stove. As Linda moved close to her, Victoria smelled patchouli and sneezed.

"I'm sorry, Mrs. Trumbull. I wasn't thinking." She set her purchases down on the captain's chair. "I'll wash my face and wrists."

She returned, scrubbed free of scent. Victoria asked, "Have you found your sister yet?"

"She's camping in a field not far from here. The police told her where to find me."

The teakettle whistled, and Victoria filled the teapot and carried it into the cookroom. Linda followed with the blue-flowered cups. "I thought I might see you at your uncle's place today," Victoria said.

"I haven't been on the Island for at least ten years. I went shopping in Edgartown and had lunch in Oak Bluffs. I met someone I knew in Vineyard Haven." She finished vaguely, "To tell you the truth, I didn't want to see the old place."

"Oh?" Victoria sipped her tea, narrowing her eyes in the steam. A cricket started to chirp. The sound seemed to come from all four corners of the room.

Linda spoke into the cricket-loud silence. "When we were children, we stayed with my uncle every summer." The cricket abruptly stopped chirping. "Then, I don't know, things changed."

"They do that. Change."

"You went there this morning?" Linda asked brightly, switching the subject.

Victoria nodded. "There's not much left."

"Is the barn still standing?"

"Yes. The fire was confined to the house. All that's left is the chimney, charred wood, and bundles of papers."

"Was that all?" Linda asked, eyes wide over the rim of her cup. "Everything gone?"

"They found mattress springs, door hinges, the kitchen stove, nonburnables. Also, they found the charred remains of his computer."

"Was the computer salvageable?"

"I would guess not, but I don't know much about computers. The outside was burned and the plastic fittings on back were melted."

"My uncle wrote me notes at Christmas. Then when he got the computer, he'd e-mail practically every week. He used it for everything, correspondence, records, bills." She ran her fingers through her hair. "I suppose it had a copy of his will on it?"

Victoria said nothing.

"Did the police take it?"

Victoria held the teapot over Linda's cup. "Would you like more tea?"

"Thank you. Did . . ."

Victoria stood suddenly. She didn't want to discuss the computer. Nor did she want to discuss Burkhardt's will. As if she had remembered something, she said, "I've got to make a phone call. I'll be right back." She went into the dining room and dialed Howland. She knew he hadn't had time to get home yet, but she wanted to stall long enough to think. She waited until his answering machine came on, said the first thing she could think of into the phone, and hung up.

She returned to Linda. "No answer. I'll try later."

"Did they find anything else at my uncle's?" Linda asked. "Evidence of arson or something?"

Victoria toyed with her cup. "I'm afraid they did find something."

"Oh? What did they find?"

"The remains of a body."

The color suddenly washed out of Linda's face, like a shade pulled down. She turned ash-gray. "Someone died in the fire? That's . . . that's horrible. That's awful." She stood up, knocked over her teacup, which skidded across the table, fell to the floor, and broke. She set both hands flat on the table and hung her head down.

CHAPTER 21

Victoria, astonished, thought that Linda might faint. She had been so cool about her uncle's death and the fire. She claimed she had gone shopping all day, and certainly she had brought back enough plastic bags with labels from fancy stores. Victoria started to get up. She would pour some ammonia on a damp facecloth and hold it under Linda's nose, that was it.

"Who was it?" Linda said softly, "Do they know?"

Victoria sat down again and handed Linda a couple of paper napkins. "Before the police can identify the body, they have to check dental records."

Linda mopped at the sodden tablecloth. Her color had returned slightly, but her face was still gray.

"When will they know?" she asked.

"I have no idea. Don't worry about the tablecloth. It was time for it to go into the wash anyway."

"The computer. I suppose it's mine now?"

"Did your uncle leave his property to you?"

"He said he was going to."

"Someone has to find his will."

"The property is mine now."

Victoria half-closed her eyes. "I don't believe anyone knows, at this time, whether he willed it to you or to your sister or to both of you." Victoria took the soggy napkins and dropped them into the trash. McCavity, who was curled up in the wastebasket, stuck his head up and yowled.

"I'm sorry, Cavvy, I didn't see you," Victoria said to the cat. She looked back at Linda. "Or perhaps he left the property to a third party."

"He left it to me. I know he left it to me."

"I can't help you." Victoria brushed crumbs off the tablecloth into her hand and dropped them in her saucer. "You should go to your uncle's place to see what's left of it. There may be some small thing you can salvage."

"I don't want to see what's left of the house." Linda hid her face in her hands.

Victoria gazed at her.

"I'm glad it's gone," Linda said.

"What happened to make you feel this way?"

Linda wrapped her hands around her stomach and rocked back and forth in her chair. "I'm sorry I broke your cup, Mrs. Trumbull. It was a lovely old cup."

"It was just a cup. You were about to tell me something."

"Nothing." Linda stood up. "Nothing at all."

A chickadee landed on the bird feeder, snatched a seed, and flitted off.

"Where's Elizabeth?" Linda asked abruptly.

"She's still at work. She has a dinner and theater date tonight, and will probably be home late."

"I wonder what happened to Uncle Jube's computer." Linda turned to watch a finch that had landed on the feeder. The feeder swung gently.

"Do you have plans for this evening?" Victoria asked.

"I was going to visit someone I know. Maybe I'll go to my uncle's before it gets dark. I probably ought to look at the old place. I'll pick up a sandwich somewhere." She cleared the remains of the tea things from the table. "I'm sorry about your cup. I'll see if I can find one like it in an antique shop."

"Please, don't worry about the cup."

"Will you be okay here by yourself? I didn't even think."

"Of course," Victoria said.

Victoria fed McCavity and made herself an omelet. She worked on the sestina she had started earlier while she nibbled at the omelet. McCavity hopped up into her lap. When she finished supper, she cleared her dishes and put away the leftover food. She was tired. She let McCavity out, and went to bed early. Her bedroom was the small west room on the second floor. She read for a while before she turned out her light. Her usual bedtime was close to midnight. It wasn't nine o'clock yet. She seldom had trouble falling asleep, no matter when she went to bed, but tonight she felt restless. Her legs itched. Scratching didn't help. The familiar creaks and moans of her old house seemed different somehow.

She thought about Elizabeth and her date, the reporter from the Cape Cod paper, a nice young man. She had a brief twinge, not of envy, but of wishing they'd invited her to go to the play with them. She loved theater. As a girl, she'd dreamed of becoming an actress. Crickets chirped in the west meadow. She heard the eerie, almost human, cry of an owl. The night wind whispered through the small screen that held the window open. She hadn't been troubled by mosquitoes this year. The summer had been quite dry, and her garden had suffered. She hadn't even felt like weeding, it had been so dry. Something banged downstairs, and she tried to identify what might have caused the noise. A shutter thumping against the front of the house? There didn't seem to be enough wind for that. One of the kitchen doors slamming? She tried to think which one it might be. Each had its own sound.

She saw, for the first time, a strange light on the ceiling, almost the shape of a tiny footprint. Was there a light on in the attic that was shining into the room? How could it, unless there was a hole in the ceiling? And a light on in the attic. Maybe it was a reflected streetlight. But the closest streetlight was at the firehouse a half mile away. Then she realized with relief—and realized that it had worried her— that the thing on the ceiling was a plastic phosphorescent footprint that her great-grandson had stuck up there when he stayed in her room earlier this summer. She laughed out loud.

She heard the banging noise again. What was causing that? She put her hand up to her neck where she felt something pressing against her. It was the shell necklace Bernice Minnowfish had put around her neck, and she'd forgotten all about it. She started to take it off and then decided not to. She rubbed the itch on her legs. Perhaps she should get up and put lotion on them. Her skin was probably dry. Maybe if she took an aspirin the itch would go away. That meant getting up and going downstairs, and that seemed like too much trouble. If she went downstairs, she could heat up a glass of milk. Then she probably wouldn't need to take an aspirin, and she could get the hand lotion from the bathroom. She needed to use the toilet, anyway. She could probably last until morning, but that was another reason for going downstairs. While she was downstairs, she would put the necklace in the box she kept for great-grandchildren's play jewels. She heard the banging noise again, and she swung her feet out of bed. She would find out what that noise was.

"Come in and meet my grandmother, Chuck. She'll want to hear all about the play." Elizabeth and her date had returned around eleven.

"Is she still up?" Chuck looked around the brightly lighted kitchen. "I don't want to disturb her."

"She doesn't usually go to bed until late," Elizabeth said. "She wouldn't leave all these lights on. She must be upstairs. You're welcome to look around." Elizabeth took the stairs two at a time. "Gram? It's me. I'm home."

There was no answer.

Elizabeth knocked on the side of the open door to her grandmother's room and went in. The light on the table next to the bed was on, and the bedclothes were thrown back as if her grandmother had been in bed. Her book was open and facedown on the table. Her clothes, the ones Elizabeth remembered seeing her wear today, were draped over the back of the rocking chair in her bedroom. Elizabeth's stomach had an awful prickling feeling.

"Grammy!"

She went to the door of the upstairs bathroom. No one there. She went from room to room. The two front bedrooms, the Indian room, the small room over the kitchen. She turned on the light at the foot of the attic stairs and went up, brushing cobwebs out of her way.

"Grammy?"

She pounded down the attic stairs, down the front stairs. Chuck looked up from examining her grandfather's war medals.

"Find her?"

"Maybe she had an attack of some kind. Maybe she fell. I should never have left her alone. I keep forgetting how old she is. I keep thinking she's my age, and she's in her nineties, for Pete's sake."

While she talked, Elizabeth moved from the library, where they'd been earlier today, to the front parlor, to the small bedroom off the dining room. She checked the kitchen again, opened each of the six doors. She looked in the cookroom, the bathroom off the cookroom. The light was on in the bathroom, and the door to the medicine cabinet over the toilet was open.

"We should have asked her to go with us. Where could she be? She's never sick. Why was the medicine cabinet open—did she fall and hurt herself? Did she have to go to the hospital?"

Chuck said nothing.

Elizabeth went into the woodshed. "Gram, are you okay?" She came back into the kitchen, and, with a sob, sat down on one of the gray-painted kitchen chairs.

"Is there someone you can call?" Chuck stood over her.

"Howland." She got to her feet. "I'll call him first. He'll know what to do." She dialed the phone on the buffet, spoke into it, and hung up. "He said he'd be here in ten minutes. He told me to call the police chief."

Casey was there in the Bronco within two minutes.

"Dojan warned me," Casey said. "I didn't listen."

Together, Casey, Elizabeth, and Chuck went through the house from attic to woodshed. They opened the cellar bulkhead doors and went down the stone steps into the cold musty interior. Nothing. The motor on the old freezer hummed. The food in it must be twenty years old, Elizabeth thought. She'd never opened it. The cobwebs had not been disturbed. They checked the small cellar on the other side of the house, the one that had the water heater and furnace. Nothing. Casey called Junior Norton, who arrived before Howland, and Casey, Junior, Chuck, and Elizabeth fanned out, searching outdoors. Under the lilac brushes. Around the Norway maples. The fishpond. The big old apple tree with branches that touched the ground. The grape arbor. Nothing. The young man who rented the garden shed next to the grape arbor was visiting his family in Maine. They opened the door to his shack and looked around. Nothing.

Casey called the hospital. Doc Erickson had been on in the emergency room all evening and had not seen Victoria. He asked around anyway. Everybody knew Victoria, all the nurses, the volunteers, the doctors. She had not been admitted.

Elizabeth was sobbing when Howland drove up.

"Do you know how to get in touch with Dojan?" he asked Elizabeth. "We need him."

"I'll call the Aquinnah police," Junior said.

"Where's Linda?" Howland asked. "She was here earlier."

"I haven't seen her all day," mumbled Elizabeth.

"Everybody sit down." Casey took over. "We'll think this through." They went into the cookroom and sat around the pine table. Elizabeth recalled Victoria sitting here at the table this afternoon, writing her poetry. She saw an envelope on the table with a few lines penciled on it. She took a deep breath and let it out.

"We'll find her," Casey said. "And when we do, I'm enrolling her in a police training course." She slapped a notebook on the table. "She's got to stop pretending she's a cop. I should never have appointed her my deputy." She turned to Howland. "What do you have to say?"

Howland shook his head.

"She would never go out without leaving a note," Elizabeth said. "Not unless someone forced her."

"What are you thinking, Howland?" Casey asked. "Better tell us."

"Burkhardt's killer may believe Victoria knows something," Howland said. "Hiram may have guessed the killer's identity and told Victoria."

"My grandmother didn't know anything. I was with her when she saw Burkhardt on the cliff and when Hiram went down to him."

"Burkhardt's dying word was 'Sibyl,' right?" said Howland.

"His computer," Casey said.

"Is it possible that there's another Sibyl, a person?" Howland looked from Elizabeth to Casey. Elizabeth shook her head. Casey looked blank.

Junior's radio crackled and he answered. It was the Aquinnah police chief.

"You need Dojan?"

"Right away," said Junior.

"Haven't seen him all day. I'll send Malachi in the cruiser, have him check Dojan's boat."

"Roger," said Junior. "Thanks, Chief."

"Has someone kidnapped her? Why? And what will they do with her?" Elizabeth ran her fingers through her hair, and pulled off the earrings she'd worn on her date. "Will they let her go when they find she knows nothing?"

"Would she have set out on some errand on her own?" Chuck asked.

Elizabeth shook her head. "Her clothes are still upstairs. She wouldn't have gone outside without proper clothes."

CHAPTER 22

Elizabeth got up. "I'm making coffee." She started to reach for the coffee grounds, but stopped and turned. "My grandmother almost never uses this overhead light. She doesn't like it because it glares."

"The light was on?" Casey said.

"The kitchen light and the bathroom light both. The medicine cabinet was open, too."

"Can you tell if anything is missing or out of place?"

"I'll check the bathroom." Elizabeth left the coffee unmade. "There's an aspirin bottle on the counter and a glass of water."

"Would that be Victoria's?" Casey asked.

"Aspirin is the only medicine she takes. She might have gone to bed early and come downstairs to get it."

Chuck took a notebook out of his inside coat pocket. "Someone may have been waiting for her downstairs."

"How would they anticipate that she would need an aspirin?" Elizabeth said.

"They may have been searching for something and she surprised them."

"Oh, my God!" Elizabeth said. "They're looking for that computer. This is awful. Poor Gram. She must feel helpless!"

"Helpless, my foot," Casey said stoutly. "I feel sorry for any kidnapper who'd tangle with Victoria."

The Aquinnah police cruiser pulled into the driveway and turned around the circle, blue lights rotating. Malachi came into the kitchen.

"Evening, Chief," he said to Casey.

"No sign of Dojan?" Casey said.

He shook his head. "I checked everywhere he might be, his mother's house, his cousin's, Tribal Headquarters, the foot of the cliffs. I checked in Menemsha to see if he was on his boat, or on

Obed's fishing boat. Nowhere. He's not in Menemsha. He's not in Aquinnah. I left messages everywhere to contact Aquinnah police if he shows up."

"Dojan intended to guard Victoria," said Howland. "She made a fuss, dismissed us. We left, since Linda was here."

"I don't know Dojan, but I've heard of him," Chuck said. "He's unusual, from what I hear. Different."

Heads nodded.

"There was a rumor that he'd been sent to Washington by the tribal council as some kind of punishment."

"Not exactly a rumor," Howland mumbled.

"Dojan wouldn't have kidnapped her, would he?"

"No. Certainly not. Not Dojan," Howland said. "Unlikely." He paused. "At least, I don't think so."

By now, it was almost three in the morning. People in uniforms, in shorts and T-shirts, in theater-going clothes, crowded in and out of Victoria's kitchen and cookroom. Elizabeth brewed pot after pot of coffee. The kitchen sink was full of coffee mugs. At one point, Howland got up, washed the mugs, and made fried egg sandwiches. Police radios crackled with static, squelched as calls came in.

There were no reports of Victoria from any of the towns. Ferries had made their last runs before Victoria disappeared, and would not start again until early morning. Casey had called the Steamship Authority and directed them to inspect every car, van, truck that could possibly hide a person. Check the trunks, the truck bodies. . . .

The hunt for Dojan had yielded nothing. No one had seen his van since early afternoon. Junior had gone down the Tiah's Cove Road starting around ten-thirty, waking people to ask if they had seen anything that might lead the police to Victoria.

An elderly woman, whose eyesight wasn't keen and who probably shouldn't have been driving, reported that she had seen a van parked on New Lane around five o'clock within sight of Victoria's, but there had been no one in it.

Elizabeth's eyes were red from exhaustion. She yawned and covered her mouth.

"Better get some sleep," Howland said. "This might go on for hours."

Chuck stood up. "I'll make sure we wake you if anything happens. Anything at all."

She shook her head.

"Where the dickens is Linda?" Casey asked for the third or fourth time.

Elizabeth yawned again. "Staying with friends?"

"I've asked Tisbury and Edgartown to look for her and her car." Casey turned to Elizabeth. "You're not helping. Lie down on the dining room couch and stay out of my way."

"I won't sleep." Elizabeth stumbled into the dining room. Chuck went with her and covered her with a blanket.

When he returned, Casey snapped. "Chuck, get out of here. Go home."

"I'm a reporter," he said. "I'll take care of Elizabeth and stay out of your way. This is a big story."

Casey glared.

Chuck saluted.

Casey turned to Howland. "Is there anything I haven't thought of? We've alerted all six Island police departments, their cruisers are out. The communications center rallied all the volunteer firemen. The Steamship Authority will search all vehicles leaving the Island tomorrow. The airport is alerted. The harbormasters in all three harbor towns have reported to their respective harbors and will check all boat activity. Anything else?"

"Boats on moorings," Howland said.

"Isn't Dojan's boat on a mooring?" Chuck asked.

"He anchors outside the harbor," someone said.

"It's not Dojan we're worried about," said Howland.

A rooster crowed. Casey looked at her watch. "It's almost four. It'll be dawn soon."

A robin caroled. Then the predawn morning was full of birdcalls, a chorus of doves and cardinals, blue jays, robins, chickadees, a flicker. Chirps and calls, songs and warbles, shrill and sweet.

After Victoria had ordered him and Howland out, Dojan had parked his van on New Lane and crept back to Victoria's, where he sat with his back to the great Norway maple at the end of the drive. The sun set in a blaze of orange and red. Linda drove away.

He could see Victoria through the kitchen windows. She took a can out of the refrigerator and divided a portion into a bowl, leaned down, and set it on the floor. Feeding her cat, Dojan thought. He watched her cook her supper and take her plate into the cookroom where she sat with her back to him, writing and occasionally picking up her fork. She looked at her watch and got up with her plate, which she put in the kitchen sink.

He listened to the evening. Crickets chirped a steady background. Above the crickets' sound he could hear the surf on the south shore. He could feel it, even here, in the center of the Island. Cicadas droned. A bird he didn't recognize made a sleepy chirp. Guinea hens hustled past him, urging one another to move on with their rusty-hinge cries. He knew where they roosted in the tall oak trees.

Suddenly his skin prickled. Someone else was watching Victoria, and was even more careful than he had been. Did they sense his presence? He turned his head slowly, slowly, and stared into the ambiguous evening light, listening for a sound that didn't belong.

Crickets, cicadas, a nighthawk. Cars went past on the Edgartown Road, tires swishing on the new paving. A mockingbird started a flood of calls. He searched for it, this unexpected sound, and located it on the uppermost tip of a cedar, an ornament against the darkening night sky. He relaxed. The mockingbird's call belonged to the night.

Victoria turned out the kitchen lights, leaving one on in the cookroom, for Burkhardt's niece, he supposed. The niece was staying with Victoria. As she turned off the house lights, he followed her progress up the stairs to the second floor, where he saw the light go on in her small west room.

His ears were full of noise. How could he strain out the noises that belonged to the night from alien sounds? He sat motionless, watching the light in the west window. Victoria appeared briefly, opened the window, put in the screen that held it up, and disappeared from view again. He heard the sound of the window scraping against its wooden frame, the scratch of the screen as it slid open, he heard the window come down again and settle with a thump on the screen. He knew, then, that he would hear those noises that did not belong to this night.

He would sit here forever, if necessary, watching and listening. A mosquito whined around his ears, a night noise. He let the mosquito land on his neck and suck his blood until it was sated. His neck itched where the mosquito had fed, and he concentrated on the sounds of the night rather than the itch.

Victoria's light went out. Cars passed on the road, casting beams ahead of them and rolling them up endlessly. Did they eat the light? Dojan allowed his mind to wander, but not far. He heard an owl cry. His ears tuned in. It was too early in the evening for an owl. The cry had a quality that did not sound right.

He waited and watched and listened.

He saw a shadow that was less than a breath flit from the shade of the maple tree that was only three or four boat-lengths from him. How could he have missed anyone? How could anyone have missed him? Was there a white man who could stalk like that? A second shadow slipped next to the first, and together, one shadow, they went to the kitchen door. Dojan raised himself from his shelter under the tree and crept across the drive, less of a presence than those intruders into Victoria's house had been.

The overhead kitchen light went on, and Dojan was momentarily blinded. He saw two forms, men or women, he couldn't tell, dressed in black, moving toward the library. Flashlight beams moved back and forth. The lightbulb in the library lamp was burned out, as Dojan knew from looking for the computer earlier. He heard a thump. The flashlight was extinguished, and the night was silent for a long few minutes. Then the flashlight flickered across the ceiling.

A car turned into the drive, and Dojan quickly moved into the shelter of the wisteria growing on the trellis by the side of the house where he could see out. The vehicle wasn't Burkhardt's niece's car. The engine had a peculiar low hum, and it was showing only parking lights. In the feeble twilight Dojan saw a small, chunky station wagon, a Jeep or GM. The car stopped, engine running, the driver still in the car. The light that should have illuminated the license plate was out.

From where he stood, he could no longer see Victoria's bedroom window. But the hall light went on, and he saw Victoria move slowly from the foot of the stairs through the front hall into the kitchen. She paused, holding her finger against her cheek, and looked up at the kitchen light. She went into the bathroom, where he could no longer see her, but he saw the bathroom light go on.

The two shadows that had been in the library slipped through the door into the dining room. In the light from the kitchen he could see they were wearing black from head to toe, ski masks, shapeless tunics that went almost to their knees, trousers. They were easing their way toward the bathroom.

Dojan leaped to his feet and charged into the house. He would tackle all of them, the people in Victoria Trumbull's house and the people in the car. He crouched, holding his arms away from himself, hands open, ready to seize them. He growled, a throaty wild sound. The two black shadows converged, and he went for them, his hands lifted to stop them.

And that was the last he knew.

Victoria heard the growl, and, startled, turned from the bathroom cabinet, which she had opened to get the aspirin bottle, and saw a figure coming toward her.

She was indignant. "What are you doing in my house?"

Things happened quickly after that. She was only vaguely aware of two figures in black coming through the bathroom door. They opened the linen closet, and the next thing she knew they had put a pillowcase over her head. They led her out of the bathroom, one on either side of her. She was wearing her long pink nightgown with embroidered rosebuds, and her knobby feet were bare.

Dawn came and the birds stopped singing. Cars swished along the road. Dump trucks and earthmovers rumbled to construction sites, driving much too fast. Howland's beard was a gray shadow. Casey's eyes were ringed with red. Elizabeth slept on the dining room couch. Chuck had taken off his linen jacket and rolled up the sleeves of his shirt. He sat at the end of the table, writing. Every half hour, Junior Norton reported back by radio to Casey. Nothing, nothing, nothing.

The radio was a continuous clatter of voices, from Chilmark, from Aquinnah, from Edgartown, Oak Bluffs, Vineyard Haven. Nothing, nothing. No one had spotted Linda's car. No one had seen Dojan. No one had found Victoria or any trace of her.

Every few minutes a vehicle pulled into Victoria's drive, a police vehicle, a volunteer fireman's car, a neighbor with food. Howland had taken over the coffee making and poured cup after cup of black coffee. He rummaged around in the refrigerator and found enough food to make a breakfast of bacon and eggs and fruit that no one wanted, that everyone ate.

Another vehicle came into the drive, and they looked up, too exhausted to care. The vehicle was a gray van like Dojan's. Everyone stood and peered out the windows. The driver's side door opened, and Dojan stepped out. In Victoria's kitchen no one moved. Dojan went around to the passenger door, and then everyone in Victoria's kitchen and cookroom poured into the narrow entry and out onto the stone steps. The noise awakened Elizabeth, who got up, blinking her eyes, red-streaked from the contact lenses she had worn all night.

Howland and Casey and Chuck and Elizabeth had stepped onto the grass by the time Dojan opened the passenger door.

He lifted Victoria out, still in her nightgown. "Put me down immediately, Dojan! I'm quite capable of walking." Victoria's voice was firm, but Dojan carried her up the stone steps past the group, who parted to let them pass. He set her down in the big captain's chair while Elizabeth and Howland and Casey and Chuck gathered around, blinking tired, blurry, burning, scratchy eyes.

Elizabeth was the first to speak. "Grammy! Are you all right? Where have you been?"

"Do we have any of that footbath left?" Victoria asked. "I'd like to soak my feet before anybody says another word."

CHAPTER 23

Casey called the communications center on the radio. She told them to notify the police departments in Edgartown, Vineyard Haven, Oak Bluffs, Chilmark, and Aquinnah. She asked them to call the airport, the Steamship Authority, and the harbormasters.

Victoria was home safe.

Casey O'Neill, West Tisbury's police chief, would report back as soon as she learned more.

Elizabeth gently worked ragged, filthy, unfamiliar gray wool socks off her grandmother's swollen feet.

"Ahhh!" Victoria sighed as she put her feet into the basin Elizabeth had set on a bath towel. Her feet were blistered and raw, scratched in places, bleeding in spots.

Howland made her a cup of tea. Chuck found a light blanket in the downstairs bedroom and put it over her shoulders.

"Well," said Victoria, sipping her tea. "I feel like quite a celebrity with all this attention." She waved her feet gently in the warm water and winced at the pain.

"The whole Island has been up all night searching for you," Elizabeth said. "We've been worried sick."

The others pulled up chairs and sat around the kitchen table, waiting for Victoria to say something.

"I came downstairs to get an aspirin and a glass of warm milk," she said at last. "I'd gone to bed too early and couldn't sleep." She looked around at her audience. "I noticed the overhead light was on in the kitchen and was annoyed that Linda hadn't turned it off. I went into the bathroom and had run a glass of water and taken the aspirin bottle out of the medicine cabinet when, *pouf!* the next thing I knew, someone put a pillowcase over my head."

"Did they hurt you?" Howland asked in a low voice.

"No, they were quite gentle. However, they didn't say a word until after they helped me into the car."

"Could you tell what kind of car it was?" Casey asked.

"The engine sounded like a Jeep, a sort of low rumble. Not a new Jeep, an old one."

"Good girl," Casey said.

Dojan was standing protectively behind Victoria's chair. He said nothing. His eyes went from Casey to Howland to Elizabeth and back to Victoria. Chuck sat at the table in the cookroom, listening, watching, and writing.

The door flew open, and Junior Norton came in, his uniform shirt rumpled, his badge awry. "Victoria! Are you okay?"

"Of course, I am," Victoria said. "I'm a bit tired and my feet hurt, but perfectly fine otherwise. A good night's sleep and I'll be back to normal."

"Go on, Victoria," said Casey.

"Well, I tried to keep track of where we were going. We went out of the drive and turned left on the Edgartown Road. Then we turned right almost immediately, so it must have been Old County Road. Then left onto Scotchman's. I was confused after that, but I was pretty sure we were heading up-Island to Chilmark, and it seemed as if we went by way of Middle Road."

"That's likely. It's not well traveled," Casey said.

"We went past Chilmark Chocolates—I could smell it. Then we drove for five or ten minutes more, not as far as Stonewall Pond, and turned right onto a dirt road. After that, I couldn't tell where we went."

"Did they say anything to you at all?" Casey asked.

"One person did most of the talking. I think I would recognize him again by his voice."

Victoria moved her feet slowly. Elizabeth felt the water with her hand, and poured fresh hot water into the basin.

"I was trying hard to keep track of time and direction and hoping to learn something about the man who spoke."

"Mrs. Trumbull," the man had said, "we won't harm you. But we need to ask you some questions."

"You could have done that at home without all this nonsense. May I take the pillowcase off? It smells like fabric softener."

"We're sorry, but it has to stay."

Victoria tried to listen for a speech pattern she could relay to Casey, or an accent of some kind. But the voice was flat, as if he were trying to disguise it.

"What do you want of me?" Victoria shifted in the backseat of the car, a Jeep she was sure. A person sat on each side of her, making themselves small because they didn't touch her and the backseat was not large. The speaker wasn't the driver. The voice came from the passenger seat.

"We hoped to search your house without awakening you," the voice said. "We didn't intend to disturb you."

"What were you looking for?" Victoria's breath felt moist against the fabric. "I'm hot," she said. Someone reached over from the front seat and fanned the bottom of the pillowcase.

"We need to locate Burkhardt's computer," the voice intoned, and when Victoria said nothing, the voice continued. "The operating unit. His computer. Where is it, Mrs. Trumbull?"

Who might she endanger if she told what she knew?

"Mrs. Trumbull?" The hand reached over and flapped the bottom of the pillowcase again.

That gave Victoria an idea. "I feel faint," she said weakly. It wouldn't hurt to act like an old lady.

"We know Howland Atherton put the unit in your library."

"I . . ." Victoria slumped slightly.

"Mrs. Trumbull, we don't mean you harm. We'll bring you home again, but we must ask you some questions."

The car stopped, the driver shifted gears, and the car started up again, veering to the left. Victoria slumped.

"Mrs. Trumbull? Mrs. Trumbull! Are you all right?"

Victoria moaned.

The driver spoke in a voice Victoria thought she would recognize again. "This isn't exactly great for an old lady."

"I told you to keep quiet," the voice said. "Mrs. Trumbull, can you hear me?"

Victoria smelled chocolate. She knew where they were now. She heaved, as if she were about to be sick.

"I'm sorry we're putting you through this," the voice continued. "If you feel sick, let me know, and I'll give you a plastic bag. I can't take the mask off."

Victoria tried to estimate the miles or minutes they had gone past Chilmark Chocolates, and thought it must be seven or eight minutes, perhaps three or four miles. That would put them close to the bridge that separated Stonewall Pond from Quitsa Pond. Would they cross that bridge into Gay Head? If so, perhaps these people were connected with the tribe somehow.

"Mrs. Trumbull, can you talk?"

"I . . ." Victoria's usually strong voice had faded into feebleness. She wanted to concentrate on where they were going, and wanted that irritating voice to stop.

"Leave her alone," the driver said. "Wait until we get there, can't you?"

"Stop talking, I tell you. We don't have much time."

But he didn't talk to her again, and Victoria continued to count the minutes and the miles. The Jeep slowed and made an abrupt right turn onto a bumpy road. Victoria wondered where they were. On this part of the Island there were at least a half dozen dirt tracks that led off the main road to isolated summer houses along the north shore. She would need to concentrate in order to remember where she was. The Jeep jounced over the road. Victoria could hear grass brushing the underside of the car, could feel the Jeep climb over large stones in the road. They turned left, toward Menemsha Pond, right toward Vineyard Sound, then down a steep hill and up the other side.

"Mrs. Trumbull, can you hear me?" The voice spoke again, and Victoria, with some annoyance, lost track of her count. She slumped against the person on her left. The person was a woman, she thought with surprise. For some reason, she had assumed all four were men. "It's not much farther, hang in there."

"For Christ's sake, Mack, she's ninety."

Victoria heard a slap, and the Jeep swerved. "Shut up," Mack, the voice, said to the driver. "Shut up, shut up!"

So his name is Mack, Victoria thought with satisfaction. She hadn't heard of anyone involved in this mess named Mack. Casey talked about sending her to a police training course? Well, she'd go, all right, if she could find someone to stay with Elizabeth. And she would ace the course. She'd show them who was an old lady. The Jeep bounced over a large rock and swerved to the left. She had lost track of the twists and turns in the road, but they were heading toward Vineyard Sound.

Another sharp turn, down a steep hill where they skidded on sand, and they came to a stop.

"Mrs. Trumbull, the driver will assist you out of the car. Just a moment."

Victoria moaned. The woman patted her gently.

"Keep your mouth shut, you understand?" Mack told the driver. "Just nod."

The front seat was pushed forward, and Victoria felt herself lifted out by strong arms. She clutched one to see if she could feel any identifying feature. All she felt was hair and muscle.

The driver held his arm around her and steered her down a sloping sandy path. She heard waves lapping on the shore. They must be practically on the beach. That should narrow down the places it could be. She smelled the iodine scent of seaweed. She could make out, through the pillowcase, the muted beam of a flashlight. The sand was chilly and moist under her feet, the way she'd remembered the beach at night when she was a child. They went up wooden steps onto a deck. She heard a knob turn, hinges squeak, a screen door open. She stepped up into a room that smelled of summer and salt, sunburned bodies, mildew, coconut oil, sun-weathered shingles, and the hard-to-describe smell of a house open only during summer.

The driver sat her down on a hard couch. "May I take this off now?" she asked.

"We'll take it off, but not yet, Mrs. Trumbull. Give us a moment to light the lamps and disguise ourselves."

Victoria smelled kerosene, heard the sound of a glass chimney being set on a wooden tabletop, the scritch of a wick turned up, a match striking, the nostalgic smell of burning kerosene. So they were not near the electric poles, or if they were, there was no electricity in this house. She scuffed her feet. There was a braided rag rug on the floor. An old one, not one made from yarns.

"Are you warm enough, Mrs. Trumbull?" Mack asked.

Victoria thought a moment before she answered weakly. "Is there something I can put on my feet?" If she could get away from here, she would prefer not to walk barefoot.

She heard drawers opening, and Mack came back with a pair of wool socks he drew gently over her misshapen toes.

"Heat up some water for soup," he ordered. She heard someone pump up a kerosene stove, heard the *glug-glug* of water poured from a jug into a saucepan, caught the strong smell of the stove.

"Would you like some instant soup, Mrs. Trumbull?"

Victoria really didn't want it but thought it might be a good idea to keep her strength up, and nodded as if it took more effort than she had.

"This was a mistake," the driver said. "You can tell the drive almost did her in. We should have left her home."

"Shut up, will you? We had no choice. I'm giving you another minute, then I'm taking the case off her head. The rest of you, out of here."

It was a relief when Victoria felt the muffling pillowcase come off her head. Once she could see again she seemed to hear better and sense things better. She must remember to act like a feeble old lady, she thought. It was her only hope of getting away from here. She tried to look around without seeming to do so. She let her bright eyes become dull. Her body sagged, her hand draped listlessly over the edge of the couch.

Mack was dressed entirely in black, and she could tell nothing at all about him. He brought her a mug of some kind of instant cream soup, and she acted as though she couldn't handle it. He was showing impatience. He spooned the soup into Victoria, who let much of it dribble down the side of her mouth the way she had seen old people eat. She let her head loll.

"Mrs. Trumbull, that trip couldn't have been that hard on you. You're a strong woman."

Victoria almost let herself rally, and told herself she was an actress, acting the part of an old lady. She moaned, and the soup dribbled out of the corners of her mouth.

"I have to question you, I'm sorry."

Her head wobbled from one side to the other. "I'm fine," she said in a way that made it clear she was not. "Ask me. Whatever I can . . ."

"Where is that computer, Mrs. Trumbull? I don't know whether you heard me or not, but we know you identified it at the fire scene. We know Atherton took it to your house and stored it in the library. It's not there now. Where is it?"

Victoria thought for a long, long time. She let her eyes go vacant while she examined everything she could see in the dark room, which was illuminated only by the one small kerosene lamp that stood on a table in front of the couch. The rest of the room receded into darkness that seemed all the darker because of the one spot of light. She could make out a table with straight chairs next to it on one side of the room, and she saw lamplight reflected in windows opposite her. She didn't dare look up, but sensed that there was no ceiling, the room went up to rafters and a dark sloping roof.

"Mrs. Trumbull!" His voice was curt. She'd better not pile it on too thickly. He was already suspicious.

"Howland put it in the library," she murmured so softly he had to move his head close to hers. She caught a faint, faint whiff of a scent coming from his face or hair or hands. Was it patchouli? Did everybody wear patchouli? Had he had some contact with Linda? She must remember to tell Casey.

"It isn't in the library, Mrs. Trumbull."

"I know," Victoria said softly. "I looked for it."

"Where is it, Mrs. Trumbull?"

His dark eyes showed through slits in his ski mask. Would Howland be safe if she told Mack where the computer was? She might learn something. Howland could take care of himself.

"Somebody stole it." She took a shallow breath.

"What! What makes you say that?"

"It . . . was . . . gone," Victoria murmured. "They . . . took it."

"Who, Mrs. Trumbull?" Mack stood up and paced. "Who? Who?"

"Dumpster." Victoria let her voice fade away.

"What!" said Mack. "Did someone throw it in a Dumpster? Who?" All rhetorical questions, and Victoria didn't answer. "Who else is after that computer? Did Atherton find it? Does he have it now?"

"I've got to lie down." Victoria leaned back against the lumpy cushions and, as if it was a great struggle, tried to lift her feet onto the couch. Mack helped her. She let one hand fall onto her stomach, where it pressed against the shell necklace she still wore, the other hand trailed on the rug.

"Please, Mrs. Trumbull. Does Atherton have it?"

Victoria moved her head from side to side as if she were too weak to answer, and closed her eyes.

"Shit!" said Mack.

Chapter 24

Mack stomped into a room to one side, and Victoria heard him say, "Everything in the world is on that computer. We've got to find it." Someone responded. Mack said, "If the fire destroyed the data, it's gone. But if anything can be recovered, we've got to get to it before anyone else does." The door between them and her shut with a click.

She heard a woman's voice, the driver's. They talked quietly, so quietly that if her hearing had not been so attuned, she wouldn't have known they were there. Mack spoke distinctly, and she could make out a few of his words.

She felt drowsy. She didn't want to lift her wrist to look at her watch in case Mack came back and saw that she wasn't sleeping. She had to be careful not to fall asleep.

Who were these people who wanted the computer? And why? Did it have to do with blackmail? Property? Motorcycles? Finances? Casinos? It was too tangled for her to sort out. Besides, she really didn't feel as alert as she'd like.

She strained to hear what was being said. She could catch occasional words. She heard "sleeping pill" and "old ladies" and "half," and she put those words together sleepily.

The door opened, and Victoria snored gently. She must not fall asleep, no matter what.

"She'll be out for a couple hours," Mack said. "Most likely the rest of the night."

"We can't leave her," the driver said.

"We have no choice. She'll be okay. She'll sleep, even if she does wake up, where can she go?"

"Don't take any chances," the driver said. "She's a smart old bird."

"She's what, ninety-two?" Someone must have nodded because he continued, "I'll lock the door on the outside."

Victoria sensed the presence of the woman, a clean soap smell, and the presence of the fourth person. She bit down on her tongue to stay awake, and pressed the back of her neck into the necklace Bernice Minnowfish had given her.

"How long do you plan on keeping her here?"

"Until we find that computer. We *must* find it."

"What if it takes a couple of days?" The driver again. "Everybody on the Island is looking for her. It's on the scanner. It's only a matter of time before they find her, and they'll accuse us of kidnapping, that's what."

"We've got to chance it. Come on, let's go."

"All of us?" said the woman.

"Everybody. She'll be okay. I'll send one of you back with food. We got nothing here except that damned soup."

Victoria fought sleep by tightening her toes in the wool socks, by biting the side of her tongue, by thinking about Elizabeth, who must be worried about her. They were looking for her. Hurry up and get out, she urged her captors silently. I don't want to fall asleep. Half of a sleeping pill? She had dribbled quite a bit of the soup down the front of her nightgown. Enough to make a difference?

They blew out the light—she could smell the burned wick—and then they left. A key turned in the lock. The Jeep started up, shifted into gear, and skidded on sand. The motor sound faded, then became louder again. Were they returning? It faded again. The Jeep must have gone into that valley and up the other side. She had to hurry. She had no idea how much time she had.

She pulled the socks up around her ankles. It would help if she could find shoes. She fumbled around in the darkness for matches, finally found some, then decided she'd better not light the lamp in case someone was watching. She put the matchbook in the pocket of her nightgown and felt her way into the bedroom, fumbled in the bare closet for shoes, didn't find any, didn't find any clothing she could wrap around herself. She had to get out of here. The wool socks would have to do.

She found her way to the front door and tried the knob. Perhaps it was the kind of lock you could open from the inside, but it wasn't. She felt around the wall until she came to the kitchen. A knife would be useful. She patted the counter until she located a drawer and a paring knife, which she wrapped in a paper towel from the holder over the sink. She found the back door, which she could unlock from inside. When she opened it, the sound of waves on the shore became louder. She must be careful not to fall. The socks would protect her feet, but they were too big and she was afraid she might trip over them or slip. She pulled them up as high as she could, almost to her knees, twisted the top of each, and made a sort of knot. She found a railing, felt for the wooden steps with her stockinged feet, and stepped down onto the sandy beach at the bottom.

The night was so dark she circled the cabin by holding one hand against its shingled wall. She worked her way toward the deck and the steps that led up to it. She looked up at the sky and could see Orion and, by turning, the Big Dipper. She would navigate by stars, the way her grandfather had taught her. The North Star was behind her. She must not go in circles, and she must conserve her energy. She ought to mark the way so Casey could find the camp. She had the packet of matches and the paring knife. Anything she could think to do with either of those, blazing trees or leaving burned matches, would take more time than she had. She could lay down a pattern of stones wherever the road branched, but that too would take too much time and the road was naturally stony. Then she remembered her necklace with its colored shells. She took it from around her neck, and cut the string carefully so she could remove one shell at a time. She dropped two shells next to the steps leading to the deck. The fluorescent shells would stand out against the grays and tans of the road.

Her feet found the rutted road, and she began the steep climb away from the cabin toward the main road. How far had they driven down that road—two miles? Three? She needed a stick of some kind for support. She made a foray off to one side of the road and picked up a fallen oak branch from among the huckleberry brush. She stopped long enough to break the stick to the right length.

Slowly, she told herself. Ten steps, then rest for a count of ten. The road was not difficult to follow. Starlight showed her the ruts and twists and turns. If she were not so concerned about the Jeep return-ing, concerned about Elizabeth and Casey, too, and if her feet were not feeling so tender, she might have enjoyed this night walk, an ad-venture that made her heart beat faster, pumping the half of the sleeping pill out of her system. She slid down, faster than she wanted to go, into what had seemed, by Jeep, like a small valley, that now was a deep bottomless gorge, and climbed up the other side, breath-ing hard. She dropped a shell every time she thought the track might be confusing.

Going up the side of the valley, she was so out of breath, she took five steps and rested ten counts. The road would level off, she re-called, and she would make better time. At the top she came to three side roads, and dropped several shells on the road she'd been on. She puzzled over the direction to take. She couldn't afford to spend energy on the wrong turn. She rested on her stick. Island roads branched like rivers, tributaries feeding the main stream at an acute angle. She studied the roads, looked up at the stars, and moved on again.

After she'd taken ten steps and waited for a count of ten so many times she'd lost track, she decided to reward herself by sitting down on the first big rock or stump or high side of the road, someplace where she wouldn't have to get all the way down, then all the way up again.

The road passed through a grove of oak trees that blotted out the starlight. Over the years the ruts had cut deeply into the sandy soil, leaving three-foot-high banks on either side. Victoria sat down on the left bank on a soft bed of moss, the height of a chair with a velvet cushion. She took a deep breath, breathed in the night air. She lis-tened to the night sounds, waves on the shore of the Sound, far away now, gratifyingly far, a bell buoy she hadn't recalled hearing before. Far off she heard a car. She listened intently and decided it was on the main road. A mile? Two miles? How far had she come, a half mile, perhaps? Up a steep hill, down into a valley, and up the other side. If she remembered correctly, there would be no more hills. But she was tired. Her feet were beginning to hurt. The cold night air seeped through her nightgown. She shivered, and started to walk again. Thank goodness for the socks. They were bulky and uncomfortable, and she had to keep pulling them up to adjust them, but think how it would be in bare feet. She must not allow herself to be tired or cold. She would think about cranberry juice laced with rum in front of the living room fire, about soaking her feet in a warm tub smelling of herbal essences. She threw back her shoulders and took fifteen steps.

Walking like a ten-year-old, she remembered, and stopped for a count of ten. Fifteen steps and rest for ten. Although the road was mostly sand, in places there were stones she couldn't see that bruised her feet. She knew there were large rocks in the road that she would have to avoid. She could not afford to stumble over one and fall. Fifteen steps and a count of ten. She looked up at the stars. They hadn't moved from where they'd been when she started. Her heading was almost due south, she figured. The road twisted and turned, but headed generally south. She stubbed her little toe on a large rock, and barely caught herself before she fell. She said "Ouch!" out loud, and lifted her foot off the ground until the pain subsided, and scolded herself for carelessness. She put the foot on the ground softly, and drew it up again with the sharp pain. If she simply ignored it and kept going, the pain would go away. Back to five steps and a count of ten.

Something rustled in the brush. She stopped. A black shape crossed the road in front of her and disappeared into the night on the other side, a skunk, its white stripes picked out by starlight. She laughed when she thought what her rescuers would think if they found her sprayed by a skunk. She moved on. The sound of waves was farther away. Not many cars passed on the main road, but when one did, she could see the glow of headlights much closer. She felt a surge of hope.

But she was shivering now. How could she avoid judgment-clouding hypothermia? She must get warm somehow. Move faster, was all she could think, and she did. She heard a car on the main road slow, saw headlights turn toward her, saw the two round dots of light. Was the Jeep coming back? Or was it someone who lived along this lonely road? She knew she would have to hide now, she wouldn't be able to act quickly enough once she identified the car. The banks along the side of the road were low, here, and the huckleberry brush was thick. She would have to find thick cover, she knew, because her pale nightgown would show up. The car's headlights jounced, at the sky, at the road. They disappeared, and showed up again, closer.

Victoria hustled into the undergrowth, feeling her way cautiously until she came to a small stand of young pine trees, and dropped down behind them. She lay on the moldy-smelling earth and covered her nightgown with as many of last year's leaves as she could scrape up. If the car's headlights did not belong to her captors, if it were someone who lived along the road, she would want to alert them. But she wouldn't be able to tell until they were almost upon her, and then it would be too late. On the other hand, if her captors' Jeep was returning, they would find her missing from the camp almost immediately, and then what would they do? Come back along the road searching for her? Should she stay hidden in the undergrowth until they passed a second time? She decided to stay hidden, if the Jeep passed, and wait until morning. She would cover herself thickly with leaves to warm herself like a hibernating creature. The headlights came closer and closer, and she realized with dismay they were not Jeep headlights. They were too high and too widely spaced.

It took her a while to stand up again. Her feet were swollen and her toe throbbed. She brushed off her leaf covering, picked up her stick, and made her way back to the road, discouraged for the first time. Rescue had been so close. Ten steps, count of ten. She heard the car go into the valley and up the other side, and then could hear it no more. Ten steps. Then she thought again. What was that car? It was heading for the camp. Was it her captors returning in a different car? Perhaps she had been wise to hide. This spurred her on. Suppose they returned, though. Victoria remembered to drop another shell. There were not many left on the string. She had to save a few to mark the turnoff from the main road.

She heard the vehicle again, and dodged into the brush, much thinner here. She hid as best she could. The steady walking had been an effort; the hiding was exhausting. This time she would stay hidden no matter what, and she would rest. She scooped leaves over her and lay as flat as she could. Headlights lit up the trees above her. She heard the engine, saw two dots of headlights. The vehicle slowed. Victoria held her breath. Surely she couldn't be seen. She pressed herself flat into the soft ground. The car stopped. The door opened. Slammed shut.

"My friend!"

Victoria tried to sit up, and couldn't.

Dojan tore through the underbrush. "Did they hurt you? Oh, my friend!" He scooped her up. She tried to pull her gown down modestly over her legs and brushed at the leaves.

He opened the front door of his van with one hand, still holding her in the other, and deposited her on the front seat.

"I will kill them!"

"No, no, no," said Victoria weakly.

Dojan slid open the side door of his van and brought out a fishy-smelling blanket, which he wrapped around her with great tenderness.

"Thank you," Victoria said, looking into Dojan's dark eyes. "How did you ever, ever find me?"

"I have spent all night searching. I saw them in your house and entered."

"I heard you." Victoria wrapped the blanket tightly around herself. She couldn't stop shivering.

"Someone hit me." Dojan gripped the steering wheel tensely. "When I came to, you were gone."

"Then what happened?"

"I was not out long. I heard the Jeep go up-Island. So I searched the roads between your house and Aquinnah."

"There must be dozens of them."

"Some had not been used lately. Those I did not follow. I followed roads that led nowhere. I saw summer cabins that were closed for the winter. I saw places with lights and people. Then I saw sandy tire tracks leading out from this road and I followed them, as I had followed a dozen others. The tracks led to the camp. There, I saw two shells, shells from the necklace my cousin gave you. I saw where you must have lain on the sofa, saw an empty cup and spoon next to it. I feared they had taken you away. Then I thought of the shells by the steps. So I found your footprints and I tracked you. I saw shells you had dropped. Where the footprints stopped, I stopped. And I found you, my friend."

It was the longest speech Victoria had ever heard from Dojan.

The night sky was lightening. Victoria could make out the horizon below a pale line of gray dawn. Dojan drove slowly so the van rocked Victoria like a cradle.

"They may come back, Dojan."

He grunted. He'd said enough.

He turned onto the paved road. Ahead of her, Victoria could see clouds emerge from the darkness, lit up with gold and silver. The van headed directly into the dawn, and Victoria's heart lifted at the beauty of it all.

Chapter 25

"If you don't mind, Patience, I'm on the phone." Peter covered the mouthpiece with his hand.

"I'll wait." Patience sat down on the couch Peter had insisted upon having in his office.

"This is a private call," Peter hissed.

"There are no private calls here. Business calls are not private. You may make personal calls from the phone booth in the corridor." Patience looked around his office. A large colored map of Aquinnah covered one wall. It was a combination topographic map that showed every hill and valley, and a soils map that showed where sand and clay predominated. It was overlaid with an enlarged assessor's map that gave every map and lot number, and showed every building. Patience couldn't help staring at the map and the detail it showed. She'd seen that map every time she'd come into his office, but had never looked at it so closely. She could see the three lots that were hers now, her property. Almost thirty acres. She thought of her grandmother's drumbeat: "Money is power." Land is power, Patience added.

Peter took his hand away from the mouthpiece and spoke into it. "Sorry. I'll have to get back to you later."

Patience waited while the person at the other end of the line said a great deal more to Peter.

"I realize that. I'll explain later. I'll call you back in a half hour." Peter stretched out his left arm so his watch emerged from under the cuff of his black silk shirt.

Patience folded her arms over her bosom and stared at the wall map. Peter had added colored map tacks in certain places, for some reason. One of the tacks was on her land. She couldn't tell what the tacks signified. Archaeological sites? She turned away from the map.

Peter was beginning to perspire. Patience handed him a tissue from her pocket. He took the tissue from her and wiped his forehead. The voice on the phone was a man's, but Patience could make out only a few emphatic words. "Don't you hang up on me," she heard, and "You agreed."

Peter said over the still-talking voice, "I've got to go. I'll explain later." He replaced the receiver, and the phone rang immediately. Patience reached across his desk, ignoring the look on Peter's face, and picked up the phone. She said nothing. The voice at the other end said, "Little, you fucker, don't you ever hang up on me again." Patience knew that voice. It belonged to a man she had thrown out of her office three months before, George Philipopoulos, a man full of his own charm.

"Thank you, Mr. Philipopoulos. He won't hang up on you again." She replaced the phone on Peter's desk.

"Would you care to discuss this with me, Peter?" She made herself comfortable on his couch, patted the soft cushions. "Nice. Leather and eiderdown. Very executive. Expensive." She paused. He squirmed. "Perhaps you have a logical reason for doing business with Mr. Philipopoulos? Or perhaps you were not doing business with him at all. Perhaps he was harassing you? In which case, I will put a stop to it for you, if you would like. Perhaps he believed he could get what he wanted by going after the weakest link?"

Peter stared at his tidy desk. He moved a letter opener to one side so it lined up with a matching silver pen. He put his hands on his desk and looked at his manicured nails.

"Do you wish to say something, Peter? Or do you choose to remain silent and let me think what I will? That you are trying to enrich yourself at the expense of the tribe?"

At that, Peter stood up. "Who's enriching whose self?" He smiled. "I don't have to listen to you."

"No, you don't. Perhaps you would like to clear out your desk. Remove your furniture to a more appreciative employer."

"You can't fire me. The tribe voted me in."

"Would you care to challenge that?" Patience smiled brightly from the soft couch, stretched her plump arm across the smooth leather back.

A hawk cried high above them. The wind riffled the bayberry leaves on the other side of the parking lot. Peter stood in front of the window, hands behind his back, staring out at the parking lot and the rolling hills beyond it. Peter's MG was parked next to Chief Hawkbill's Cadillac, Patience's battered red Ford pickup was next to his MG.

"I've got my supporters," he said finally.

"I'm sure you do." Patience melted further into the soft leather. "Shall we see who has more? And do you think yours will still support you when they learn the source of your wealth? That your connections have nothing to do with tribal advancement, but everything to do with the advancement of Peter Little?"

Peter swiveled around. "Sounds like the pot calling the kettle black."

"Let me number the votes. On your side are Littles and Minnowfish. Can you count on support from them? Dojan is a Minnowfish. He is, what, third or fourth cousin?"

Peter shifted in his chair.

"On my side are VanDykes and Hawkbills. Also on my side are the off-Island Wampanoags who know nothing about Peter Little. Shall I demand a recall vote?"

Peter's voice was tightly controlled. "I'm sure your supporters will be interested in hearing about the land you've somehow managed to acquire. Secretly. Looks great for someone who's always crying poor-mouth. You planning to build trophy houses? Or will your land be suitable for the casino you want so badly? That would explain a lot of things, wouldn't it?"

Patience looked up, surprised.

"Bought by the Quahog Trust, not by poor Patience VanDyke, who drives a fifteen-year-old pickup." Peter laughed. "You thought you could keep a secret like that on this Island?"

Patience sat up straight. "I like a challenge, Peter. You against me isn't much of a challenge. Gather your supporters. See how far your tactics will get you. The Wampanoags have been led by strong women for generations. Do you think they will trust a silk-shirted boy with a fancy sports car? And silver desk ornaments? They understand land, Peter, and I understand them."

Peter stared at her for long moments. He turned toward the parking lot, his MG and her pickup. He turned back, folded his hands on his desktop, and smiled. "All right," he said. "What do you want of me?"

"I do not need you working against me, Peter. Why don't you tell me what you and Mr. Philipopoulos were concocting between you."

Peter bowed his head and examined his fingernails.

"As I recall, he represents a shipping firm, right?"

Peter said nothing. His back was to the window, his face in shadow. The light reflecting from the hood of Chief Hawkbill's Cadillac flickered in Patience's eyes. She moved to the other side of the couch and settled herself again.

Patience lifted herself slightly to straighten her skirt under her. Her heavy breasts swayed under her gauzy cotton blouse. She smoothed her skirt over her knees, bent and tugged the fabric around her ankles. She wore clogs with thick soles and thick heels on bare feet. She couldn't see Peter's expression but suspected it was one of distaste.

She sat up and spoke sharply. "Well, Peter, how much are they paying you?"

Peter swiveled his chair so he faced the parking lot again, and said nothing.

"How much are they paying you? Or do we ask the federal government to look into your income and the taxes you pay? I assume you pay federal income taxes. How do you afford leather office furniture and silver desk appointments on the salary I pay you? Inherited from the Little side of the family? No. Certainly not the Minnowfish side."

Peter still said nothing.

"I suppose it's too much to ask that you cooperate with me in getting a government grant?"

Peter stood and faced Patience. "Federal funding is not the way to go," he said.

"Because you won't get your rake-off?" Patience laughed. "It is easy to see through you, Peter. Mr. Philipopoulos's bosses want a floating casino, and are paying you well to lobby for it, aren't they?"

"A floating casino makes sense. It will wipe out Islanders' greatest argument against a gambling casino. It would not be built on the land. No worries about traffic, ferry tie-ups, liquor, noise, children going astray." He laughed. "Tribal members will captain vessels, not spin red and black wheels."

"Your points are well taken, Peter. Why have you not discussed this freely with me and with the tribal council?" When he started to answer, she held up a plump hand with rings on each of her fingers. "We know why, don't we? You like the good things, don't you, Peter? Mr. Philipopoulos is able, through his employer, to provide you with the stipend, or, shall I say, bribe, that allows you to indulge yourself. You do not want to see that source of money dry up, do you, Peter? Which it would if you cooperated with me." She sat forward on the couch. "You were working with Mr. Burkhardt, too, weren't you? To slow the granting of permits. Was Mr. Burkhardt also getting money from Mr. Philipopoulos?"

Peter toyed with his paperweight, a heavy glass dome containing a chunk of clay from the cliffs.

"Mr. Philipopoulos is a fool. However, he does not work for fools. Has the money and its power corrupted you so much? Was it your cohorts, Peter, who kidnapped Mrs. Trumbull last night?"

Peter dropped the paperweight on his desk with a thump. "What about Mrs. Trumbull?"

"You needn't pretend to be astonished. Everyone on this Island, with the possible exception of Mrs. Trumbull, has a scanner. You included. Where were you last night, Peter?"

"It's none of your business."

"You're right, where you go at night does not concern me. However, the police are likely to be interested. I suggest you think up a credible alibi."

Victoria refused to go to bed, but Elizabeth ran a warm bath for her. When Victoria emerged, pink and herbal-scented, wearing her gray corduroy trousers and a moss-colored turtleneck, Dojan helped her lift her feet up onto the couch. Within seconds she was snoring softly.

Elizabeth covered her grandmother with a blanket, and tiptoed into the kitchen, where Casey was stacking papers and Howland was rinsing dishes.

"Who would have kidnapped her?" Elizabeth was wiping the dishes. "Why my grandmother? They said they wanted Burkhardt's computer. How many people are after it?"

"A lot." Howland wiped his hands on a dish towel and put clean cups in the cupboard above the sink.

Dojan was sitting in the captain's chair by the door, his eyes half-shut.

Casey, rumpled and tired-looking, her hair disheveled, stepped up from the cookroom. "I'm beat, you guys. I'm going home to bed. I'll talk to you later." Chuck shrugged into his linen jacket, and gathered up his notes. "Anything I can do before I leave?"

Elizabeth smiled at him. "Thank you for a nice evening."

Dojan sat up abruptly and hooted. "First date?"

In the dining room, Victoria slept soundly, and Elizabeth, Howland, and Dojan tiptoed into the cookroom.

Howland scratched his unshaven chin. "An earthquake wouldn't disturb her."

"The kidnapping has to be tied to Burkhardt," Elizabeth said. "Were they the killers? Were they bikers? Wampanoags? Casino financiers? Maybe Linda's buddies?"

"Where is Linda, by the way?" Howland asked.

"I haven't seen her since yesterday. I have no idea where she is." Elizabeth looked around. "She didn't come home last night. Did she?"

Dojan had moved from the captain's chair in the kitchen to the bentwood armchair in the cookroom. He sat stolidly at the head of the table, his arms crossed over his chest, his bare feet flat on the floor, his eyes closed.

Howland took a pen and a lined pad of paper from the table below the wall phone. "I'll make a list of facts and assumptions." He drew two vertical lines on the paper and wrote in the first column.

"I'm too tired to think," said Elizabeth.

"Right." Howland tossed the pen aside and yawned.

Elizabeth pushed her chair away from the table. "Is anyone else hungry? I feel as if we've been eating all night, but I'm starved."

Dojan opened his eyes and stood. "I will fix food. You talk." He went into the kitchen, and Elizabeth heard the refrigerator door open. Soon she smelled bacon frying.

She sat back again, put her elbows on the table, and rested her chin in her hands. "You know the weeder my grandmother and Dojan found?"

Howland nodded.

"My grandmother has one just like it. I tried breaking up quahog shells with it yesterday. Quahog shells are really, really heavy."

Howland nodded again.

"I smashed the shells as though they were eggs." Elizabeth shuddered. "It wouldn't take a strong person to crush a skull."

Howland leaned back in his chair and yawned again.

"Don't let Victoria see you lean back like that."

Howland set the chair down on all four legs.

In the kitchen, Dojan clattered dishes and utensils, and soon after, came in with a dish of Indian pudding—a kind of cornmeal spoon bread—a platter of bacon and sausage, and fried green tomatoes.

"I put some in the oven for my friend," Dojan said. Elizabeth reached into her back pocket, took out pieces of broken clamshell, and set them on the table. "I was wondering what felt so uncomfortable."

CHAPTER 26

Howland was still yawning over the notes he was writing when Victoria awoke a little before noon. Elizabeth had set her grandfather's slippers next to the couch, and Victoria eased her sore feet into the soft lamb's wool.

"I must have fallen asleep," she said to Elizabeth, who had been sitting in the cookroom with Howland. "I didn't mean to. Where's Dojan?"

"Here, my friend." Dojan rose from the captain's chair, where he had been dozing.

"Something smells good." Victoria's eyes brightened when she saw what was on the plate Dojan set out for her. "I haven't had Indian pudding for years."

"Would you recognize any of the people who kidnapped you if you should see them again?" Howland asked after she had finished her late breakfast.

Victoria set her fork on the side of her plate. "I heard the driver call his boss 'Mack.' He had a voice I'd recognize."

"The kidnappers worked together," Howland said. "Were they tribal members?"

"I had no way of knowing. Mack was disguising his voice. He was tall and didn't seem heavy, although it was hard to tell because of his loose clothing. The driver had muscular, hairy arms and was much shorter." She thought some more. "One of the others was a woman. The fourth may also have been a woman or a smallish man."

"Anything else you can recall?" Howland asked.

"When Mack leaned over me, he smelled of patchouli."

"Patchouli?"

"It's a perfume made from some East Indian plant," Elizabeth explained. "It's popular with touchy-feely types."

"Could it have been his shaving lotion?"

Victoria shook her head. "I don't think so."

"Patchouli is a woman's perfume," said Elizabeth.

Victoria glanced around. "Where's Linda? Did she come home last night?"

"Not while we were here," said Howland, pushing his chair away from the table.

"I hope she's all right." Victoria frowned. "I was bothered by her reaction to her uncle's death and the fire. Almost no reaction. Yet she was shocked, out of proportion, when she heard that we'd found a body in the house."

"That *is* pretty shocking," said Elizabeth.

"No more so than her uncle's murder," said Howland.

"She made quite a point of asking about the computer," said Victoria. "She insists that it's hers."

"Burkhardt's heir hasn't been established yet," said Howland. "The courts will have to establish whose it is. Unless, of course, someone finds a will."

"Linda wants to see who gets the eighteen million. There's bound to be a copy of his will on it. If her uncle didn't leave his property to her . . ."

"She might do something about it?" Howland finished.

"Linda didn't kill her uncle," said Victoria.

Elizabeth snorted. "I wouldn't put it past her. Money. Everything comes down to money."

Victoria shifted her feet slightly and winced.

Elizabeth got up quickly. "Another footbath, Gram?"

"I'm fine, thank you," said Victoria.

Elizabeth sat down again.

"What about Hiram's friend?" Howland asked.

"Tad was more than just a friend," said Victoria.

"I assumed so," said Howland.

Victoria cleared her throat. "At some time in the past, before Tad came into the picture, Hiram and Jube Burkhardt were lovers."

"Ah!" said Howland.

"You knew Burkhardt threatened to expose Tad if Hiram didn't sign the phony noncompliance papers?"

"And Hiram went along with the scam," said Howland. "Yes, I'd heard."

"Where's Tad now?" Elizabeth asked.

"On his way home to Nebraska," Victoria replied. "He called Hiram on his cell phone from the ferry."

"He could have been anywhere," said Howland. "Tad had an excellent motive for killing Burkhardt. And opportunity, assuming he wasn't calling from the ferry."

"He was driving his car back to Nebraska," said Victoria. "The Steamship Authority will have records."

"Good point." Howland jotted something in his notes.

"We told you about the 'Fatal Error' message on Burkhardt's computer, didn't we?"

"You did," said Howland.

There was a loud snort from the end of the table, and all three looked at Dojan, who'd been so quiet they'd forgotten he was there. He had fallen asleep, his arms folded across his chest, his head bowed. The feather in his hair bobbed with his breathing.

"We should move into the other room," Elizabeth whispered.

Howland yawned. "We're not likely to disturb him."

"Dojan had a rough night," said Victoria.

Howland smiled. "So did almost everyone on the Island."

Victoria continued in a low voice. "The morning after Jube's murder the killer must have gone to Jube's house to see what was on his computer."

"Burkhardt's computer was an antique," said Howland. "If the killer tried to erase certain files, but didn't know how, he would get that 'Fatal Error' message."

"Hardly an antique," said Victoria. "I don't believe Jube had owned his computer for more than ten years."

"Ten years!" muttered Howland. "Even a computer nerd might not understand codes that ancient."

"Ancient!" said Victoria.

"I bet Hiram went to Jube's for the same reason," said Elizabeth. "To delete whatever he could from the computer."

Victoria started to say something, then stopped.

"What were you about to say, Victoria?" Howland asked.

"The killer must have been in the house when Hiram got there."

"Go on," said Howland.

"Hiram saw the computer running and suspected something was wrong. Jube wouldn't have left it on. That was when Hiram called me. The killer undoubtedly heard Hiram leave that message on my answering machine."

Howland nodded. "Hiram may have seen the killer."

"I guess it was hopeless to think we could recover anything from the computer," said Elizabeth. "I wish we could have known what was on it."

"Be right back." Howland went out to his car and returned with a disk in a plastic case. "Here you are."

"You got it?" Elizabeth shouted.

Dojan woke up with a start and shook his head.

"Most of it," said Howland. "Once I pried the case off, the insides were intact. I removed the hard drive and installed it in my own computer."

Elizabeth picked up the disk gently.

"I made four copies," said Howland. "One's at my house, one's in my safe deposit box at the bank, I gave one to Chief O'Neill, and this is the fourth."

"Have you seen what's on it?" Elizabeth asked.

Howland nodded. "Everything. Just like his house. He kept everything. Financial records, every e-mail sent to him, a database I haven't deciphered yet, and file after file of who knows what. It's going to take weeks to go through Burkhardt's files."

"Fools!" rasped Bugs. "You fools! You stupid shits! What in hell possessed you to do that? What in hell did you think you were doing?" He pushed his glasses back onto the bridge of his nose.

The four bikers stood silently before him, scowling, three men and a woman.

Bugs loomed over them, his large hands clenched in hammy fists, muttering something with his lips that never came out as words. He stalked away from the shade into the sunlit field and kicked at a clod of earth.

The four, all dressed in black leather trousers, jackets, and boots, glared at his back. The shortest man spat off to one side. Bugs walked into the field, sending a shower of dirt over goldenrod and Queen Anne's lace. He circled back to them. The woman was cradling a black and white helmet. She lifted a tangle of hair off her neck with one hand.

"Sit!" Bugs ordered.

"Who you talking to?" said the redhead.

The girl snickered.

"Sit," Bugs said again, much too quietly, and pointed to the bench attached to the picnic table.

They hesitated. Bugs moved a half step forward, and all three sat, backs to the picnic table. Bugs stood over them, working his mouth.

Finally he spoke. "I assume this was your idea, Mack?"

The three bikers looked at Mack.

"Yeah."

"Why? Tell me why?"

"She surprised us. We didn't expect her to come downstairs."

"What in hell were you doing in her house?" Bugs's heavy glasses slipped down his nose, and he pushed them back.

"We needed to get that computer."

"And why, may I ask?" Bugs's voice was tight with sarcasm. "I suppose you think it's got nasty comments on bikers? Burkhardt had a right to his opinions. First Amendment, after all." He stabbed a finger at Mack. "Free speech, in case you don't remember."

The girl, at the end of the bench, moved her helmet into her lap, and looked down at it. The chunky redhead shifted something in his mouth and continued to chew. The smallest man gazed beyond Bugs into the field, where yellow butterflies flitted over a patch of budding asters. Mack looked down at his hands.

"You look at me, not your hands," Bugs ordered. "All of you. And you answer me."

They slowly raised their eyes to his.

Mack cleared his throat. "It wasn't about his biker complaints. It was something else."

"Well?"

The girl straightened the strap on her helmet. The redhead chewed. Mack opened his mouth as if to say something and shut it again.

Bugs moved a step forward, closing in on them. All four leaned back against the table. A breeze passed through the trees above them, a soft sigh of rustling pine needles. "It was personal," Mack said finally. "Nobody else's business."

"It's not personal when you break and enter with intent to burgle. That's against the law, in case you didn't know. Did you think of that? Did you?"

They looked down at the ground.

"You think it's a game when you kidnap an old lady, a ninety-two-year-old lady, for Christsake, in her nightgown and bare feet and rough her up?"

"We didn't treat her rough," the redhead said.

Bugs swiveled on his heels and stalked a few paces away from the four, then swung back again.

"You know you go to jail for kidnapping. And they throw away the key. Did you think of that? Did you?"

Mack started to say something, but Bugs continued. "Prehistoric Neanderthals with undeveloped brains. Roaring around country roads on motorcycles, raping and pillaging. A bunch of assholes, that's what you are." He stopped for breath.

"Nobody was raping nobody," said the redhead, sullenly staring at the ground.

"You look at me!" Bugs rasped.

He looked up.

"First the cute little race with the cops."

"That wasn't us," said the smaller man.

Bugs swung around to face him, and the redhead leaned back against the picnic table.

Bugs turned on Mack again. "And now this, one hell of a lot more serious than playing tag with local cops. Personal, eh? Nobody else's business, eh? In the next five minutes, you tell me what you had in mind, before I turn you over to that same local cop you thought was so cute. You'll see how cute she is. Talk." Without taking his eyes off them, Bugs reached over for one of the white resin chairs, pulled it under him and sat. He folded both arms over his chest.

Mack darted a glance at the other three, who were trying their best to look unconcerned.

Bugs glanced at his watch. "Four and one-half minutes."

"Burkhardt had stuff on his computer," Mack blurted out.

"Obviously," Bugs said. "So what?"

Mack started to stand up.

"Sit!" Bugs pointed to the bench, and Mack sat again.

"His will and stuff."

"What's his will got to do with you?"

Mack was silent. A chickadee landed on a pine branch above them, showering the picnic table with brown needles. The bird called its mournful late summer *pee-wee*.

"Four minutes," Bugs rasped.

"I've been seeing his niece."

Bugs stood abruptly. "That goddamned two-timing bitch . . ."

"No, no," Mack said. "Not Harley, Linda."

Bugs thumped back into his chair, speechless.

"I been seeing Linda. She didn't want her uncle to know she was dating a biker. Her uncle was leaving his place to her because of Harley dating a biker, and all?"

Bugs's face reddened.

"She thought her uncle found out about her and me, you know?"

"So she killed him." It was a statement.

Mack shook his head vigorously. "She didn't kill him. She wouldn't have killed anyone."

Bugs's eyes were fixed on Mack. "Well?"

"She wanted to find out what was on his computer, that's all. If he changed his will again."

"Money." Bugs turned partway in the chair, faced away from the four on the picnic bench with a look of disgust.

"He was always changing his will, she said."

Bugs stared at the others, who avoided his eyes. "Why the rest of you? Why'd you let him euchre you into this?"

The redhead said, "We didn't know what it was all about."

Bugs turned on him. "You didn't, eh? You got black hoods, a get-away car, and a hideaway cabin at the end of a two-mile-long dirt road, and you thought this was fun and games?"

"We didn't know we was going to take the old lady," the redhead said.

Bugs stood again. He whacked the side of his head with his hand. He paced away from the four at the picnic table into the field of golden and white and purple flowers, and yellow butterflies. He paced back, passed the table, strode into the shadowy grove of pines, and stopped at the Indian pipes. Half of the waxy translucent plants had turned black.

"Corpse plants. You know that's what they call them, corpse plants." He laughed silently. "You got to take your medicine, all of you." He came back to the white resin chair, and, still standing, put his hand on its back. "First of all, we go to see Mrs. Trumbull. You guys better take one huge bouquet of flowers. And apologize until the cows come home. Understand?" He stared at them and they looked away. "Get down on your knees and beg her pardon, understand? Grovel."

The girl played with the strap on her helmet. The redhead chewed and stared steadily at Bugs. The smaller man took out a soiled handkerchief and blew his nose. Mack started to stand, apparently thought better of it, and settled back on the bench.

"Then you are going with me to the police chief, that local cop you think is so cute, and throw yourself on her mercy. You tell her everything, understand? I hope to hell she throws you in jail until you rot." He put on his helmet and fastened the strap under his chin. "Get on your bikes, and follow me."

CHAPTER 27

The day after her uncle died, Linda had gone to his house on the Great Pond with Mack, riding on the back of his Harley. Linda had a feeling of relief she couldn't account for. Perhaps it was the brilliant day, the way sunlight flickered on the pond, the luminous golden light that took away some vague sinister quality of the house. Uncle Jube was dead. Should she feel sorry? When she got off the bike, she stretched her arms out wide and breathed the bright air in as deeply as she could.

"Nice spot," Mack said.

"When I was little, it was like paradise," she said. "But when I was twelve, the place began to seem creepy." She shuddered.

"Someone walking on your grave?" Mack asked.

She smiled weakly. This was a day to exorcise evil spirits. The blue sky, the puffy white clouds, the green trees across the pond, the yellow barrier bar. The breeze, so soft it felt moist, the cry of gulls. The sound of water lapping sleepily on the shore.

"I might as well go inside," she said. "See what the place looks like now."

"You need me, I'm working on my bike," Mack had said.

And then it happened.

When she stepped onto the sun-warmed granite stone outside the back entry, when she opened the door and the familiar smells of mildew and old rubber boots and oilskins washed over her, when she put her foot on the familiar worn linoleum, which crunched with a sound she remembered from childhood, when she saw the same kayak paddle, the fishing rods, the same oilskins, the same boots with moldy laces, it flooded back to her, that last summer. She could still hear her mother's raised voice, shouting at Uncle Jube. She could still feel the caned seat of the rocking chair sticking to the back of her bare legs in her sister's attic room. She could see her sister's scared face over the book she'd been reading to her. She remembered how the sky outside her sister's window was full of fluffy white clouds, like today, lamb clouds, she and her sister had called them, dazzling white and clean in a dazzling summer sky.

The smothering blanket of time suddenly lifted. She hadn't wanted to see what had been hidden for so long. But it flooded back anyway.

She rushed out of the entry, stumbled over the granite stone, and fell on her knees in the brittle grass, her arms straight in front of her, head down.

"Hey, girl, what's with you?" Mack had been in the barn, crouched over his Harley, wiping it gently with an oily rag. He stood.

Linda's mouth was open, her face twisted, her blue eyes wide and hazy.

"Hey, cool it! What happened in there?"

She couldn't talk at first. She was shivering.

Mack stood with the oily rag in his hands, his booted feet apart, wiping his hands on the cloth. His face was a mixture of puzzlement and concern.

"It's come back," she said finally.

He finished wiping his hands, and put the rag in the saddlebag.

"What's come back, hey?"

"I killed him." Linda's eyes focused on something beyond him.

Mack looked over his shoulder, then back at Linda. She continued to shiver.

"Let's get outta here." He had taken his leather coat off the hook in the barn where he had left it, and wrapped it around her. He wheeled the bike out of the barn, led her to it, helped her aboard, and fastened his extra helmet under her chin. He roared out of Uncle Jube's place as if something was after them. Down bumpy dirt roads, down thinly paved tar roads, along the up-to-specs state road. White stripes whizzed below their feet. Linda had not seen the cars they passed.

When they reached the other side of the Island, ten miles away, he turned onto a narrow asphalt road that bordered the Sound, slowed going up a hill, stopped at the East Chop lighthouse gate, parked his bike beside the turnstile, and helped Linda off. She stumbled.

"Can you walk okay?" he asked.

She nodded.

He led her to a bench at the foot of the white lighthouse. In front of the bench, a grassy slope ended in a fringe of wild rosebushes at the top of a high bluff. Nobody was around. He perched beside her, watching her. She unfastened her helmet and laid it on the bench between them.

Mack looked down. "You skinned your knees," he said. "I should've made you wear long pants." He stood. "I'll be right back with the first aid kit."

"Don't leave me," she said.

Mack sat again.

The Sound spread out below them, dotted with fishing boats trailing long wakes and clouds of gulls. Sailboats heeled in the breeze. A cluster of small boats was drifting near the shoal, where a froth of fish broke water.

After a while, Linda spoke. "I'd buried it forever."

"Meaning what?" Mack said.

She took a deep breath. "When my sister and I were growing up, my mother took a long vacation every summer, and we stayed with Uncle Jube. He had a rowboat, and my sister and I used to row out on the pond and just sit there, you know? Watching clouds and trailing our hands in the water. Uncle Jube didn't have electricity, not until years later."

"Yeah?" Mack shifted the helmet that lay between them and put his arm around her.

She was quiet for a long time.

"Yeah," Mack said finally. He stroked her shoulder through her leather jacket.

"In the evening we used to sit around the table reading by the light of the kerosene lamp, all four of us. Uncle Jube was like our father. He'd play with us and tickle us like puppy dogs, and we'd roll in the grass laughing until my mother made him stop."

"The funny uncle," Mack said.

Linda shuddered once and looked up at him. "Yeah."

Below them, the ferry whistled. They watched it round the point, pass in front of them, and become a white dot trailing a comet tail of wake.

"So, go on," Mack said.

"Uncle Jube went from being warm and friendly to being scary, and I didn't know how to stop him or what to do because it was my fault I had let him go so far and I couldn't tell my mother because, after all, I'd let him, and . . ." Linda sucked in her breath with an asthmatic wheeze.

"Bastard," Mack said. "And your goddamned mother, she should've known."

Linda took a long breath and went on. "One night my mother came into my room to say good night, and that's when she found out about Uncle Jube."

"And you heard them fight, and that was the last time you were on the Island."

"I hated him. I didn't know why until . . ."

"You went into that house."

"I came back to kill him."

A breeze riffled the grass in front of them, bringing the scent of pine. A seagull flew over, heading for the Sound. A string of motorcycles roared by on the road behind the lighthouse.

"Somebody beat you to it."

She shook her head. "I hate that house."

"Can't say as I blame you, girl."

Linda turned on him. "Don't call me 'girl.' I hate that!" She pounded her fist on his thigh.

He grabbed her fist. "Okay, okay, Linda. Sorry."

"Everything about that house is rotten, from the floors to the roof. And all that garbage. I couldn't stand being in it, even fixed up."

"Cool it, Linda. There's nothing you can do about the past. He's gone."

"That house, it's not worth saving," she said.

"I don't know. It's a real old house. Historical. Worth one hell of a lot of money."

"Not to me, it isn't."

"Come on, Linda. When you get it cleaned up, all that shit can go in the rubbish. You can sell it to someone who never knew your uncle."

"You're not hearing me."

"Yes, I am."

"I'm going to kill that house. Like I killed him."

"Don't talk nonsense."

"Do you love me, Mack?"

He tightened his arm around her.

"You said once you'd do anything for me."

"I'll say it again. I would. I'd do anything in the world for you, Linda."

"I want to kill everything about that house."

"What the hell are you talking about?"

"Purify it. Burn it to the ground."

Mack removed his arm from her shoulder and stood up. "You can't do that."

"Why not? It's my place. Practically. I can do whatever I want with it."

"That's arson. You don't torch a place because you don't like it."

"Will you help me or not?" Linda's eyes were wide and as bright as the sky. "There are other guys, plenty of other guys, who'd be happy to help me. Especially knowing it's my property. Especially knowing what it's worth."

He walked to the edge of the bluff, plucked off a bright red rose hip, tossed it toward the Sound, and returned to her. Linda sat huddled and fragile, small and vulnerable in his big leather coat. She watched him with her innocent blue eyes.

"Linda, whatever you want. I'll do whatever you want."

CHAPTER 28

From the study, where she sat at her computer the next morning, Elizabeth could look out the small-paned window at the Norway maple at the end of the driveway. Its branches hung low, almost hiding the pile of stacked firewood and the compost heap beyond. The tree had a faint tinge of yellow. Summer was almost gone.

When she heard Howland's distinctive footsteps on the stairway, she glanced up.

"I'll hook up my ZIP drive to your computer," he said. "Then you can print out what we need."

"I don't know what a ZIP drive is."

"It lets you copy a lot of data onto a small space in a short time. I'll show you how. Without it, I'd have taken days to copy what's on Burkhardt's hard drive."

Elizabeth gave him her seat. A short time later, she heard her grandmother's shoes squeak on the painted stairs.

"I don't suppose I can help?" Victoria asked.

"I'll show you how to use the computer if you'd like," Howland murmured with a faint smile. "It's simple."

Victoria moved a chair close to the desk where Howland was working. "Never mind."

Elizabeth stood behind Howland, watching him work.

"He was well organized, I'll say that for him," Howland said when the screen finally showed lists of files and directories. "This is his word-processing program, an old one. Not many people use it these days." He stood up. Elizabeth sat down and read off the list of files.

"Correspondence, Finances," she said. "Legal, Personal, X. Shall I check the X-file?"

"We need to start somewhere. X is as good as any."

Elizabeth tapped keys, and a list showed on the screen.

"It doesn't make sense." Elizabeth scrolled down. There were about fifty items on the list.

Howland leaned over and looked. "It's coded," he said. "Burkhardt probably encrypted those files. Try to get one up on the screen."

Elizabeth tapped keys. PASSWORD, the screen demanded.

"Well, well, well." Howland leaned over Elizabeth and tried another item on the list. PASSWORD, the screen read.

Victoria leaned forward to see the screen. "Is there any way to get around that?"

"There are three or four decoding methods I can try. If they don't work, I can go to my Washington DEA experts, but that will take time."

"Perhaps we can guess his password," Victoria said.

Howland shrugged. "We can try. Most people use something simple, like their names or birth dates. Mother's maiden name. Any thoughts, Victoria? An eight- or fewer-letter word." He turned back to Elizabeth. "Try Burkhard, without the *t*. Or Jube. Try Engineer."

Elizabeth typed the words into the space for PASSWORD. The computer beeped, and each time, the screen read: THIS ISN'T THE CORRECT PASSWORD."

Howland straightened up and put his hands in his pockets. "We're wasting time. Let's check the other files. He could have used anything for a password."

"Try 'Mitchell,'" Victoria said. "That was his mother's maiden name, his house was the Mitchell place, and it's eight letters."

Elizabeth typed MITCHELL. A file popped up on the screen. She scrolled down, then back up again. "It's nothing but gibberish."

"He was certainly protecting whatever he's got here." Howland frowned. "That entry looks like a name. This," he pointed, "is probably an address and phone number."

"That might be a dollar amount," said Victoria.

"I bet this is his blackmail list." Elizabeth scrolled down. "There are a half-dozen entries with figures next to them."

"He probably used a simple code he could access easily," Howland said. "Print the entire file, Elizabeth. Two copies. One for Chief O'Neill, and we can attempt to decode the other."

When the printing was finished, Elizabeth set the hard-copy pages of the X-file to one side.

"Now start from the beginning of the directory." Howland pulled a chair next to Elizabeth. "We can make a quick run-through, then check everything later in detail."

"Is there a file where he'd have stored his will?" Victoria said, examining the list of directories. "Or at least his attorney's name. She or he would have the original executed will, I imagine."

"Unless he drew it up himself," Howland said.

They checked Correspondence. Letters to Sears, to a plumbing supply company. Nothing stood out except for a sizable file of letters to Smith College.

The directory titled Finances listed banks and financial institutions and was cross-referenced to an accounting program. They went on to Legal.

Elizabeth felt a surge of anticipation as she brought up the files in the legal directory. It was not a long list, perhaps a dozen files in all. Three lawyers' names were listed, and in each file were letters of inquiry about real estate, fees, and Wampanoag rights.

One of the letters in the legal file, dated three years earlier, was to Montgomery Mausz, the attorney for the tribe. Burkhardt had asked his fee for preparing a will. Letters to other attorneys also requested their fees for preparing a will. Elizabeth printed the letters.

"Shopping around for a lawyer, all right," Howland said. "But no will. Try Personal."

Elizabeth brought up the directory labeled Personal and scrolled through the files. Letters to his nieces, mail orders for clothing, hardware, computer supplies, and at the end of the files Wills. "We got it!" Elizabeth tapped ENTER and the file appeared.

Victoria leaned forward.

"The first entry is dated two years ago," said Elizabeth.

The morning sun streamed through the south window, reflected off the papers stacked on the windowsill. Elizabeth shaded the screen with her hand. Howland got up and pulled the shade partway down. Victoria moved her chair closer.

"A lot of legal stuff," said Elizabeth. "He leaves everything in equal shares to Harriet and Linda."

"Is there a more recent will?" asked Victoria.

Elizabeth continued to scroll down. "The next is dated a year ago, and he leaves everything to his niece Harriet. The one everyone calls Harley." She kept scrolling down. "Here's one dated three months later, and he leaves everything to his niece Linda."

"Nice guy," muttered Howland.

"Here's another. Looks like the last one, dated three weeks ago. He leaves all his property, house, barn, and land, to the Conservation Trust, with a hundred dollars to each of his nieces."

"Well!" said Howland.

"That's it," said Elizabeth.

"I'm glad this isn't my problem," said Howland.

Elizabeth, Victoria, and Howland looked at one another.

"Someone needs to find a signed, witnessed, notarized copy. It's likely his attorney has it on file," Howland said. "He probably lists his attorney in there somewhere."

"What if he didn't use an attorney," said Victoria. "Anyone could have written the wills on his computer."

Howland shrugged. "Anyone who had access to his computer and his password."

"Whoever caused the 'Fatal Error' message?"

"The computer will have the dates they were written. I'll print out copies of the wills for Casey and us."

While the files were printing out, three motorcycles roared into the driveway and parked under the maple tree. One carried two people. The bikers got off and started toward the house.

"Looks as though we have callers," said Victoria.

CHAPTER 29

"I'm fed up with all of you," Bugs growled at the three bikers who stood before him in the shade of the pines at the field's edge. The last Indian pipes had shriveled and turned black. "I'm sick of this whole nursery. Macho bikers? Horses' asses, that's what you all are."

The tents behind them were dappled with circular spots of sunlight filtered through the trees.

"What happened to Mack and them?" Harley asked.

"They're at the police station, doing one hell of a lot of explaining to Chief O'Neill, that's what."

Harley shifted her helmet from under her right arm to under her left. "You said you wanted to see me."

Bugs took off his horn-rimmed glasses, put them in their case, and snapped it shut. He squinted at Harley while he took a pair of mirrored sunglasses out of his pocket and hooked the earpieces around his ears. Harley could see her reflection, her purple hair with metallic orange glints.

"You find your sister and talk to her, you understand?" Bugs said. "There's stuff going on that you and she have to work out between you."

"I tried to meet her, Bugs, honest I did. I hitched into Oak Bluffs early this morning to meet with her. She never showed." Harley's voice had a whiny edge. "She left me a message that she'd be at the Flying Horses."

"How'd you get the message?" The bug-eyed mirrors turned on her. Wherever she looked, she saw her face, fat in the thick prescription lenses, with a halo of purple and orange.

"She left a note with somebody at Alley's. He said he'd deliver it here to me, and he did."

"All right. Go on."

"That's it, Bugs. Toby and I went by Victoria Trumbull's house yesterday, you know, where my sister's staying. Her car wasn't there."

Bugs stared down at her. "Put on your helmet and get on the back of my bike. We're finding your sister if it takes us all day. God-damned mother hen," he muttered. "Mack doesn't know where she is, and he's got his own problems right now. He'll spend eternity locked up in jail until someone straightens out that mess." He put on his helmet. "What kind of car does she drive?" He fastened the strap under his chin as he spoke, one finger against his throat.

Harley swung her leather-trousered leg over the back of the Indian and seated herself behind Bugs. "A blue Ford. Small. I don't know what kind it is."

Bugs grunted. "Where's she likely to be?"

"Who knows?"

"Did you know she had a thing going with Mack?" Bugs turned his head to look at her.

"No, I didn't. Honest." Harley sounded bitter. "Uncle Jube cuts me off for hanging around with a biker, and that sneak . . ."

"Would she go shopping? Bird-watching? The beach?"

"Shopping. Definitely."

"We'll try Vineyard Haven first. Then Oak Bluffs. Then Edgar-town. Got your helmet fastened?" He kicked the motor into life and turned his head to check. The pipes spit out a puff of blue smoke.

Harley put her feet up on the footrests behind Bugs and held onto the backrest in front of her.

The engine was quiet enough so that she could have heard Bugs above the noise, but neither of them said a word. The gang on Alley's porch swiveled their heads in unison. Bugs snorted. A laugh, Harley guessed. They went past the Parsonage Pond and the cemetery, across the narrow bridge. Through Middletown. Down the hill past Tisbury Meadows, the Land Bank property. Into Vineyard Haven.

Bugs turned onto Main Street and cruised slowly past cars angled in to the curb. They looked up the streets that fed into Main Street— Center Street and Church Street. No small blue Ford. Bugs turned right onto Union Street toward the steamship wharf, and they wove through a crowd of people in the parking lot. He turned again onto Water Street and cruised through the Stop & Shop lot. No blue Ford.

He turned onto Beach Road, and they skirted the Vineyard Haven harbor. Harley could see two ferries passing, the *Islander* arriving from Woods Hole, trailing a curving white wake, and the *Governor* taking off for the mainland. They crossed Lagoon Pond bridge over the steel grating that hummed under their wheels.

They passed the hospital and drove down New York Avenue into Oak Bluffs. The road had been named New York Avenue a hundred and fifty years ago, when ships from New York docked at the foot of the street. The docks were long gone. They passed the Oak Bluffs harbor, humming with boats—cabin cruisers, outboard motorboats, Scarabs, sailboats under power. The water shimmered in the noon light. They drove past the Camp Meeting Grounds. Pastel-colored gingerbread houses circled the wrought-iron Tabernacle where revival meetings were once held. Now it was rock concerts. They drove slowly up Circuit Avenue and around the streets behind it where there were more shops. No small blue Ford. They turned right before they got to the Flying Horses, and Bugs gunned the motor. Harley felt the puff of hot exhaust from the pipes beneath her legs. They raced along the road that led to Edgartown, following the sweep of Nantucket Sound.

A flight of Canada geese flew in a tidy V low over Sengekontackett Pond to their right. Harley could hear them honk over the sound of the Indian's motor. To their left, a long line of cars had parked along the bathing beach. Beyond the cars, banks of rugosa roses blanketed the low dunes. Narrow sand paths led through the thorny roses to the beach. Red and white flowers dotted the low green bushes, mingled with bright orange rose hips, fruit of early summer blossoming. Beyond the roses sunbathers lay on bright towels. In the water, close to shore, swimmers' heads were shiny black dots, like muskrats or otters. No small blue Fords were parked along the long stretch of beach.

Bugs leaned into the turn that led into the village, and slowed for the tourists who wandered from one side of Edgartown's Main Street to the other. He drove to the harbor, and when he'd checked for the blue Ford and found none, he swung back to North Water Street, slowly so they could look at every car. Nothing, nothing. Bugs went up one street and down another, past trim white houses with black shutters and rose vines climbing over white-painted picket fences. No blue Ford.

"What about lunch, Bugs?"

"This is not good. We've got to find her."

"She'll show up. She always does."

"No lunch," Bugs rasped. He skimmed through town and turned onto the West Tisbury Road, the same road that, in West Tisbury, was called the Edgartown Road.

He gunned the motor and they dodged between cars heading up-Island.

"Where to?" Harley shouted into the wind.

"Your uncle's." The wind blew his words back to her.

"You know the way?"

Bugs grunted.

They sped past Victoria's house and turned onto New Lane. Bugs's silence began to worry Harley, and she tightened her grip on the handhold behind his seat. On the rutted road they kept to the left-hand side. Grasses swished against her right leg, branches and shrubs whipped against her left. A branch deflected by Bugs's jacket stung her cheek, and she felt a trickle of blood.

They came out of the woods into Burkhardt's open area. The burned ruin faced them. A breeze stirred up a cat's-paw on the pond, and wafted toward them the stink of half-burned plastic and wood. Harley felt a brief wave of nostalgia for her lost attic room. She could still feel that morning breeze that sifted through the screen, moving the curtains, the offshore breeze that blew every morning from land to sea until the land warmed in the sun and the wind shifted.

Bugs stopped the motorcycle, turned off the engine, kicked down the stand, and leaned the bike on it. Harley swung her leg over the back and stretched out the kinks in her arms and legs.

The barn door was ajar. It swung with a low moan as a slight breeze passed over them.

"There it is," Harley said, pointing. "On the other side of the barn."

She could see only its light blue trunk from where she stood. She called out. "Linda? Hey, Linda!"

Bugs strode over to the car, and Harley followed close behind him. He stopped abruptly, but she could see around him. The driver's side door was open, and the dome light was on, a feeble pale blotch.

"Whoa!" Bugs held an arm out to stop her, but she went around him.

Linda was slumped in the driver's seat, her seat belt still fastened. Her head hung limply on her chest, and below her neck was a bib-shaped blotch of dark brown. Her left arm dangled almost to the ground.

"She's not dead?" Harley whispered.

Bugs lifted Linda's hand and felt her wrist. "Long gone. Shit," he said. He unzipped his leather jacket and removed his cell phone and dialed 911. "Hope this damned thing works from here," he said.

CHAPTER 30

Harley sat down suddenly in the grass in front of the barn and leaned against the weathered shingles. "Now what?" She took off her helmet and shook out her spiky hair. She wiped her hand across her forehead, where it was beaded with cold sweat.

"We wait, that's what," said Bugs.

Victoria was looking up a word in the library's big dictionary when she heard the police siren. She hurried into the dining room and saw the police Bronco racing down New Lane, lights flashing.

"Why didn't she stop here?" Victoria murmured. Then, "Let's go, Elizabeth." By the time her granddaughter realized what was happening, Victoria had pulled on her sweater, picked up her cloth bag, and hobbled out the door on her way to the car.

They arrived at Burkhardt's and pulled up next to Casey, who was standing by the Bronco talking on her radio.

"Why didn't you pick me up?" Victoria asked, hurt.

"This was an emergency."

"My house was on your way."

"Sorry, Victoria." But Casey didn't sound sorry.

The door of the blue Ford was still open, and Linda's dead hand dangled, limp and gray. The dome light was out.

Bugs sat astride his Indian in the shade of a pine tree, his sunglasses in place, cleaning his fingernails with a penknife. Harley was sitting on a stump, her hands between her knees, her eyes blank.

Elizabeth took a quick look at the slumped body in the blue car and hustled down to the edge of the pond, where she sat on a driftwood log and lowered her head.

"The state police are on the way," Casey said to Bugs. "I need to ask you a few questions, probably the same ones the state guys will ask."

Bugs nodded.

Victoria limped over to the barn, careful not to step on any marks the killer might have left. She peered through the open door without touching anything. In the dust on the barn floor she could make out footprints, partially swept away. A freshly broken pine branch with bunches of long needles lay next to the door.

Casey finished talking to Bugs and joined Victoria.

"Someone was here," said Victoria. "Waiting for her, unless she took him by surprise."

Casey knelt to examine the blurry prints. "Maybe the state lab can make something of them. Not much there."

They turned away from the barn.

"What, exactly, killed her?" Victoria asked.

"Her throat was cut."

Victoria put her hand on her own throat. "With what, a knife? Razor?"

"Doesn't look like a knife or razor cut," said Casey. "More like a wire garrote. Doc Jeffers is on his way here."

Victoria leaned against the Bronco.

"Do you want to sit down?" Casey asked. "Your feet must still be tender."

"I'm all right, thank you. I'd rather stand."

Casey, too, leaned against the police vehicle. "Now I've called the state cops, everyone on this Island knows we have big-time trouble here. There's no possibility of keeping anything quiet."

"Why would you want to?" said Victoria.

Casey shrugged instead of replying.

Victoria nodded toward the blue Ford. "Linda's seat belt is still fastened. Which means she was killed immediately after she opened her car door and before she unbuckled her seat belt. The killer must have been quick."

"Yeah," said Casey, studying the Ford.

"From the way the car is parked, it would be impossible for someone to steal up behind her without her seeing him. The killer was somebody she knew and trusted."

Casey said nothing.

"Linda had some reason for coming here. I wonder what it was?

199

I'm sure she set the fire, but I don't think she intended to harm any-one. She was horrified when she learned there was a person inside."

"We'll never know, now," Casey said.

"From what she told me about her uncle, I gathered there were some goings-on when she was a girl."

"He molested her?"

Victoria nodded.

"Kids bury those memories. Deep." Casey kicked at the dry grass and a puff of dust rose. "Bunch of scum." She shook her head. "While we're waiting, we can check out the back roads you told me about, if your feet can take it. See if the killer might have parked along one of them."

Three roads led from Burkhardt's. The most commonly used one followed Tiah's Cove, another skirted the shore of Long Cove, and a third ran down the middle of the point. Victoria knew them all. Two of the roads were overgrown now with brush and grasses.

"You okay with walking?"

"Fine." At that, Victoria stepped on a rough spot in the grass. "Ouch!"

Casey looked at her with concern.

"Here's Elizabeth now." Victoria called out to her granddaughter. "You can leave now if you want, Elizabeth. Casey will see that I get home."

"I'll put your things in the Bronco," said Elizabeth.

Victoria and Casey walked slowly down the middle track, Victoria leaning on her walking stick. "We're looking for car tracks and footprints?"

"Right."

"This road doesn't seem a likely place," Victoria said. "A car would have crushed these sticks. And the branches along the sides would be bent or broken."

"The killer may have parked farther along and walked the rest of the way."

Fall was not far away. Late summer acorns had dropped into their path. Tall grass growing between the overgrown ruts had turned rus-set and pale gold, and huckleberry leaves were already dark bur-gundy. The air was pungent with oak and pine and sea salt. A hawk circled high overhead with its mournful cry, "Scree!"

They retraced their steps to the barn, then followed the old road that skirted the cove. From here, they could see across the pond to the opening in the bar.

Three or four times a year, storm winds and tides swept sand across the opening, closing it. Then the pond level would rise, fed by streams and groundwater, covering the edges of the pond. When the level was high enough, townspeople would cut a new opening, in the old days with a team of oxen, now with a bulldozer.

Where the pond level had risen earlier this summer, it had left a rim of seaweed, driftwood, and small shells. Fat brown seedpods of wild iris rattled as they brushed by.

"Here's a print!" Victoria sang out.

"Mark it with sticks or something."

They found another print, and another. Partway along the track, where it passed under oak trees, they found traces of a vehicle.

"One question answered." Casey wrote in her notebook, slipped it back in her pocket, and started back.

"Wait," said Victoria. "Farther on, the road follows the top of a bluff that overlooks a lily pond. It would be easy to dispose of a car by pushing it off the bluff."

"Hiram's van?"

Victoria nodded.

The bluff rose about fifteen feet above a closed-in arm of the cove. The pond was covered with pale pink water lilies. Victoria inhaled. The scent reminded her of clean babies, of the powder she had smoothed onto her daughters' legs and arms, chafed by scratchy wet wool bathing suits.

Casey examined the grasses and shrubbery that grew close to the edge of the bluff, then called to Victoria, who limped over.

"Look." Casey pointed to the surface of the pond. Almost hidden by lily pads was a partially submerged vehicle, only its back window showing.

CHAPTER 31

Victoria awoke to a gray day with low clouds hanging over the west pasture. After breakfast, she and Elizabeth headed into the village to get gas at the filling station.

"Drop me off at Alley's," Victoria said. "I'll pick up the mail while you get gas."

As Elizabeth pulled over to the curb, a few drops of rain splashed on the windshield. Lincoln Sibert had parked his pickup behind them, and they went up the steps together.

"Looks as if we're in for a nor'easter," Victoria said.

Lincoln nodded. "Red sky this morning. Going to the casino meeting this afternoon, Miz Trumbull?"

"I expect so. And you?"

"Everybody on the Island is going. They're serving free booze. Draw a crowd every time."

"Then I'll see you there," said Victoria. She walked to the back of the store, past groceries and racks of postcards, to the bank of mailboxes on the back wall.

She was sorting through letters and catalogs when someone behind her said, "Hello, Mrs. Trumbull."

Victoria looked up and smiled. "Why, hello, Patience. We don't often see you in West Tisbury."

"I'm posting last-minute meeting announcements," Patience said. "I hope the rain doesn't keep people away."

"I wouldn't think so. This is an important issue." Victoria tossed a catalog into the cardboard box below the mail slot. "I wish they wouldn't waste so much paper."

"Entire forests of trees," Patience agreed. "We'll see you this afternoon, won't we?"

"I hope so."

"Can I give you a ride?"

"No, thank you. Chief O'Neill is taking me."

"We'll see you later, then." Patience paid for a newspaper and a box of chocolate chip cookies and left through the back door. She held the newspaper over her head, opened the door of her red pickup, lifted her voluminous skirt, and climbed in. She slammed the door and drove off.

Victoria watched the truck until it was out of sight around the side of the store, and tried to recall what the red truck reminded her of.

After lunch, Victoria put on her raincoat and her tan hat, pulled her rubber boots on over her wool socks, and walked slowly down the road to the police station. She sat in her usual chair, misted with rain and out of breath.

Casey looked up from her computer. "I was going to pick you up, Victoria. You need to favor your feet."

"I like walking in the rain. Besides, I don't want my feet to atrophy." Victoria opened her raincoat and fanned herself with it. "What time is the meeting?"

Casey looked at her watch. "We have plenty of time. It's not until two o'clock."

"Who's giving the presentation?"

"The tribe is sponsoring it, but the presentation itself is by Casinos Unlimited. They've invited the three up-Island police chiefs. We'd be the ones involved if some old lady has a heart attack over hitting the jackpot."

"I wouldn't mind trying my hand at the slot machines."

Casey looked up quickly from her work with a grin.

"Elizabeth doesn't seem to think most members of the tribe support a casino," said Victoria.

"Doesn't much matter what they think. Patience gets what Patience wants. I got to give her credit. She's done a lot of good stuff for the tribe." Casey turned back to her computer. "I'll close this file, and then we can go."

Victoria glanced around the office while she waited. The page of this month's calendar featured a basket of kittens tangled in colored yarn. She examined Casey's cluttered desk and the obsessively neat desk Junior Norton shared with the two patrolmen.

She looked out at the millpond. Rain pockmarked the surface. The swans and their three half-grown cygnets sailed with no apparent effort on the dimpled surface. Snapping turtles had dragged four of the swans' seven cygnets under, and killed and eaten them, one at a time. The animal control officer told Victoria she had seen one cygnet disappear underwater, and had waded into the pond in her good leather boots and jeans to try to save the baby. But the turtle had gotten away, leaving a trail of bubbles that led to the middle of the pond.

Victoria was musing on the violence within the quiet pond, and suddenly had a thought. "I know how we can trap the killer," she said out loud.

Casey looked up and waited for Victoria to say more. She turned off her computer and stood up. "Well?" She looked at Victoria again, reached for her heavy belt that was slung on the back of her chair, and fastened it around her waist.

Victoria hadn't followed up on her trap comment.

Casey took her yellow rain jacket from the closet, and they both went out the door. Victoria turned in time to see the chief make a face at the door as she pulled it shut.

"Are you going to tell me who you think the killer is, or do I have to guess?"

"I don't know who the killer is," Victoria said.

They climbed into the police vehicle, and Casey backed out of the parking area.

"What's this trap you're planning to set, then?"

"It's going to sound foolish to you, unless I can explain my thinking."

Casey glanced at Victoria, whose face was half-turned toward the open window. She was smiling.

"Victoria," said Casey, "I wish I were as young as you look at this moment. Smartest thing I ever did was to appoint you my deputy."

Victoria turned, still smiling.

"But," said Casey, and Victoria's smile faded, "we're supposed to be a team. You've got to stop doing stuff on your own. What is this trap you're planning to set?"

Victoria cleared her throat.

Casey kept her eyes on the road ahead of them. "I'm sorry I didn't pick you up last night when Bugs found Linda's body. I wasn't being a team player, was I?"

Victoria pulled down the sun visor and looked at her reflection in the small mirror. She was wearing her baseball cap with gold stitching. She pushed the visor back against the overhead, took a small notebook out of her cloth bag, and started to make a list.

Casey glanced away from the road briefly.

"Suspects," Victoria explained. "I have a list of eight. Seven." She crossed out Burkhardt's niece Linda. "All of them except Tad Nordstrom are likely to be at the casino meeting this afternoon."

Victoria was perspiring from her walk to the police station. She was glad for the occasional spray of rain blowing in on her through the open window.

"Who are the seven?"

"Hiram's friend, Tad Nordstrom. He had the strongest motive of all. Jube was blackmailing him. He may have felt Hiram had deceived him about his and Jube's affair."

"And Linda's death?"

"Linda's death puzzles me."

"I'll check with the Steamship Authority to see if Nordstrom was on the boat he claimed to be on," said Casey.

Victoria scribbled something. "Next strongest suspect is Harley. She had a good reason for killing both her uncle and her sister."

"Eighteen million is a pretty good motive."

"Hiram got in the way, so she had to kill him." Victoria wrote something. "Then there's Toby, her boyfriend. Harley could have promised him a share of the money, if he killed her uncle and sister. Linda was on my list, but obviously, we have to eliminate her."

"Someone did," said Casey.

"Linda's boyfriend, Mack is a likely suspect."

"Whatever possessed him to come up with that crazy kidnap scheme? Stupid, really stupid. What did it get him? A long time in prison, that's what."

"He wanted to find out, for Linda's sake, who her Uncle Jube named as heir. He thought I would tell him where to find the computer."

"Anyone can type a will," Casey said. "Even if we find a will on his computer, it won't hold up in court."

"No, of course not. They needed to know what was *in* the will," said Victoria. "And the name of Jube's lawyer."

"I can picture not-so-bright Mack killing Jube and Hiram without considering what he's doing, but not his girlfriend Linda."

"She could be quite aggravating," said Victoria. "When the arson team found Hiram's body, she may have blamed him. Told him she was through with him. After he'd killed two people for her, he'd have been angry enough to kill again."

"That makes four suspects, if we include Tad."

"Both Patience and Peter had good reasons for wanting to get rid of Jube. He was playing one against the other, holding up permits, and threatening to sabotage both Peter's and Patience's casino plans. A casino would mean a lot more money than eighteen million dollars."

"That makes six," said Casey. "The seventh?"

"I don't have a name for the seventh. A man with a shipping company is involved with Peter. I have a feeling he'll be at the meeting this afternoon."

"You left off two prime suspects."

"Dojan? He's not the killer," said Victoria, stoutly.

"You sure you're not influenced by the fact that you like bad boys?"

"Of course not. Dojan is not a killer."

"Ha!" said Casey.

Victoria wrote Dojan's name on her list, and immediately crossed it off. "Dojan is not the killer."

The winding road led up into the Chilmark hills, where stone walls hemmed in irregular fields. Rain had dampened the gray-green lichens that covered the stones, and enhanced the colors of the grasses.

"And what about Bugs? A motorcyclist whose name is on Burkhardt's short list."

"Bugs is a professor. He wouldn't kill anyone."

"Professors kill people all the time," said Casey.

They went around a bend and suddenly there was the sweep of

the gray Atlantic beyond the sheep pasture, a view that always put matters into perspective for Victoria.

"Okay, what about your trap?"

Victoria was holding her hand out the window to catch the flying raindrops. "I've just realized something," she said. "There may have been two killers, and Linda might well have been one of them."

CHAPTER 32

They passed stone walls covered with wild grapevines, gray shingled houses, stark against the dull sky.

"Jube was taking money from the pro-casino, the anti-casino, and the floating casino people," said Victoria. "A lot of money was involved. He seemed to be taking cash, and he must have squirreled it away somewhere."

"If it was in his house, it's gone now," Casey said.

"He mentions a safe deposit box in some of his letters. But no one knows where he kept the key."

Casey slowed as they came to a dirt road branching off to the right. Oak trees overhung the road, which was dry underneath the leafy branches.

"Look familiar, Victoria? There's your escape route from the kidnappers."

"They weren't bad people," Victoria said. "They apologized."

"It's out of your hands. The state does not approve of kidnapping. Nor do the feds."

"They didn't know any better."

"You can say that at their trial, if you want. The state will expect you to testify."

Victoria was silent as they went down the hill to the bridge that separated Stonewall Pond from Quitsa Pond. Casey slowed at the overlook where the hazy expanse of pond, village, and Sound was grayed by the drizzle.

"We're almost there. Are you going to tell me about the trap before we get there?"

Victoria didn't answer directly. "If I say something strange at the meeting, don't think I've lost my mind."

Casey said, "I'd never think that, Victoria." She grinned suddenly and looked at her deputy.

The parking area at Tribal Headquarters was full. Casey let Victoria off by the front door, and Victoria went in with a group of people, many of whom she didn't know.

"Getting nasty out there," someone said.

"Victoria Trumbull!" Chief Hawkbill, wearing a beaded headband, greeted her. He escorted her down the broad stairs into the community room, which was set up with rows of folding chairs. "I have saved a seat for you in the front with other dignitaries."

A heavyset bearded man rose from his seat as they approached.

The chief said, "I don't believe you've met Dr. Jandrowicz, have you?"

Victoria started to say she hadn't when she looked up at the tall man and recognized Bugs. She smiled. "Yes. I met Dr. Jandrowicz first at the cliffs, then he brought my kidnappers to my house with armloads of flowers, and then, apparently, carted them off to the police station."

Bugs bowed. "Flowers and apologies are hardly enough."

The chief murmured something about greeting other guests, and backed away.

"Won't you have a seat?" Bugs indicated the chair next to his and they both sat.

"Are you interested in casinos, Dr. Jandrowicz?" Even sitting down, Victoria had to look up at Bugs. He was a very large man, she realized. And beamy, like a catboat.

"Indirectly," Bugs said, once they'd adjusted their folding chairs and Victoria had stowed her scuffed leather pocketbook beneath hers. "I'm making a survey of Island butterflies. What we learn may affect any casino site."

"You teach, don't you?" Victoria said. "At Smith College?"

Bugs nodded.

Behind them Victoria heard the sounds of a gathering audience. Chairs scraped, neighbors greeted one another. People speculated about the presentation.

"Have you found any interesting or rare butterflies?"

"Not as yet. The habitat is right for two or three endangered species. It would be a triumph for my students to find one of those species here."

"Would that affect casino plans?"

"Under the state endangered species law, construction would be held up while a survey is made," said Bugs. "However, if an endangered species were to be found on tribal lands, who knows?" He shrugged. "The Wampanoags are considered a sovereign nation, and as such, they do not necessarily need to adhere to federal or state laws. The tribe's rights to bypass state and federal law are being tested in the courts."

"I understand Mr. Burkhardt found some rare specimens on one of the proposed properties."

Bugs grinned. "There are no secrets on this Island, are there? Mr. Burkhardt planted some preserved specimens on the property, then asked me to identify them." He laughed. "The specimens were long dead, preserved, faded with time, and had pin marks in them. Obviously from somebody's collection. Mr. Burkhardt offered me a large sum of money to verify his discovery."

"Were they a rare species that you hoped to find?"

"Yes. Mr. Burkhardt had done enough research to know the site was the right habitat for his dead specimens, and he knew that finding them would have been a major scientific discovery."

Chief Hawkbill bustled up to the front row and sat on Victoria's right. "We're about to begin," he said.

Victoria looked around. The hall was filled with people. People were standing along the side walls. Tribal members were setting up more folding chairs in the back.

The lights blinked off and on again, and Patience made a dramatic entrance through black curtains behind the stage, stepped up to the podium, and lifted her hands. She was wearing a black dress that hung loosely from her shoulders to her feet, concealing her considerable weight. A double string of wampum beads hung around her neck. She, too, was wearing a beaded headband, hers was purple glass, the same color as her wampum necklace.

"She looks quite regal," Victoria whispered to Bugs.

The audience hushed. Patience made a few remarks, then introduced the speaker from Casinos Unlimited.

The speaker showed a big-screen movie that was full of economic statistics and toothy, smiling people, and had a musical background, inoffensive rock underlaid with drums.

After that, there were questions, some decidedly hostile, which Patience and the Casinos Unlimited spokesman answered politely. Finally, Patience, looking around for more questions and finding none, said, "We can continue our discussion over drinks upstairs in the conference room." She made some small joke about Indians and firewater, there were a few polite snickers, and the meeting broke up.

"Professionally done," said Bugs with respect. "May I buy you a drink, Mrs. Trumbull?"

It took several minutes to wade through the crowd. Neighbors greeted Victoria as if they hadn't seen her for some time. Victoria looked around anxiously for Casey, and wiggled her fingers when she saw her. Casey nodded, her eyebrows raised quizzically.

"Is there someone you'd like me to find for you?" Bugs asked courteously.

"They're probably upstairs, congregated around the bar," Victoria said, so they climbed the stairs.

She saw Peter Little first, looking more saturnine than usual. His sullen expression changed slightly when Victoria waved at him. He started toward her through the crowd. As he did, Victoria saw the young woman with spiky purple hair she'd seen at the cliffs. The girl was accompanied by the tall man with long dreadlocks and blue-black skin Victoria had seen with her.

"Is that Harley?" Victoria asked Bugs, who was staying next to her. "Jube Burkhardt's niece?"

"Harley and Toby," Bugs growled, and turned away from her so she couldn't see his expression.

"With her sister dead, I wouldn't think she would want . . ." Victoria didn't finish.

"The two weren't close." Bugs abruptly changed the subject. "Would you like me to get you a glass of wine? Or something stronger?"

"White wine, please."

Harley and Toby worked their way toward Victoria. Peter, a martini glass in hand, was approaching at the same time. Victoria looked through the crowd, noisy with cocktail chatter, and saw Patience. Patience held up a wineglass and pointed to it with a questioning look, apparently asking Victoria if she'd like a glass. Victoria shook her head. She could see Casey, eyeing her from the side of the conference room. The conference table had been moved to the end of the room and had been set up as a bar. The great tree trunks that held up the arched roof seemed like living trees in a forest.

Casey was talking with the Aquinnah police chief and sipping from a tall glass, which, Victoria knew, held only tonic water.

"Excellent presentation, Patience. Here's to you." It was Chief Hawkbill, who'd joined the circle. He held up a champagne glass as he spoke. "I can only toast you with ginger ale, but the sentiment is the same."

"Hear, hear," Peter said with a trace of irony, and held up his martini glass. "Good God, here comes the apparition."

Victoria looked in the direction Peter indicated and saw Dojan working his way through the crowd to the knot gathered around Victoria. When he reached her, he nodded, and moved behind her. The others around Victoria chattered about the worsening weather, the fine quality of the hors d'oeuvres, the presentation, the size of the crowd. No one mentioned what everybody else on the Island was talking about—the murders.

Chief Hawkbill brought up the subject first.

"Victoria Trumbull, you know more than anyone else on the Island about the murders. Are we any closer to knowing who the killer is?"

Victoria turned to the chief, her hooded eyes bright. "Yes, indeed. We've had a major breakthrough."

"Oh?" Peter stopped, his glass halfway to his lips.

"You mean, my sister's killer?" Harley had worked her way into the circle that surrounded Victoria. Toby stood behind her.

Casey moved next to one of the tree trunks, out of sight but within hearing distance of Victoria.

"I found something in the barn that I am sure will wrap everything up," Victoria said. "It's only a matter of hours now before we make an arrest. Thank you," she said to Bugs, who had handed her a glass. She sipped her wine and gazed around the circle of people who closed in on her.

Behind Peter, Victoria saw the Aquinnah police chief signaling to Casey. The post blocked her view of Casey, but the Aquinnah chief smiled and moved away.

"Tell us more, Victoria Trumbull," Chief Hawkbill said. "We are all ears."

Victoria felt Dojan shift behind her. Peter sipped his martini. Patience opened her eyes wide. Bugs thrust his hands into his pockets. Toby put his arm around Harley's shoulders. Harley leaned against him.

"I've probably said too much already."

"What sort of evidence did you find?" Peter said.

"Footprints? Tire tracks?" Harley breathed.

Toby tightened his grip on her shoulders.

"Mrs. Trumbull is wise not to tell us too much," said Patience.

Chief Hawkbill's glasses had slipped down his nose, and he lifted his head to look through them at the cluster of people around Victoria.

The noise level in the conference room had grown to a dull roar, interspersed with occasional laughter. The room was warm, and the warmth was releasing a jarring mixture of perfumes.

"Well," Victoria said, dabbing at her moist forehead with a paper napkin. "I don't want to say too much more until I have a chance to talk with the police."

"Haven't you told Chief O'Neill?" Peter scowled.

"Not yet. I intend to talk to her first thing tomorrow. I suspect it might help solve all three murders."

"Wise," said Chief Hawkbill. "Very wise."

"Was it a thing?" Harley said. "You know, like a cigarette lighter or a handkerchief with initials on it?"

"I'd better not say," Victoria said. "I'm sure it will be in the paper, maybe as early as next week's edition."

Victoria caught a glimpse of Casey's uniform shirt behind the pole. Both the Aquinnah police chief and the Chilmark police chief were standing near her. Finally, Casey came out from behind the tree trunk, and Victoria noticed that her cheeks had flushed a becoming pink. Her coppery hair reflected glints of the overhead lights.

Victoria held up a finger, as if she were summoning a taxi. "I think I see my ride." She handed her half-finished glass of wine to Peter, who took it dumbly, and smiled at the group around her. Harley moved aside to let her through, and Victoria swept out of the conference room, trailed by Casey and the hum of conversation.

When they were outside, Victoria said, "How did I do?"

"You ought to go onstage," Casey replied. "But when this is over, I'm asking the selectmen to send you to the police academy. You can't do the stuff you're doing."

"I don't know why not," Victoria said. "You do think I was convincing, don't you?"

"Wait here while I get the Bronco," said Casey.

Victoria stood under the shelter, greeting people as they left, while Casey darted into the rain, and drove up a few minutes later, tires swishing on the asphalt.

"Now you've set the trap, how do you intend to spring it?" Casey asked as they pulled away from the building.

"I'll pack a picnic supper and some blankets, and we'll go to Jube's place and wait."

"The police vehicle is pretty obvious."

"We'll hide it."

"I like that 'we,'" Casey said.

"Most people don't know the middle road to Jube's place exists. No one will see a car parked along there. The killer most likely will use the back road, the one overlooking the lily pond."

"I'll call Junior Norton, have him row across. He can hide his boat along the shore, and be available if we need him. What about Dojan?"

"Let's go back and get him."

"No, I'll call the Aquinnah police chief. He can contact Dojan."

214

CHAPTER 33

Casey turned into Victoria's drive, slowed for the puddles, and pulled up in front of the stone steps.

"After that performance of yours, Victoria, you won't be safe. I don't think your trap is a great idea."

"We'll catch the killer tonight, I'm sure."

On the way home from the meeting at Aquinnah, Victoria had explained her idea to Casey. While Victoria waited in the barn loft, Casey, Dojan, and Junior would hide where they could see the barn doors and hear Victoria if she called.

"I'm guessing we have at least an hour before we need to be there," said Victoria.

Casey looked at her watch. "I've got to finish up some stuff in the station house, so the sooner I get started, the sooner I'll be back."

"I'll put together a picnic, and will be ready to go when you finish."

"Dojan is on the way. Where's Elizabeth?"

"At work. She'll be home around six."

Casey checked her watch again. "An hour and a half. I'll be back way before then. Take care, now, Victoria."

Rainwater dripped off the roof into the gutters and gurgled down the drainpipe. A slight gust of wind blew the maple tree, and a shower of water pattered onto the ground.

Victoria waved airily as Casey pulled away, but in truth she felt a bit nervous. A cold-blooded murderer now believed she held the key to his identity. If she thought about it too much, she felt butterflies in her stomach. That made her think of Bugs. Was it just possible that he had been so outraged by Jube's butterfly deception that he killed Jube and Hiram? Linda, too? And had reported Linda's death so he seemed innocent? She could picture Bugs as killer, after all.

Victoria checked each of the four doors that led outside. None of them could be locked. She didn't have keys. Rain fell steadily. She moved back to the kitchen and placed eggs into the egg cooker to hard-boil. Soon she forgot about the killer. She brought two pillows and two down comforters from the upstairs bedroom, and set them by the kitchen door, in case she and Casey had to spend the night. She buttered bread for egg sandwiches, made a pot of coffee, and was reaching into the refrigerator for ginger marmalade when she heard a loud *snap* that startled her. She slammed the refrigerator door and heard something fall inside. Then she realized the snap was the egg cooker turning itself off. She laughed and patted her chest, where her heart seemed to be pounding loud enough to hear.

She looked in the refrigerator to see what had fallen and found that it was the bowl of fish chowder left over from several nights ago. She had been meaning to throw it into the compost bucket, but although the chowder was not quite fresh enough to eat, it hadn't spoiled yet. Now the lower shelves of the refrigerator were coated with fishy-smelling goo.

She cleaned it up and went back to making sandwiches. Ginger marmalade and cream cheese would serve for dessert. Apples and a handful of hard candies.

Out of the corner of her eye, she saw something move to the east of the house, behind the fishpond. She stopped what she was doing to see what it was. While she watched, she saw the tall irises in back of the pond part, and the neighbor's black dog trotted out. He put both front legs into the pond and lapped up water. Then he looked up, pink tongue hanging out, a dog-smile on his face, and shook himself. Water drops flew around in a swirl. Victoria put both hands on the kitchen counter to steady her nerves, and laughed to herself.

She finished packing sandwiches, napkins, apples in the picnic basket, closed the lid, slid the bits of bamboo into the loops that held it closed, and set the basket inside the west door where it wouldn't get wet.

As she straightened up, she thought she saw a figure flit from behind the Norway maple tree into the shadows. It was only chance that she'd seen it at all.

She said, in her mind, that if a stranger should dare come into her house, she could easily evade him. A stranger wouldn't know the nooks and crannies of the house, the secret hiding places, the multitude of doors.

She decided to go upstairs to the second-floor attic, the room above the kitchen, where she could look out the window without being seen. She crept quietly up the steep back staircase. Perhaps her imagination was getting the better of her. Perhaps nobody was there behind the maple tree. Perhaps she was being overly dramatic.

She looked at her watch. Casey should be here in another five minutes. If someone was out there, Victoria thought, she could elude them for that five minutes, at least, until Casey showed up. If someone should come into the house and come upstairs, she could go down either the front stairs or the back stairs, make her way out of the house through the front door, and flag down a passing car. She found herself breathing heavily and perspiring.

The phone in the upstairs study rang.

At first, she couldn't decide whether to answer it or not. Surely it would be something innocent, like the League of Women Voters telling her about a meeting. Or the Garden Club asking her to bake cookies. After three rings, she snatched up the receiver.

"Victoria? This is Casey. I've been delayed another ten minutes. Are you okay?"

"Of course." Victoria's voice sounded thick to her.

She hung up the phone and went back to the window. Might someone have crept across the yard while she was on the phone? Had she imagined that figure by the maple tree? She checked her watch. Now it would be twelve minutes.

She'd be foolish to escape by going up to the big attic on the third floor, she thought. It had only one stairway and she would be trapped. The closet in the west room had a back that led into another, smaller, bedroom. When she was a child, she pretended it was a secret passage. She could hide in the closet and escape through one door or the other.

She told herself she was being ridiculous. She looked at her watch. Only three minutes had passed since Casey had called. Nine more minutes. If only Dojan and Casey hadn't made her feel so vulnerable. She saw a movement near the maple again. Was it a shadow from wind-blown branches? Or the black dog marking territory on its way home? Certainly it couldn't be a person. No one would hide like that.

Or could it be? She thought again of the trap she'd set. One of the people in that circle around her this afternoon, she was sure, had killed three people. If that person thought she, Victoria Trumbull, had found evidence, what would stop that killer from coming after her? Someone must be feeling panicky now and might take risks in order to stop Victoria Trumbull from telling what she knew. She had assumed the killer would go directly to Burkhardt's place to get rid of the evidence she had said was in the barn, but now that she thought about it, it made sense for the killer to come after her first. Why had she so lightly dismissed Casey? Pride, she told herself. I really should start acting my age. Six minutes until Casey got here. Perhaps she would be early.

Victoria saw the movement again, too large for a dog, too solid for a shadow. If she stayed here at the window, she would have enough warning if the person—if that's what it was—crossed the yard. And if Casey showed up in the police Bronco, the person would never dare appear.

But if it was the killer, wouldn't Casey's Bronco be a warning that Jube's place was being watched?

Victoria shook her head to clear it, and stood by the side of the window, out of sight, where she could watch for movement near the Norway maple.

The Bronco pulled into the drive. Victoria dabbed the perspiration off her forehead and eased her way down the back stairs. The steps were steep and slippery and there was no railing, so she braced herself with a hand on either side of the narrow walled-in stairwell.

Casey was already in the kitchen. "Sorry for the delay, Victoria. Was everything okay?"

Victoria told her about her small frights, and laughed.

Casey looked somber. "I should have thought about that myself, that you might be in danger. I'll check behind the maple tree and see if there's a trace of anyone."

Victoria was gathering up her cloth bag and the picnic basket when she heard Casey shout. Then she heard Casey's voice, louder and louder, higher and higher. It sounded as if she were angry. Victoria went to the entry and looked out. Dojan, head hanging down, was following Casey, whose face was thunderous.

"You're supposed to guard her, not scare her to death," Casey was saying. "What were you thinking of?"

Before Casey could say more, Victoria put down her basket and her cloth bag and held out her hands to Dojan.

"Thank you," she said. "I'm glad it was you, Dojan. I was afraid that if the killer had seen the police vehicle, we would never have been able to spring our trap."

Casey, standing with her fists on her hips, turned on Dojan. "I want you down at Burkhardt's, right now. Watch for anyone walking or driving, probably down the road next to the lily pond. Don't let anyone see you, you understand? We don't want the killer alerted too soon. Don't leap out and capture someone who is innocently walking along the road. You understand me, Dojan?"

He looked at his bare feet and traced circles in the sand of the driveway with his toes. He nodded, his feather bobbing in his hair, turned, and disappeared down the path that cut across Victoria's property to the Tiah's Cove Road. The viburnum and raspberry canes that almost blocked the way closed in behind him.

"Goddamn!" said Casey, kicking a stone out of the driveway onto the grass. "What goes on in his mind?"

"He was guarding me."

"Guarding? He's like a kid playing cops and robbers."

"Cowboys and Indians," said Victoria.

"Get in. We've got to set your trap."

As they approached the turnoff to Burkhardt's place, Casey said, "How do you get onto that middle road?"

"As I recall, there's a big rock on the left, which is unusual because there aren't many rocks on this part of the Island. It's mostly sand. And there was a bent sapling."

Casey turned at a fork Victoria indicated, and the Bronco moved slowly along the brushy road.

"A vehicle has come through here recently." Casey pointed to broken branches and broken sticks in the track.

"This leads to the lily pond," Victoria said. "Fishermen use this road sometimes."

"Not often, from the looks of it," Casey said. "Here's a rock. And there's your bent sapling." She pointed to an oak tree, its trunk a foot-and-a-half in diameter. The trunk bent sharply, three feet off the ground, then grew straight up to a leafy crown.

Victoria leaned out to look up at the tree. "I'd never have guessed a tree would grow up so quickly."

"Quickly?" said Casey. She shifted into four-wheel drive, and they plowed over bushes and small trees.

"I'll park a bit farther on, out of sight. We can go the rest of the way on foot." Casey inched along another hundred feet, and pulled the Bronco off to one side, the thick undergrowth snapped back to conceal it.

Victoria reached into the back of the Bronco for her stick. "I'll be in the barn."

"No you don't, Victoria. Let's think this through."

"I have thought it through. You stay close enough so you can hear me when I call. If I'm right, the killer will come down the back road by the lily pond, will park in the same place as before, and will enter the barn. That's where I'll be, lying in wait."

As they walked along the track, wet branches slapped against them, sprinkling them with rainwater.

"Victoria, this is a bad idea. As soon as I see someone, I'll move in and make an arrest. We can wait in the Bronco and eat our picnic supper until they show."

"What could you arrest them for? No, that's not the way to do it." Victoria shook her head. "After what I said at the gathering this afternoon, almost anyone might come here out of curiosity, someone entirely innocent. We have to wait before we can spring the trap."

"With you as bait? No way. If we need someone to wait in the barn, I'll do it."

The rain had let up briefly, but the trees overhead dripped water as if it were still raining. With every slight breeze, it pattered down on the huckleberry leaves below.

"Don't you see," Victoria said, a trifle impatiently, "an innocent

220

person seeing me there will be surprised, but will say something like, 'Just came by to have a look.' On the other hand, if the killer believes I've come by myself, that person will try to get me out of the way, and we can catch them red-handed."

"Yeah, after they've garroted you, Victoria."

"I wore my turtleneck," Victoria said.

"Not funny, Victoria. We're not playing games. There's a killer loose."

Victoria held her hands in gnarled fists by her side. They had stopped briefly so Victoria could catch her breath. The trees shook raindrops onto them. "I planned this trap and I intend to set it. The only way we can catch the murderer is in the act. If they see you, a police officer, the killer will be all innocence. We have to take a chance."

"Victoria . . ." Casey started to say.

"Your responsibility is to capture the killer, it's not mine. I'm simply bait." Victoria started walking again toward the clearing and Burkhardt's place.

"Suppose I'm a half second too late, Victoria?" Casey strode along next to her.

"You won't be. Dojan will be on watch, so will Junior."

Casey threw up her hands. "Look at it from my viewpoint, Victoria. I'm a trained cop. You're not. I've gone to school for this stuff. You haven't. Suppose something happens to you? I'll never be able to live with it, never."

"It's time you learned to listen to your elders." Victoria set her mouth stubbornly, reached into her cloth bag, took out her blue baseball cap, and set it on her head.

"Okay, okay, you win. If anything happens . . ." Casey didn't finish.

"If anything happens to me, there'll be no doubt about the killer's identity, will there?"

The track ended at the back of the barn. The road had once been used to haul hay. A long beam protruded from the roof peak above a wide window. At one time there was a pulley to lift the hay up to the window.

"I can always get out through the window," Victoria said. "It's not a long drop to the ground, and there's still a mound of old hay as a cushion."

Casey stood for a few moments, still doubtful.

"You'd better hide in case someone shows up," Victoria said. "Otherwise, all this will have been in vain."

Casey shook Victoria's hand gravely and moved out of sight into the wet woods.

Victoria walked around to the front of the barn, where the wide door faced the charred ruin of the old house. She had to tug hard on the wooden handle to open the door. The wood had swollen with moisture. The hinges squealed. A barn swallow flew out.

She carefully put one foot after another on the dusty floor inside the barn, and looked behind her to make sure the footprints showed clearly. As she moved toward the back, where a ladder led up to the hayloft, she heard a rap on the back boards.

"Can you hear me?" It was a loud whisper. "It's Casey."

"Yes. I'm climbing up to the loft."

"Do you need help?"

"No," Victoria hissed.

"Be careful."

Victoria had never liked heights, even when she was a girl, and the loft looked high above the barn floor. She studied it for a few minutes. The ladder seemed sturdy. She debated whether to take her stick up with her, and decided it would be worth it. But how would she get it up there?

While she was thinking, the barn swallow swooped back into the barn through the partly opened door, and flitted high up into the rafters in a flash of forked tail and pointed wings.

She decided the best way to get her stick up into the loft was to tie it with the belt from her raincoat, and then tie the belt around her waist. Awkward, but she could climb with both hands free. She held the sides of the ladder, her right foot on the bottom rung. Was the ladder fastened securely? she wondered. It seemed to be. She was glad she was wearing tough walking shoes. Elizabeth had cut a hole in the uppers for her arched-up toe. The soles had a sort of pattern that would keep her feet from slipping. She brought up her left foot. She paused a moment, then moved her hands up a bit, one at a time. Then her right foot on the next rung, her left beside it.

Another swallow darted through the door and landed with a chirp near a nest she could see in the rafters.

She looked down. She wasn't far off the ground, only about as high as a chair seat. She looked up. The loft still seemed awfully far above her. She moved her hands. Right foot. Left foot. She wouldn't think about anything but how she would get herself over the edge of the loft floor. She wondered if the floor would hold her weight, after all these years.

She used to play in this loft with the Mitchell children, Jube's mother and uncle and aunts. The rain had started again, and she heard it patter down steadily on the roof. Somewhere she heard the sound of running water, a leak in the roof, probably, that was letting in rain.

One foot, another foot. She remembered the sweet fresh smell of hay when she had gone haying with the Mitchells. In the hay field, long windrows of hay would dry in the sun. Mr. Mitchell and Asa Bodman's father would pitch the hay from the windrows into the wagon with long two-tined pitchforks, and the children would stamp it into the corners of the wagon. The horse would move on. Finally the hay would be high above the wagon bed, higher, even, than Mr. Mitchell's hat, and he would turn the horse toward home. The horse would walk, she remembered, between the bent sapling and the rock, and would trudge along the middle road, which had open pastures on both sides. The grown-ups, with much shouting, would haul the hay up into the barn with ropes and the pulley on the beam.

As children, they had jumped out of the window onto the hay. She supposed she still could, if she had to.

Only two more rungs to go. Victoria wondered where she would put her hands when she got to the top. Were there handholds nailed into the floor? She was tired. She knew how the conquerors of Pike's Peak must have felt. Her hands trembled from holding the ladder so tightly. When she reached the top, she found the sides of the ladder extended several feet above the last rung. She had forgotten that. She held on tightly, hands aching, until she could step onto the loft floor, which she did gingerly, feeling for soft spots in the flooring. The floor seemed solid.

The loft was dark except for a spill of light that seeped around the edges of the big hay-loading window. Perhaps she could push the window open a bit for more light. She felt her way across the floor, poking her stick ahead of her as if she were blind. A large mound of hay, dry and still sweet scented was heaped at the back of the loft. She reached the board-covered window, and pushed hard against it. The window didn't budge. Then she recalled that the window opened inward, so she tugged it toward her. She was exhausted from the climb and was breathing heavily. She was afraid she might not have enough strength left, but the window swung in easily, letting in light and a gust of damp air. She closed it again, partway, and then looked around.

What would the killer do? Was the barn door through which she'd come the entrance he'd use? She remembered there was another door. She scolded herself for not thinking of it sooner and making sure it was locked before she made that climb up into the loft. She could never, possibly, get down to lock it and then get all the way back up again. She could only wait and see what happened. Casey and Dojan and Junior were all watching. At least, she was out of the rain; all three of them must be soaking wet by now. She scooped out a hollow in the sweet hay, a hollow with arms and back like a low easy chair. She spread her coat over it, and, using her stick as a prop, lowered herself into her nest. She tried to imagine how she would get up in a hurry if she needed to, and realized it would not be easy. She decided to rest for a bit, then she would think of a better place than this low cozy spot to wait for who knew what. Someplace where she wouldn't be at such a disadvantage. She took her notebook and pen out of her coat pocket and started to write in the dim light from the partly opened window, a few lines of the sestina she had been mulling over. The rain drummed rhythmically on the roof over her head.

She hadn't meant to sleep. She had simply closed her eyes to rest them. The next thing she knew, she was wide-awake, wondering where she was, then wondering what had awakened her. The rain was still drumming on the roof. She heard a twittering from the barn swallows. Her eyes had grown accustomed to the dimness in the corners, and she could see the barn owl perched on a beam over the main part of the barn, looking like a lump of feathers. She heard a slight scratching that must have been caused by field mice. How pleasant it was here on the soft hay with the sounds and smells of childhood around her.

But what had awakened her? Dimly, she had heard a sound that didn't belong. She listened, wide-awake now, her eyes and ears attuned to the quiet of the barn.

She heard it again, rusted hinges creaking. The sound didn't come from the main door, through which she'd entered, but from the side door. She had a brief moment of panic when she wondered if Casey and Dojan and Junior knew about the side door. They must, she thought. Carefully, she rolled over onto her knees, helped herself up with her stick, so quietly she didn't even disturb the swallows. She crept over to the edge of the loft and peered down into the darkness below. She could see a line of light on the barn floor that widened, then narrowed again. She heard a creak as the door shut, heard soft footsteps on the floor below. She could see the beam cast by a flashlight, could see it swing back and forth and stop when it picked out her footprints.

She had decided not to identify herself right away. Someone might just possibly have an innocent reason for being here. She didn't think so, but she would wait to see what happened first. Her footprints had showed up in the flashlight beam, she knew. She couldn't tell what sort of person was holding the light, man or woman. Would the person climb the ladder into the loft supposing that she was up there? She couldn't hope to defend herself against anyone determined to hurt her. Yet she hoped the person would threaten her enough so she would know, and Casey would witness, without a doubt, that she had trapped the killer. She knew how a circus performer swinging from one trapeze must feel when he has only an elusive instant to catch a partner who has leaped confidently from the safety of another trapeze to his outstretched hands. Timing, she thought. She wiped her moist hands on her worn trousers.

The soft footsteps moved across the floor. Victoria could hear, but still couldn't see, the person who was holding the flashlight.

"Hello! Anybody here?"

Victoria began to tremble. It was not the voice she had expected to hear.

CHAPTER 34

The voice at the foot of the ladder was light and casual, entirely matter-of-fact, as if someone were stopping by a construction site to watch a concrete mixer at work.

It sounded so normal, Victoria wondered for a second if she weren't mistaken. Sweat trickled down her back. This was not the way she had expected this encounter to be.

"Hello? Anybody here?"

Victoria made her decision. It would seem odd for her not to identify herself when her footprints so obviously led only one way. She called down from the loft. "Hello, hello, down there, Patience."

Patience moved toward the foot of the ladder.

"Hello, Mrs. Trumbull."

"Have you come to see what I've found?"

"Yes. When I heard you talking about evidence this afternoon, I decided I'd better have a look."

She's going to spoil everything, Victoria thought. Of course she would want to come by to have a look. Victoria debated about calling down to warn Patience about the trap that she hoped to spring. It might be better to wait until Patience came up to the loft. Then Victoria could enlist her to help with trapping the killer.

"What are *you* doing here, Mrs. Trumbull?"

Victoria suddenly realized with a jolt that she had guessed wrong. She could smell the fear scent of her own clammy sweat. "I wanted to check to make sure I was right about what I said this afternoon."

"Are you sure now, Mrs. Trumbull? Have you found something up there?" Patience stood at the foot of the ladder, her face in shadow. Victoria couldn't see her expression, but she could make out the dark costume Patience had worn this afternoon.

"How did you get here, Mrs. Trumbull? Did your granddaughter bring you?"

Victoria was not a good liar, so she said, truthfully, "I like to walk."

"A long walk for a woman your age," said Patience.

"This isn't as far from my house as it seems by car."

"I'm sure that must account for your extraordinary health," Patience said pleasantly. "You don't happen to have seen Chief O'Neill around, have you? I'd like to give her a copy of this afternoon's program."

"Not at the moment," Victoria said, truthfully. "She told me she had paperwork to do this afternoon."

"Interesting. I didn't see the police car when I came by the station a few minutes ago."

"I don't know," Victoria said.

There was a moment's silence.

"What are you doing up there?" Patience looked up. "Have you found what you hoped to find?"

"To tell the truth," Victoria said, "I fell asleep."

"How pleasant," Patience said. "In the hay, I suppose. Will your granddaughter pick you up?"

"She didn't know I was coming here," Victoria said. "She doesn't get off work until six."

Patience looked at her wrist. "It's about half-past five now. Do you need help up there? I'd be interested in seeing what you've discovered."

Victoria's first reaction was panic. Then she thought about her trap. She hoped Patience wouldn't smell her fear. She said, as calmly as she could, "That would be nice. It was more of an effort to climb up here than I expected. I wasn't looking forward to coming down again."

"You did it before, though, didn't you, Mrs. Trumbull?" Patience tucked the skirt of her flowing black dress under her belt and put her foot on the first rung of the ladder.

Victoria wanted to call out. To Casey, to Dojan, to Junior. Please help me, she wanted to say. I'm not brave after all. But she held back. It was still possible she had been right, that Patience was not the killer. If so, it would be embarrassing for everybody if she sprang the trap too soon. And if she was dealing with the cold-blooded killer after all, she might alert her too soon. Either way, Patience would say she had come, as an interested town official, simply to see what Victoria had been talking about. She must convince Patience that she'd told nobody else, and that she'd come alone. She had to trust Casey, Dojan, and Junior to rescue her at exactly the right instant, neither before nor, she shuddered, too late.

She peered over the edge at Patience, who was on the third or fourth rung and climbing steadily.

"I played in this loft when I was a child." Victoria hoped her voice didn't sound as quavery as she felt.

"Interesting." Patience looked up. Her head was below the level of the loft floor. "So you know this barn well."

"There aren't too many places left on the Island for barn swallows to nest," Victoria said.

Patience was halfway up the ladder. Her intense eyes were level with the floor now. Victoria stepped back and picked up her lilac stick, which was lying against a stack of hay. She leaned on it.

Patience reached the top of the ladder and, holding the uprights, stepped onto the floor of the loft. Victoria felt the floor dip slightly under her weight. Patience was breathing heavily. She shook her loose black skirt down around her ankles, around the high black moccasins she wore. In the dim light of the loft, the effect of her pale face framed by her black hair above her black clothes was like a dream of a disembodied head floating in the hay-scented loft with the patter of rain on the roof. Victoria had an instant of terror, as if she were seeing a head on a pike.

Patience's head looked around and spoke. "What was it you found up here, Mrs. Trumbull?"

Victoria stalled. "It's interesting. I didn't want to show it to the police until I had another look."

"What is it, Mrs. Trumbull?" Patience's voice had an edge of irritation.

"I don't think I should tell anyone but the police."

"You're being a tease." Patience smiled and moved toward her. "I don't think you found anything at all."

"It won't mean anything to anyone but the killer or the police." Victoria leaned on her stick. She had gotten over the momentary fright, but it was replaced with a feeling of unreality, as if she were observing herself from above, playacting with a make-believe killer. She couldn't quite convince herself it was real. Things would work out all right. Casey would come in time. Dojan wouldn't let anything happen to her. She smiled up at Patience's head, and Patience's eyes stared back at her like the obsidian Indian tears her daughter Amelia had collected out West.

"We seem to be at an impasse," Patience said.

"Impasse?"

"You aren't going to tell me what you found?"

"I think the police need to know about it first."

Patience stepped forward. "You haven't told them yet?"

Victoria inched back, toward the partly open window. "I intend to as soon as I get home." She sensed her smile was annoying Patience, so she wrinkled up her face with a particularly irritating, she hoped, false smile.

"If you found nothing, Mrs. Trumbull, you should not bother the police with your fantasies."

"I really mustn't say more," Victoria said, stepping back again as Patience moved forward. "By the way, I hadn't realized you drove a red pickup truck."

Patience stopped and took an audible breath. "What do you mean by that, Mrs. Trumbull?"

"Nothing, I'm sure. I saw a red pickup truck drive away from here the night Hiram Pennybacker was murdered."

"You couldn't have seen it."

"Perhaps Elizabeth and I were mistaken," Victoria said. "We both commented on that red pickup truck, but who knows?"

"You're making that up, Mrs. Trumbull. You are lying."

"I don't lie," Victoria said stiffly. "I think it's time I left now. I have a long walk ahead of me. And I'd better see if I can climb down that ladder." She smiled at Patience. "I may need your help getting down."

She heard, rather than saw, the rustle of Patience's dress, and she was aware that Patience had removed something from her pocket.

This has to be it, Victoria thought. Patience moved toward her. Victoria backed up.

"What are you afraid of, Mrs. Trumbull?"

"Help!" Victoria called out. "Help!" Her voice sounded feeble to her.

"There's no one to hear you, Mrs. Trumbull." Patience held something between her hands. Victoria couldn't see what it was, but she could guess. It must be a garrote, a wire Patience had used to cut Linda's throat. She put both gnarled hands up to her wrinkled cheeks so her arms protected her throat. "This won't hurt, Mrs. Trumbull. But it's necessary. Perhaps you are faking, but I can't take a chance. You seem to know too much. My grandmother taught me about power. I can't have you robbing me of power now I'm so close. After all the work I have done."

She moved forward suddenly. Victoria retreated, and fell into the hay behind her. She quickly lifted her arms again to protect her throat, and kept them there as Patience dropped to her knees. Victoria could see, now, that she held a shiny wire between her hands, as lethal as a knife.

Victoria's mind raced. Where are they? This is that split second when I need them. The time seemed to move slowly around that split second.

"Help!" she cried out. She never realized how weak her voice was. "Help!"

Victoria saw the wire come nearer and nearer. She held her hands tightly against her face.

Patience let go of a handle on one end of the wire to tug Victoria's hands away, but before she could grasp the wire again, Victoria's hands were back, her arms a barrier against that shiny wire. It is the end, after all, Victoria thought. Something had happened to Casey. Casey would come, but it would be too late. There would be no doubt about the killer. Victoria thought about her little joke only an hour before. But I don't want to die. I want to be around to see what happens next.

She felt the wire press against her arms, felt Patience tug her arms again.

"You can't fight me forever, Mrs. Trumbull. You're an old woman.

You don't have much time left, Mrs. Trumbull. Take your hands down. It won't hurt you, I assure you."

Victoria felt the floor yield beneath her, heard a howl that sent prickles down her back. Patience was lifted up, and her screams joined the howl, wild animal sounds, the likes of which Victoria never wanted to hear again.

Victoria felt more movements on the floor. She had closed her eyes with Patience's scream. Now she opened them again and saw Casey and Junior Norton.

"Put her down, Dojan," Casey said. "Put her down. Victoria's safe now. I'll cuff her. Put her down."

Junior bent over Victoria, his drooping eyes concerned.

"Are you okay, Mrs. Trumbull?"

"Of course," Victoria murmured, sitting up. She turned over so she could get to her knees. Now that it was over, she started to tremble. The trembling extended from her stomach, where it started, to her arms and legs and hands. Her teeth chattered.

"Dojan, help me get Mrs. Trumbull down that ladder. She's had a tough time."

Junior retrieved her walking stick, and she took it in shaking hands. "You are one hell of a brave woman," he said.

"You heard me call out?" Her teeth were chattering so that she could get only one word out at a time.

"Everybody in West Tisbury must of heard you. They probably heard you up to Alley's."

"Get Victoria down safely, Junior. Then come back for this . . ." Casey jerked her head at Patience, whose face still looked disembodied. She writhed and spat. Casey had handcuffed Patience with her back to one of the barn's upright posts, hands behind her. Together, Junior and Dojan carried Victoria tenderly down the ladder.

"I'll get you for this, Victoria Trumbull!" Patience screamed. "I'll get you if it's the last thing I do on earth."

CHAPTER 35

The northeast wind swirled rain around the front of Alley's store. It shook early-changing leaves onto the road, where they lay flat and yellow and slick.

Joe parked his pickup across the road in the usual spot under the elm, tousled Taffy's ears, settled his cap on his forehead, and darted across the road, looking both ways.

"Nasty day," he greeted Lincoln Sibert, who was sitting on the bench next to Donald Schwartz. "Where's Sarah at?"

"Who knows? Lotta stuff going on up to Aquinnah."

"What's the latest?" Joe asked.

"You heard what happened yesterday?" Lincoln said.

"Couldn't tell much from the scanner. Something over to Burkhardt's place, I take it."

"Here she comes now." Donald looked up as a Jeep pulled into Alley's parking place. He stood up. "May as well spring for a cup of coffee."

Sarah, covered by an oversize yellow foul-weather jacket, dashed from her car to the shelter of the porch. She threw back her hood, unzipped the jacket, and shook off the beaded rainwater.

"Ugly out there. Where's Donald? I thought I saw him."

Donald appeared at the door with two steaming cups. "You don't take cream or sugar, right?"

"Right. Thanks." Sarah reached for the paper cup and took a sip. "Ugh!" She made a face. "This stuff must have sat all afternoon."

"Grow hair on your chest," Joe said.

Lincoln moved to give Sarah room on the bench. She sat next to him and her yellow slicker dripped water onto the slats of the bench and the porch floor beneath.

"So what's happening?" Joe said after everyone had settled back into position—Joe leaning against the porch post, Lincoln next to Sarah, and Donald propped against the rusty red Coke cooler.

Sarah studied her fingernails, which she'd recently painted black. "The usual," she said brightly.

"Oh shit." Joe turned his back to her and spat off to one side.

"Ain't you cute."

"All we know is what we hear on the scanner," Lincoln said, "and that's not much. Something big must of happened last night. Nobody's saying a word."

"Well." Sarah drew out the word. "I guess you heard Mrs. Trumbull almost got killed?"

Joe stopped chewing. "No shit! The old lady?"

Sarah nodded.

"What happened?" Lincoln crossed one ankle over the other, and put his hands in his pockets.

"She set a trap for the killer and caught guess who?"

"Come on, come on." Joe gestured with both hands.

"Patience." She looked around at the three men who were frozen in position. "Patience VanDyke. Tribal chair."

"Yeah, yeah. We know who she is," Donald said.

"Patience?" Lincoln said.

"*She* killed Burkhardt?" Donald asked.

"Burkhardt and Hiram. And Linda." Sarah smirked with satisfaction. "And almost got Mrs. Trumbull."

Lincoln uncrossed his ankles. "Why?"

"I always thought she was a nasty bitch, but I didn't see her killing anybody," Donald said.

"Well, she did."

"What for? She had everything going for her."

"It looked that way. Only she was stealing from the tribe to buy all that property, like millions of dollars. She lined up everybody who owed her little favors and they were all ready to vote in favor of a casino."

"Send her property values through the roof." Donald swirled the remaining coffee in his cup and watched it eddy.

"So who blew the whistle—Burkhardt?" Joe said.

"Sort of," Sarah said. "He told her the shipping people were offer-

234

ing him more money than she was paying him for septic permits. He was about to ruin her."

"So she said to Burkhardt, 'Why don't you come with me, honey, I've changed my mind, we can look over a nice site for a dock,' " Joe said.

"And killed him there." Donald sipped the last of his coffee and folded the cup in on itself.

"She thought she'd killed him. But he crawled up the cliff to that rosebush, you know? Where they found him?"

A car went past, its windshield wipers slashing, its tires swishing, trailing a long motorboat wake.

"Anybody ever find out why it was so important he had to get up that cliff?" Lincoln asked.

Sarah looked up. "He shoved an envelope under the rosebush."

"Well?" Joe beckoned with both hands. "Go on."

"It was a letter from the state archaeologist saying there's an Indian burial site on his property."

All four exchanged puzzled glances.

"What's the big deal?" Donald mused.

Sarah shrugged. "Guess we'll never know."

In the distance below Brandy Brow there was a low rumbling growl.

"Jee-sus Christ. I forgot all about the motorcycle rally," Joe said. "Surprised anybody's out. They'll be drowned rats, day like today."

"Not much fun," Donald agreed.

"All Burkhardt's to-do over nothing." Lincoln shook his head. "Washed out. What was his trouble with them, anyway?"

"Noise." Sarah stuck her forefingers in her ears.

"It had to have been more than that," Lincoln said.

The rumble came closer, and they waited to see what would appear around the bend at the top of the hill.

"I heard his mommy wouldn't let him have one as a little boy," Joe said. "Had it in for bikers ever since."

"Probably true," Donald agreed. "Good Lord Almighty. Who's this coming?"

A huge glittering motorcycle materialized out of the rain and mist around the curve on Brandy Brow. Joe stared. It was the giant of all motorcycles. Blue and silver sparkles on its fenders and flank picked up the dim rain light and cast it around the bike in a misty metallic aura. The rider was wearing a matching metallic blue and silver helmet with great Pegasus wings that had tiny flashing blue lights across the front. He wore a trailing silver poncho that streamed out behind him. Silver and blue metallic tinsel rippled from the handlebars, which the biker clutched in his silver-gauntleted hands. He was wearing heavy leather boots festooned with chains. All this they could see as the motorcycle approached. As the silver cape flapped in the wind, they could see a black leather bag strapped to the seat behind the biker.

"Holy smokes!" Joe opened his eyes wide. "Batman."

"He's a local product," Donald said. "You know who it is, don't you?"

Sarah looked at him and shook her head.

"It's Doc Jeffers."

"Yeah?" Joe said.

As the biker continued toward Chilmark, they could see, embroidered on the back of his cloak, a caduceus, the physician's winged staff entwined with two serpents. "He's the only doc on the Island who makes house calls."

The motorcycle faded into the distance on its self-made cloud. The silver cloak floated behind the biker, the wings on his helmet flashed with tiny blue lights.

"Live and learn," said Joe.

The state police took Patience to the county jail, awaiting transportation off-Island.

Back at Victoria's house, Elizabeth and her grandmother ate supper at the card table set up by the parlor fire.

After supper Casey came by, and so did Junior, Dojan, and Howland. Fluorescent coals shimmered beneath the back log and the fire hissed and crackled. Outside, rain pattered against the windows. Victoria sat in the mouse-colored wing chair, and Elizabeth brought out drinks for everyone. Cranberry juice with rum for Victoria, Scotch for Howland, plain juice for Dojan and the two police officers.

"I have a couple of questions," Elizabeth said when she sat down again next to the fire, her own drink in hand. "What about the two sets of motorcycle tracks in the barn? Who left them? And who swept them clean?"

Victoria set her glass down on the coffee table. "The first was made by Mack and Linda. She wanted to look over her uncle's house. Her house, she thought."

"And the second set?"

"Mack and Linda, again," said Victoria.

Casey was rocking gently in the parlor rocking chair. "Mack confessed that they set the fire at her uncle's."

"So they're the ones who swept the tracks out?" asked Elizabeth.

"Patience did, to conceal her footprints that led to the loft," said Victoria.

"Then Patience stole the computer from here?"

"She was in the barn when the arson investigators were there," said Casey. "She must have known Hiram's body would be found. And she must have suspected the computer would be found, too."

"She was up in the loft when Gram opened the door?"

"Right," said Casey. "When she saw your grandmother, that gave her the first clue that Victoria knew something."

Victoria lifted up her glass to Howland and Dojan. "Thank you, both of you. Howland for his magic with the computer, and Dojan for rescuing me, not once but twice."

Howland's mouth turned down in his characteristic smile. Dojan held up his juice glass.

Junior and Casey told Elizabeth in detail about her grandmother's trap and her close call, and about Dojan's terrifying wild howl. They talked and laughed and congratulated Victoria and one another and drank to Victoria's health until Victoria's head nodded and her eyelids drooped. Finally, Howland, Casey, and Junior slipped away, followed by Dojan, and Victoria went up to bed.

She slept late the next morning, warmed by the three cats who took up most of her bed—McCavity, Burkhart's calico cat, and Hiram's gray longhair. She didn't get up until almost ten, when McCavity, vigorously cleaning the other two cats, shook her awake. Howland and Elizabeth were in the upstairs study, working on Burkhardt's files.

"Morning, Gram. We brought you a cup of coffee."

"While you were otherwise engaged yesterday, Victoria, I found Burkhardt's safe deposit key." Howland held up a small silver key. "The bank let Harley and me look at the contents of the box. No one can take anything out, yet."

"Where was it?" Victoria asked.

"Taped to the inside of the computer case. When I removed the case to get at the hard drive, I found the key. The fire didn't even damage the duct tape."

"Sibyl," Victoria murmured, half to herself. "That was why Sibyl was important." She looked up. "What was in the safe deposit box?"

The rain beat down on the roof outside the study window, ran down the shingles in a stream, and poured into the wooden gutter, where it burbled toward the downspout.

"One hell of a lot of money. Cash. Big bills. Close to fifty thousand dollars. Deeds to his and other properties, a dozen compromising letters, a stack of compromising photos."

"Did you find his will?" Victoria asked.

"Yes."

Rain slashed against the windows. A leaf hit the window, stuck briefly, slid off.

"Who gets his property?"

Elizabeth had been working on the computer while Howland and her grandmother talked. She looked up at mention of the will.

"When Burkhardt found out that Linda was also dating a biker, he apparently decided to sell the property. There was a signed sales agreement in there."

Elizabeth stopped typing.

"Who did he plan to sell it to?" Victoria asked.

"Who do you think?"

Both Victoria and Elizabeth shook their heads.

"Patience."

Victoria and Elizabeth looked at each other, then at Howland. "Surely, that can't be right?" Victoria said.

"Burkhardt had accepted a sizable deposit from Patience. Nonrefundable."

"How strange," Elizabeth murmured. "Was that why Patience killed Linda? To ensure her ownership of Burkhardt's property?"

"Not entirely," said Howland. "Linda may have learned about the land deals. Was she hoping to blackmail Patience, just like her uncle?" Howland shrugged. "We'll never know. Linda was a threat to Patience, so she killed her to shut her up. What was one more death?"

Elizabeth shuddered.

"Patience had been acquiring land in Aquinnah under a real estate trust, using tribal money to pay for it," said Howland.

"Intending to pay it back later, I suppose," Victoria said.

"Exactly. Burkhardt would salt a prospective piece of property with Indian artifacts. That would trigger the state law that requires an archaeological survey."

"Which would hold up construction almost indefinitely," Elizabeth added. "And that would drop the land value, and Patience would buy the property at a price below market."

"Jube was working against Patience at the same time he was working for her," said Howland. "He planted butterfly specimens on the casino site, hoping that Bugs would think the rare butterflies had been found there."

Victoria watched the steady stream of rainwater pour into the gutter. "Patience wasn't in any hurry, I suppose. She knew that eventually the archaeologists would determine there was nothing of significance on the site."

Howland nodded. "She expected that once the casino was in place, land values would skyrocket, and she could easily pay the money back to the tribe. No one would even need to know she had borrowed it."

"No wonder she was opposed to the floating casino," said Elizabeth.

"Burkhardt, of course, knew her ploy, since he was the one planting bones and potsherds," said Howland. "He didn't want eighteen million dollars for his property. But he was nasty enough to try to keep his nieces from getting their hands on the money."

"So why the deal with Patience?" Elizabeth asked.

Howland laughed. "He put a stipulation in the sales agreement that if an actual archaeological site were found, the property would go to the Conservation Foundation."

"That was the beneficiary on his most recent will," said Elizabeth.

"What are you laughing at, Howland?" asked Victoria.

"The state archaeologist had already investigated what Burkhardt thought was a burial site on his property. Overlooking the lily pond, actually."

"And was it a burial site?" Victoria asked.

Howland lifted his shoulders and held out his hands, palms up, in a Gallic gesture. "But of course."

"You said Patience would not get the deposit back?"

"That was the way Burkhardt worded it. She didn't think there was a chance in hell that anything was on the property, and was willing to gamble. She forfeits the money, not that it would do her any good considering she's not likely to be released, ever. And the property looks as if it's going to the Conservation Foundation. I imagine Harley gets the cash in the safe deposit box."

CHAPTER 36

Chief Hawkbill had convened a meeting of the tribal council, which now consisted of only three members—the chief, Peter Little, and Obed VanDyke. The three sat solemnly around the end of the long table.

The chief spoke. "I have invited Victoria Trumbull to this meeting." He nodded to Victoria, who was sitting next to Obed. "I also invited West Tisbury's Chief O'Neill. Mrs. Trumbull has helped the tribe more than once over this difficult time."

Victoria lifted a hand from her lap in acknowledgment. Chief Hawkbill nodded to Dojan, who was sitting next to Peter. "I invited our Washington representative, of course."

Dojan stared straight ahead.

Outside, the chilly wind-driven rain beat against the large windows of the headquarters building. The polished surface of the conference table reflected fluorescent lights that had been turned on to cut the gloom.

From where she sat, Victoria could look out the rain-streaked windows and see the misty softness of the ocean beyond.

"Who's going to serve as tribal director now?" Peter asked.

Obed looked up. "Right to the point, aren't you, Peter."

"The tribe needs a new leader. With all due respect to Chief Hawkbill," Peter's lips formed a thin smile, "he is not a leader."

The chief glanced impassively at Peter through his thick glasses before he answered. "I will appoint an individual to fill the position on a *pro tem* basis. "With Patience's 'departure,' tribal management reverts to me."

"Until the tribe holds an election."

"Yes, Peter." The chief nodded. "Until we have an election."

Obed toyed with a ballpoint pen, clicking the point in and out, in and out. A gust of wind slashed a sheet of rain against the window. The chief turned to Peter. "Just so you understand, I did not plead our sovereign nation status when Patience VanDyke was taken away."

"Ha!" Peter turned insolently to Dojan, who returned his look with his unsettling eyes.

The chief held up his hand. "Dojan's situation was not comparable to Patience's. Put that out of your mind."

Dojan continued to stare at Peter, who finally dropped his gaze.

"The United States authorities had no intention of prosecuting Dojan. Tribal laws took over in Dojan's case. He will work for the tribe in Washington until I determine that his time is up." The chief continued to look steadily at Peter. "I want this understood, Peter. The matter with Dojan has been settled by the tribe. The matter with Patience will not be. She murdered coldly, for money and power. I want to hear no more, Peter. Do you understand?"

Peter did not look up to meet the chief's gaze, and the chief repeated his question.

"Do you understand, Peter?"

Peter nodded, looking at papers in front of him.

"We must not abuse the status of sovereign nation. The courts have already ruled that we need not uphold United States laws banning discrimination. That was a wrong issue for us to challenge. I have fought discrimination all my life. Now the courts say we may practice it against others?" He shook his head. "I digress."

It had rained all afternoon the day before, all night, and all morning. It would rain for another day at least. The hill below the tribal building sloped into grayness, where gray sky met gray sea. The horizon had washed into the wet sea. Close to the building at the top of the hill the black of wet bayberry bushes contrasted with vivid russet and pale grasses, gray reindeer moss, burgundy cranberry leaves. A gust of wind shook the building. A brown oak leaf slapped against the window and stuck.

"To business." The chief straightened a pile of papers in front of him. "The first order of business concerns you, Peter Little."

Peter looked up expectantly with a slight smile. Obed frowned and continued to fiddle with his pen.

"I am releasing you from your tribal duties as of today."

Peter's mouth opened slightly. Obed and Victoria looked up. Dojan continued to stare straight ahead.

The chief held up his hand. "I am aware, Peter, of your dedicated work on behalf of a floating casino." The chief's eyes, the gray of the sea and the sky, were magnified by the lenses of his glasses. "I understand you are still on the payroll of the shipping company. Your work was on behalf of them, not on behalf of the tribe. It was for you, yourself. The shipping company pays you handsomely. I believe you will serve yourself, the tribe, and the company better if you work for only one master."

Peter pushed his chair back slightly from the table.

"I have in this stack of papers"—the chief shuffled through them—"a prepared resignation. You may wish to sign it." He slid a paper down the table toward Peter, who clutched the arms of his chair.

"Or, if you prefer, we will fire you. Don't look so surprised, Peter. It is common knowledge that you have been working against the tribe. That cannot be tolerated."

Peter's pale face flushed. "I was not working against the tribe. A floating casino makes sense."

"You are a paid lobbyist for the shipping company, Peter, the same company that runs the *Pequot* from Vineyard Haven to its casino in Connecticut. I have said enough. Do you have a pen? Perhaps Obed will lend you his."

Peter pulled the paper toward him, read it quickly, reached into his pocket for his silver pen, and signed with a flourish, drawing a curved line under his name. He slid the paper back to the chief, who studied it for a moment and set it to one side.

"I'm sure you need to make arrangements to clear out your office. You're welcome to make a statement. However, if you have nothing further to say, you may leave now."

Peter shoved his chair back and stood up. "Fuck you. All of you!" he spit out, and swept out of the conference room, through the door that closed behind him with a hiss and a click.

The rain spattered against the window and the oak leaf that had been plastered against the glass slid down a few inches.

"Our next order of business," said the chief calmly, "is to appoint a *pro tem* tribal chairman. This, as Peter Little pointed out, is only until the tribe holds elections. Obed, I am asking you to take that job."

"But . . ." Obed looked around desperately. Victoria smiled. The chief sat impassively, his hands folded over his stomach.

Obed said, "A woman has always held the position of tribal chairman. Since the beginning of time."

"Times change." The chief moved another paper to one side. "The next order of business is to announce that the federal government has approved a grant submitted by you, Obed VanDyke, to fund a three-million-dollar shellfish hatchery you proposed."

Obed stood up and thrust his fist into the air. "All right!" He sat again, grinning.

The chief lifted his head slightly so he could look at Obed through his glasses, which had slipped down again.

Victoria moved her chair back so she could see Obed better. "Congratulations!" She offered her hand, and he shook it, still grinning.

"Was it Dojan who got the grant approved?" Obed asked.

"Dojan has been working hard in Washington." The chief nodded toward Dojan, who stared out at the rain as if he hadn't heard.

"Now for the next order of business." The chief shifted more papers. "I have in front of me the results of the survey we sent to all Aquinnah residents. We had an eighty-five percent response, almost unheard of. We asked how residents felt about a gambling casino. Only five people out of almost three hundred said they wanted a casino." The chief moved a paper to one side. "That, too, will have to be voted on. But we know now, for a certainty, the sentiments of the tribe."

"Thank the good Lord," Obed murmured.

"Lastly," the chief went on, "all of us, with the exception of Victoria Trumbull, know why I asked her to this meeting."

Obed and Dojan turned to face Victoria.

"It is my pleasure to give you this certificate, appointing you an honorary member of the Wampanoag Tribe of Gay Head/Aquinnah." The chief faced Victoria.

Obed and Dojan stood. Obed reached into his pocket, brought out a package wrapped in tissue paper, and presented it to Victoria. She opened it to find a wampum necklace of sea-smoothed quahog shell teardrops set in swirls of antiqued green copper, wrapped like a vine around a leather thong. Obed fastened it around her neck. Her lavender turtleneck matched the purple wampum.

"Thank you," she said softly. "Shouldn't we smoke ceremonial pipes now to commemorate this?"

"Indian pipes, Mrs. Trumbull?" Chief Hawkbill laughed. "As I said a moment ago, times change. This is a smoke-free campus."

044789446